"You really are a nice guy, aren't you?"

Before she could stop herself, Paige walked across the yard and grabbed hold of his arms; solid, muscular arms that tensed at her touch. Looking up at Fletch, memorizing every inch of his handsome face, from that slight twitch as he fought a grin to the amused glint in his sea green eyes, she stopped thinking.

Without breathing, without worrying, Paige stretched up on her toes and very softly, very carefully, pressed her lips to his.

What she'd thought was an expression of gratitude shifted in the blink of an eye, in the flex of his fingers. She held on to him even as his hands moved and settled lightly on her hips. He didn't take; he didn't demand. He let her lead wherever she wanted to take them.

Until she realized she couldn't go where she wanted.

D0424702

Dear Reader,

Welcome back to Butterfly Harbor. I've been looking forward to writing Paige and Charlie Cooper's story since they first walked into the Butterfly Diner back in book one (*The Bad Boy of Butterfly Harbor*). They were both a surprise, characters I never expected to exist. When they stepped onto the page they did so with a wink, a smile and most definitely some secrets. Above all, they arrived searching for what so many of us want: a place to call home. But Charlie wants a bit more than that. She wants a dad, and this determined eight-year-old has her sights set on Deputy Fletcher Bradley.

Whenever I begin a story, I'm usually pretty certain whose story it is: the heroine, or in this case, Paige, a woman doing her best to protect her only child from the mistakes she's made. Or maybe it's the hero, Fletcher, who struggles with being thought of as a hero, especially when his own failure as a young man changed his family's future forever. There's usually a leaning one way or the other. But as I wrote, I realized this was the first story where a third person was equally important: a little girl desperate for the same family stability her best friend has. She wants—she needs—someone other than her mother to count on, to love her.

I'm a firm believer in family, and not just the kind we're connected to by blood. My friends are my family, and they're who I think of whenever I come back to Butterfly Harbor. I love that we can choose our tribe, that we can thrive in communities we might not have been born into but that we find along the way. Taking that one unexpected turn (or in Paige's case, a highway turnoff) can give you all you've ever wanted—and needed—in life. I hope you enjoy Paige and Fletcher (and Charlie's) journey to their happily-ever-after.

Anna J.

HEARTWARMING

A Dad for Charlie

———

USA TODAY Bestselling Author

Anna J. Stewart

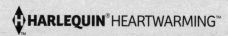

HARLEQUIN® HEARTWARMING™

Recycling programs
for this product may
not exist in your area.

ISBN-13: 978-0-373-36847-1

A Dad for Charlie

Copyright © 2017 by Anna J. Stewart

Printed in U.S.A.

www.Harlequin.com

Bestselling author **Anna J. Stewart** can't remember a time she wasn't making up stories or imaginary friends. Raised in San Francisco, she quickly found her calling as a romance writer when she discovered the used bookstore in her neighborhood had an entire wall dedicated to the genre. Her favorites? Harlequins, of course. A generous owner had her refilling her bag of books every Saturday morning, and soon her pen met paper and she never looked back (much to the detriment of her high school education). Anna currently lives in Northern California, where she continues to write up a storm, binge watches her favorite TV shows and movies and spends as much time as she can with her family and friends...and her cat, Snickers, who, let's face it, rules the house.

Books by Anna J. Stewart

Harlequin Heartwarming

Recipe for Redemption
The Bad Boy of Butterfly Harbor
Christmas, Actually
"The Christmas Wish"

Harlequin Romantic Suspense

Reunited with the P.I.
More Than a Lawman

For all the Charlie Coopers

May you find your forever dad.

CHAPTER ONE

"WHAT DO YOU think that's all about?"

From where he sipped his beer, Deputy Bradley Fletcher pulled his attention from the besotted bride and groom and followed his fellow deputy's curious gaze across the expansive—and newly landscaped—roundabout of the Flutterby Inn.

Every nerve ending in his body fired against the cool Pacific breeze coming in off the ocean beyond the nearby cliffs. Over the din of conversation and the ever-so-faint tunes of a four-piece string quartet emanating from inside the landmark hotel, the nerveracking sound of waves crashing against the rocks echoed in his ears. He shifted position, his knuckles going white around the bottle. How, after over fifteen years of living in the oceanside town of Butterfly Harbor, could the sound of the ocean still fill him with dread?

As he caught sight of Gil Hamilton chatting it up with a neighboring town sheriff, the anxiety and unease slipped to the back of his mind.

If there was one talent Fletch had honed in his thirty-one years it was his ability to know when someone—especially a suspicious someone—was up to something.

And there were few people in Butterfly Harbor more suspicious than their very own mayor.

"Excellent question." Grateful for something to concentrate on other than his personal demons, Fletch straightened and tugged down the edge of his rented tuxedo jacket.

"Heard Mr. Mayor is getting a little anxious about the upcoming election," Ozzy said in his own lowered voice. "With more than a year out, I don't think Gil expected Luke to declare his intention to run for sheriff again quite this soon."

"Gil isn't a fan of anyone he can't manipulate and control." One of the reasons Luke Saxon had earned Fletch's respect within his first few hours on the job had been the way he'd stood up to their former classmate turned boss. The onetime Chicago Bomb Squad officer didn't take anything from anyone; not even the mayor who had reluctantly appointed him over his personal choice of the man he was currently speaking to. "Gil might put on a good show, but he hates the fact Luke's approval ratings are higher than his. Even in a town this small."

"You think Gil wants to talk Sean into running? You think Gil's coming after Luke?"

"He wouldn't be his father's son if he didn't." Far across the manicured grounds of the iconic landmark hotel, Sheriff Sean Brodie gave the mayor a toothy grin. His chuckle carried across the breeze of the perfect late summer day and rankled the last nerve Fletch managed to hold on to. "Timing can't be a coincidence," Fletch said. "Not with Luke heading out of town on his honeymoon. I recognize an ambush when I see it."

"What kind of ambush?"

"Another excellent question." Fletch toasted his fellow groomsman and took a step away to grab two more bottles. "How about I go find out?"

"Fletcher." Ozzy's wide eyes grew even larger in his round face. The youngest and most rotund of Butterfly Harbor's three deputies might be the smartest of them when it came to all the advancements in law enforcement, but he wasn't exactly the diplomat of the group. Not that Fletch was much better, but he had half a lifetime of experience with their head politician.

"Don't worry, Oz." Fletch patted Ozzy on the shoulder. "I won't do anything to cause a scene." His only goal was to stave off any potential controversy that would mar Holly and Luke's wedding. As best man, it was his job to make sure the happy couple's day went off without a hitch.

As Butterfly Harbor's longest-serving deputy, it was his obligation to protect the town and everyone in it.

Fletch maneuvered his way around people he'd known ever since he and his sister had come to live with their grandfather right before freshman year of high school. Shop owners and residents turned friendly faces, smiled at him and waved as he passed, the gushing comments and well-wishes echoing in his ears. There was little Bradley Fletcher enjoyed more than a big community event like the celebration today. Unless it was watching two of his favorite people find their way to happily-ever-after.

Not that he'd ever voice that out loud. Closet romantic that he was, Fletch would be more than content to take that particular character quirk of his all the way to the grave.

As he approached the two men—both of whom he'd had the displeasure of traversing his dodgy teenage years with—Fletch caught a flash of suspicion in the mayor's eyes. Yep. Gil was definitely up to something.

When the suspicion faded and slipped into that familiar, over-wide, simpering smile on the face of a man who, by all rights, should be chilling out on a surfboard riding the waves far below them, Fletch shifted into what some of the kids in town would have called super-hero mode.

Sans billowing red cape, of course. Fletch didn't do capes.

"Mr. Mayor. Sheriff." The title nearly caught in Fletch's throat, but he was going to play nice with their neighboring town's head of law enforcement. For now. "Pretty good turnout, wouldn't you say?" He handed them each a beer and lifted his own in a mock toast. "Don't think anyone stayed home today. Always great to see how much the town supports its local heroes."

"I wouldn't call almost getting himself blown up by a psychopath being a hero." Sean Brodie's dark eyes narrowed as he took a long drink. "Rex Winters did have some friends, you know."

Fletch forced a smile onto his lips. So much for playing nice. "As difficult as that is to believe, yes, I am aware. I've been meaning to talk to you about Winters. Some of those firearms Rex had in his possession, we haven't been able to trace where he got them. Any ideas?"

"I really don't see where this is the time or place to discuss closed cases," Gil interrupted. "Whatever Rex Winters was up to died with him. Was there something you needed, Deputy?"

"Mmm-hmm." Fletch nodded as he drank. "Yes, actually. Luke mentioned you scheduled a meeting with him on Friday. Something about the string of break-ins and vandalisms we've been having."

"With both Luke and Sean here, I did, yes." Gil barely twitched. "I think it best to be kept up on the ongoing investigation, especially given these crimes are affecting both our communities. I was sorry to hear Luke won't be able to make the only time I have open."

"You mean because he'll be on the honeymoon he planned a month ago and you only asked him to meet two days ago? Yeah.

Funny how that worked out." Fletch's fingers tightened around the neck of the bottle. There was the spin he'd been waiting for. "Would you excuse us for a moment, Sean?"

"Of course." A coolness crept into Sean's shifty eyes.

"I have to hand it to you." Fletch managed to maneuver the mayor to a clear spot away from both the steep stairway down to the beach and the throng of party guests. As his ears cleared and his mind eased, he slipped into uniform mode. "You never cease to amaze me, Gil."

"How's that?"

Funny how Fletch could see that rich-kid "I dare you to stop me now" face in the eyes of the man Hamilton had become. Fletch didn't like Gil any more now than he did the first day he'd met him. Of course Gil and his buddies had been in midbully session and slamming one of their smaller bespectacled classmates into a bank of lockers at the time. That didn't make for a good first impression. "You never have any problem going behind people's backs to get what you want. Yet here you are, celebrating Luke's wedding and the entire time you're commiserating with your longtime buddy about how to oust Luke while he's on his honeymoon."

"I think you're reading a bit too much into two men talking," Gil said without looking at him. "If Luke isn't able to make the meeting—"

"You want an update on the case you should talk to me, seeing as I'm the one in charge of it." Fletch watched Gil's eyes widen at his lie. "Luke handed it off to me a few days ago. Must have slipped his mind to tell you with all he's had going on. He wants to make sure someone will follow through while he's gone. So if you had thoughts of bringing your buddy in to take over our side of things, you can forget it. I'm more than capable of keeping Luke's seat warm for him."

Gil tilted his head and looked at him for a good five seconds before saying, "If I didn't know you better, I'd think you were vying for Luke's job yourself."

"But you do know me, Gil." The last thing Fletch wanted was a promotion. He was more than happy in his current position despite the sudden necessity to be anything other than honest. If there was one thing Fletch couldn't abide, it was a liar. And he was standing in front of one of the best in the business. "You also know the lengths I'll go to in order to protect my friends."

Gil's face went blank. "I assume you and Luke have discussed the case in detail then. You know he's only a few pieces of evidence away from issuing an arrest warrant for Jasper O'Neill?"

"Of course." Fletch swallowed more beer along with the sudden unease. Jasper O'Neill? Okay, how had that kid's name come into this? Jasper was an odd one for sure. And he'd had a few run-ins with them over the years. A few breakings and enterings, loitering and other nonviolent charges. But nothing that led Fletcher to believe he'd do something of this magnitude. The destruction of property alone would carry a felony charge.

Then again, one of Jasper's best friends was currently doing an eight-month stretch in juvenile detention. Who knew what vacuum that left in their, for want of a better term, social circle. Fletch didn't want to believe Jasper was involved in anything that would put more stress on his family; the O'Neills had been dealt more than their share of hardships lately.

But what Fletch got to believe and what was the truth… Well. He knew better than most you didn't always get to choose which came out on top.

Fletch glanced over his shoulder to where his boss and friend smiled at his new bride. Why hadn't Luke said anything to his deputies about his suspicions?

"Luke and I are completely on the same page." Fletch pushed the words out of his mouth before he changed his mind. "I plan to follow the evidence while he's gone wherever it leads. If Jasper's responsible, I'll make sure he's punished for it."

"It's good to know our sheriff is leaving the town in excellent hands," Gil said. "Wouldn't want the failure of one of his deputies affecting the election."

"No, we wouldn't want that." How was it the urge to sink his fist into Gil Hamilton's solar plexus didn't diminish over time?

"Of course, it's still early," Gil said. "There's plenty of time for damage control should things go awry."

"You would know about damage control. Speaking of jeopardizing things." Fletch glanced to his right and raised his glass in acknowledgment of Harvey Mills, the local hardware store owner who was commiserating with a group of town volunteers working out their next community fundraiser. "I hear you're just about ready to decide on the final site for the butterfly sanctuary. A lot of people aren't overly pleased with your preferred choice of location. Duskywing Farm could be a destination spot on its own. You don't have to encroach onto its property to enhance your own agenda."

"You do hear a lot." Gil had become the master of the unreadable politician's expression. "No decision has been finalized as of yet. The town council will get their say. Making unpopular choices is part of the job of an elected official, Deputy Bradley. I'll do what's best for Butterfly Harbor. Always have."

"Like when you kicked more than a dozen families out of their homes last year? Yeah, sounds like what's best to me. You know what wouldn't be best for you?" Fletch leaned in close, much in the way he'd seen Sean Brodie do earlier. He lowered his voice, enunciated every word so there was no mistaking his meaning. "Ousting a sheriff everyone in the county limits loves. Just something to keep in mind as you move forward." He clinked his bottle against Gil's. "See you Friday morning."

"MOM, DO YOU think next week we can finally go look for those ocean caves Mrs. Hastings told me about?"

"What? Charlotte Rose, don't you dare!" Paige Cooper steered her almost eight-year-old daughter away from the wedding cake before a baby pink rose found its way onto Charlie's finger. "We'll have to see about the caves." Paige's schedule these days barely gave her enough time to breathe, but she knew at some point she'd have to find time to quell her daughter's curiosity about one of Butterfly Harbor's more mysterious legends. Something about ocean caves, a treasure box and your heart's true desire. She supposed it was only a matter of time before her normally practical, well-reasoned daughter had her head turned by a fairy tale. No treasure box could solve life's problems. "The caves aren't going anywhere." Wherever they were.

Charlie sighed in a more dramatic way than normal. "You always say we'll see. School starts pretty soon and I want to see them before…oh. Hey, Mom? Why's Willa crying?"

"Where do you see Willa?" Paige cast a cursory glance around Flutterby Dreams, the recently renovated restaurant turned reception hall for the day, but saw nothing but familiar friendly faces crowded together.

"Over there, by the window. With Mrs. O'Neill." Charlie flashed that cheeky gaptoothed smile that always hit Paige dead center of her heart. "And why can't I have a flower? I'm the flower girl. Holly won't mind. I helped pick out the cake, remember?"

Paige remembered. She also remembered the techno-colored puke fest that followed and proved her sweet-toothed child had a sugar threshold after all. "Choosing a cake doesn't give you frosting flower privileges." She tugged Charlie into the corner of the room and stooped down to poof up the daisy yellow dress that had been accentuated with tiny embroidered monarch butterflies by, of all people, Willa O'Neill. What that young woman could do with a needle was pure magic.

Paige's chest tightened as she located the young woman bending down to straighten the lightweight blanket around her mother Nina's thin legs. As she stood, she swiped an angry hand across her damp cheeks. Nina pressed her hand against her daughter's cheek, her lips moving in what Paige assumed were words of comfort from her wheelchair.

Paige fought the desire to inquire as to their distress even as she reminded herself it wasn't any of her business. But how could she not ask? Helping people was second nature to Paige—a compulsion. A compulsion that had gotten her into trouble most of her life. That said…Paige pursed her lips. She didn't like to see anyone upset, especially not on a celebratory day like today.

Paige gave her daughter another once-over. With a crown of carnations and daisies in her long red hair—it had taken bribing Charlie with a trip to the bookstore to get her to forgo her trademark pigtails—her little adventurer was pretty as a picture. Tears misted Paige's eyes as she glanced down at the new neon pink sneakers on Charlie's feet. Her kid definitely had personality plus.

"Mom, you're doing it again." Charlie rolled her eyes at what she called Paige's "sappy" expression. "Can I go find Simon now?"

"I think they're still taking pictures." Pictures Paige had been trying to avoid for the last hour. She took a long, steadying breath as the knots that formed in her chest last summer tightened to the point of suffocation. Two months to go. In two months she could stop looking over her shoulder; she could stop worrying about having her picture showing up…anywhere.

All she had to do was keep her head down, stay off everyone's radar and ride out the consequences of the worst decision of her life.

Not that she could avoid the photographs forever. Holly deserved the perfect day, no matter Paige's previous lack of judgment. "Hey, there's Calliope and Stella." Paige gestured to the bell-laced gypsy-like woman and her much younger sister maneuvering through the town residents who had turned up for the long-awaited nuptials. Between the crowd inside the inn and the group outside, Paige was pretty sure just about everyone in town had come out to join the celebration. "Why don't you head on out and I'll catch up."

"'Kay." That her daughter was immediately engulfed by compliments on her stellar flower girl performance had Charlie flying almost as high as her favorite winged insect.

If Paige had any doubts about extending their stay in Butterfly Harbor, she only had to look at Charlie to dismiss them. Her daughter had always been a friendly kid, but she'd blossomed in the months since their arrival. Moving on was always difficult. Moving on from Butterfly Harbor—if they had to—would be downright impossible. Not to mention heartbreaking, especially for Charlie. Speaking of breaking hearts…

Paige bit the inside of her cheek as she gave in to temptation and shifted around guests toward Willa O'Neill.

"Smile!" Melina Sorento, her mass of tight black curls bouncing around her round, curious face, snapped her camera phone and caught Paige unaware. "Thanks, Paige. We're featuring the wedding in next weekend's edition of *The Monarch Gazette*. Nothing Butterfly Harbor likes more than a party, right? Especially one that closes down the entire town!"

"Right." And there was nothing Paige detested more than being a headline. Then again, she didn't have much to worry about considering the town paper's circulation was limited to the guests in attendance. No one back in New York would ever know. Paige swallowed hard. She hoped.

"Willa?" Paige placed a gentle hand on the young woman's arm; not gentle enough apparently, as Willa jumped, color popping into her cheeks as she spun to face Paige. "I'm so sorry I startled you. Are you all right? Nina? How are you doing today? I'm so pleased to see you here."

"Nothing was going to keep me from seeing Holly Campbell get married." Nina brushed a nervous hand over her tropical-colored-scarf-encased head. The months of chemotherapy had taken their toll, from what Paige had been told. In the little time Paige had known the family, she'd seen a serious decline in the older woman's health, the result of a late-stage breast cancer diagnosis. "I was just telling Willa how nice it is to be out among friends. I feel almost normal."

"You look beautiful." Paige rested a hand on her frail shoulder and gave a slight squeeze. "I don't mean to pry, but is everything all right?"

"Mmm-hmm." Willa pressed her lips into a thin line and nodded once. "Everything's great."

Paige glanced from daughter to mother. Nope. Not buying it. "Is there anything I can do?"

"It's Jasper," Nina said and earned a huff of frustration from her twenty-something daughter. "Willa, you know this situation is getting beyond our control. Paige might have some ideas as to what we should do."

"I'd be happy to try to help," Paige offered. "How about we find a quiet place where we can talk?" As well-meaning as their fellow Butterfly Harbor residents tended to be, they definitely had a talent for whipping up the rumor mill where anything potentially scandalous was concerned. Knowing what Paige did about Willa's brother Jasper, scandal could very well be a possibility. "Have you seen the updated kitchen yet?" She shifted her way behind Nina's wheelchair, released the brakes and pushed her around the edge of the room toward the double swinging doors. "The new owners really did it up nice."

"We haven't, but we've heard it's beautiful." Nina tugged at the edge of her scarf.

"It's definitely a stunner. Willa, would you mind?"

"Of course." Willa pressed her slight frame through the doors first, stepping back to let Paige push Nina through.

Pale yellow bridesmaid gown tucked into one hand, Paige headed toward the side porch exit, offering a smile to resident chef Jason Corwin, who was bent over the counter. "Hey, Jason. Don't mind us. Just passing through."

"Wasn't going to." Jason glanced up from where he piped salmon mousse into delicate phyllo dough cups. With shorn dark hair and eyes as sharp as the edge of a knife, Jason looked more like a magazine cover model than a onetime celebrity chef. "Mrs. O'Neill." He nodded politely at Nina then Willa. "Hey, Paige, when you see Abby, would you send her back? I need a taster for one of the appetizers."

"What am I? Chopped…" She grinned when his brow arched in her direction. "Chicken. I was going to say chicken. I'm an excellent taster." She motioned for Willa to open the door.

"Uh-huh." Jason grinned. "Keep moving. You're not getting your hands on any of my new recipes."

"That's what he thinks," Paige whispered to Nina, who let out a soft chuckle. What Paige wouldn't give to pick the brain of one of the country's top food artisans. The midafternoon breeze welcomed them as she situated Nina's wheelchair by the narrow bench overlooking the ocean. She took a deep breath, let the pure salt-caked air refill her lungs and clear her mind. "Now, tell me what's going on. No one should be crying anything but happy tears at a wedding."

Willa wilted onto the bench beside her mother. She was a tiny thing with one of the kindest natures Paige had ever encountered. She also had a spine of steel. Rarely did Paige see Willa with anything other than a brilliant smile on her thin face despite the weight of responsibility she carried on her shoulders.

"Sheriff Saxon called asking if he could come by to talk to Jasper again," Willa said. "About those break-ins."

"Again?" Paige sat beside her and, because Willa seemed to need the added comfort, took hold of her hand and squeezed. "Why?"

"He wouldn't say. Exactly. You know the sheriff," Nina said when Willa shook her head. "He's very nice about it, very under-standing, but this time, I don't know. I got the feeling they haven't moved past thinking Jas-per's somehow involved. Last time he asked Jasper to account for his whereabouts on a bunch of different evenings."

"And was Jasper able to?" Paige asked.

"No. In fact he was out almost all those nights," Willa said with an air of defiance that had Paige's insides jangling. "He's out most every night. Jasper might have his quirks, but this isn't something he'd do. He knows the last thing we need is for him to get into trouble."

"You said Luke only talked to him," Paige said. "He didn't say anything about a warrant or being there to arrest him?"

"No. But I'm sure that's what's about to happen. He's only sixteen, Paige. He can't afford to get into serious trouble if he hopes to apply for scholarships and grants for college. They look into all that." Nina seemed to be taking the situation better than her oldest daughter. "This puts his entire future at risk."

Paige squeezed her hand. "What do you think of Luke's idea he's involved with the break-ins?"

"I'm his mother," Nina said, her pale face losing what little color it possessed. She tucked her trembling hands under her blanket. "I don't want it to be true. But I'm also a realist." She straightened in her chair, the bright blue of her dress catching against the sun. "He's been through a lot these last few years. It's…changed him. There are times I think he's just so angry, withdrawn. And he's never kept company with the best of influences."

"He's always got his nose in a book. Or he's in his room watching those gruesome videos," Willa explained when Paige inclined her head. "I suggested he look for a job, but he doesn't think anyone around here will hire him. And he's probably right. He rubs people the wrong way."

"That doesn't mean he's so far gone he'd take to damaging property and vandalism," Nina said. "He wouldn't do that to me. To us. Not now. The last thing we can afford is bail, let alone a lawyer."

"That's the second time one of you has said 'not now,'" Paige said, recognizing grief when she heard it. "What's changed?"

Willa's eyes filled as she looked at her mother before glancing away.

"My latest test results came back last week," Nina said after she cleared her throat. "They say the cancer's spread to my lymph nodes. The chemotherapy didn't do as much as they'd hoped, so they're putting me on an experimental regimen. But that means going to San Francisco and being admitted for four to six weeks." Nina shook her head as if to clear her own tears. "It'll be tough. Willa will have to take on even more than she already has. Maisey's only ten. I want her life as disrupted as little as possible. She's a dream and little trouble, thank goodness, but—"

"Jasper being under suspicion with the police is only adding to the strain." Paige nodded. Oh, boy. She'd heard this before. She should have followed her instincts and stayed far, far away. The last thing she should be thinking about was getting involved with anything having to do with the police. "Did Luke give you any more information about the crimes themselves? Maybe if I talked to Jasper…"

Mother and daughter looked at each other again. "We haven't seen or heard from Jasper since we got Mom's results," Willa said. "He took off. I don't know what Luke's going to think if he shows up trying to talk to him in person. I'm sure he'll take that as more evidence of his guilt."

"If Jasper did these things, he did them," Nina said. "It's something we need to come to terms with. We'll deal with whatever happens."

"And what if he is innocent?" Willa asked. "Mom, what if he's a convenient scapegoat? There are plenty of bored kids around town, not to mention frustrated adults with just as many grudges," Willa added as Paige assumed she was talking about the still new teen community center. "Why are they focused on Jasper? Because he's different? Because he sees things in a way different from the rest of us?"

Because Jasper O'Neill walked around Butterfly Harbor looking like death's less optimistic minion? Paige had met Jasper only a handful of times. He was quiet, sure. Introspective, one might think. But if appearances were any indication, there was also the way he embraced the black clothes and had jet-black hair that covered equally dark eyes. And then there was the attitude he wore like a second skin. Yeah. Paige could understand why he was at the top of the list. That didn't mean he was guilty.

"If this was anyone other than Luke Saxon we were talking about I'd be inclined to agree with you." Paige had little to no faith in law enforcement, but that was because of her own personal bias. Luke was one of the reasons she still had some. "You know Luke's own history. He'd never railroad someone just because they look the part or it's the easy way out. He goes by the evidence." What that evidence might be, however, was the question. She could probably find out. A few questions here and there, if only to put Nina's and Willa's minds at ease…

What was she thinking, getting involved? Just moments ago she'd been reminding herself to keep her head down, and now she was considering poking around an active criminal investigation?

She should get up and walk away. Luke was a good man. He wouldn't do anything to hurt this family; not if he could help it. And yet…

Paige wasn't one to turn her back on people who needed help. She could do this. Carefully, quietly. Yeah. She tucked a strand of hair behind her ear. She could do this. "I have some pull with the groom." Paige's heart leaped ahead of her brain. "Let me poke around a little. Maybe it's not as bad as you think. Maybe they've found something that exonerates him and just haven't let you know yet."

"We can't ask you to do that," Willa said. "You have so much going on already."

"You're not asking, I'm offering. And I always have time for friends," Paige said. "Your family has a serious fight ahead of you. The last thing any of you need is a distraction. All your energy needs to be going to getting you better, Nina. If I can help make things a little easier, that's what I'm going to do."

"You'll talk to Luke for us?" Willa's disbelief scraped against Paige's heart. "You'll try to convince him Jasper's not involved?"

"I'll do my best." A promise she felt pretty confident she could keep. Dealing with Luke was easy enough, and thankfully he'd taken the lead. Now, if she had to try to extricate information from Deputy Fletcher Bradley…

Paige shivered. Oh, well, that would be a whole other story.

Handsome, attentive, charming Deputy Bradley Fletcher. How many times had she felt herself getting sucked into the attraction vortex that seemed to develop whenever she got into his orbit? She'd gone out of her way to avoid him, especially after realizing he was just as interested in her. Not that he'd pushed or tried to insert himself into her life; just the opposite. He seemed to respect the fact she wanted to keep her distance. Which, of course, made him all the more appealing. The kicker was he was so good with Charlie; he flipped all those switches inside her that made her wish everything about her life was different.

Nope. Paige gave herself a hard mental

shake. That train of thought needed to be derailed immediately. As uncertain as Paige was about a lot of things in her life, she knew one thing for sure: no matter how appealing the good deputy might be, anything other than a cursory friendship was absolutely impossible.

Because a lawman like him would never understand a fugitive like her.

CHAPTER TWO

"FASTER, DEPUTY FLETCH! Spin me faster!"

Charlie Cooper's demanding squeal lightened Fletcher's heavy heart. Taking the political hit for his friend was one thing; needing to go after a member of an already overburdened family he'd known most of his life was another. The O'Neills had so much to deal with already. How could he even think about sacrificing one of their own to save his friend's career?

No wonder Luke hadn't said much about the investigation. He probably felt as conflicted as Fletcher did.

"I think that's fast enough." Fletch found himself laughing as Charlie released his hand and tottered dizzily on her sneakered feet. He caught her around the waist before she fell into the lush flower bed in front of the Flutterby Inn. He steadied her and glanced up as Paige Cooper exited the inn. She stopped short on the edge of the porch, her knowing, beautiful blue eyes glistening almost as brightly as her recently changed hair. The now strawberry blond tresses with hints of fire matched those of her daughter's, except where Charlie's was razor straight, Paige's tumbled around her shoulders in thick, glossy waves. She was girl-next-door pretty, with that radiant smile of hers and a small dimple in her left cheek. All of that seemed so surface, but it was all he had. Despite the overwhelming desire to know more.

Every time he saw her was like the first time. And that first time…

Whew. He felt the rush of heat in his face. That first time it was as if Fletch had been tackled by the entire defensive line of his high school football team. He did his best and tried to maintain his cool and keep a straight face around her. He wasn't a man prone to feeling, well, flummoxed.

And Paige Copper definitely flummoxed him.

He also found her utterly fascinating. She was always helping people, always doing something. She wasn't one to just sit back and wait for things to happen. She made them happen. His interest confused him, but that was the case with any mystery that crossed his path. How could he be so fascinated and yet so…in the dark? Talk about a puzzle begging to be solved.

The air around him stilled and she released the soft yellow of her summer bridesmaid dress, the gauzy fabric draping over her pretty form.

He blinked. There were times he wanted nothing more than to pull her into his arms and kiss her. Then there were others where all he wanted was to talk to her; get to know her, learn about her. Discover whatever secrets he was convinced she had.

That she did just about everything she could to avoid him should have stung. Instead, it was like honey to a bee and he couldn't resist the pull. But he respected her enough—and whatever ghosts she carried with her—to do as she silently asked and kept his distance.

He was a man who not only followed the rules, he lived by them; possibly the only thing stopping him from running a simple background check. Somehow that felt like an invasion; something that if she were to ever find out, she'd never forgive him for. He might not know a lot about her, but he had little doubt she was the kind of woman who valued honesty and truth above all else. He wasn't about to violate either. He sighed.

So be it. At least Charlie seemed happy to be in his company, and being around Paige's little girl definitely kept a smile on his face.

Paige's sparkling gaze landed on him and sent his racing thoughts skidding to a halt. Until she looked past him to where Luke stood watching his wife and her maid of honor hamming it up in front of the camera. Fletch's smile dipped as Charlie darted out of his grasp. Gil Hamilton wasn't the only one up to something today.

Paige walked down the stairs and beelined for the sheriff. "Luke? May I have a quick word with you?"

Luke turned, his dark eyes heavy with celebratory happiness. He blinked, nodded. "Sure. What about?"

"It's about Jasper O'Neill and these break-ins," Paige said. "I was just speaking to Willa and Nina—"

Luke shifted to full attention, his brow furrowing. "I don't think—"

"Paige, I need to talk to you." Fletch locked his hand around Paige's wrist and spun her toward him. "Wedding stuff. We'll be back in a second." He tugged her toward him, ignoring the brief look of panic on her face as he pulled her to the edge of the narrow path leading up to the lookout point. He stopped just shy of being able to see the foam spraying off the crashing waves. He didn't need that nightmarish roar of the ocean any louder in his ears on top of dealing with Paige.

"What do you think you're doing?" Paige shivered as a cold breeze shot over them.

Fletcher shrugged out of his jacket and draped it over her shoulders. "Today isn't the day to talk about Jasper O'Neill, Paige."

"Thank you." Even as he saw her debate rejecting the offer, she clasped her hand around the edges and drew it closed across her chest. The thin gold chain and butterfly charm glistened against the sun and the hollow of her throat. Paige's eyes narrowed. "Since when is it any of your business what I talk to the sheriff about?"

"Since the break-ins are my case." For a man who didn't lie, he seemed to be setting a world record. "Luke asked me to take over. You want to talk about Jasper, you get me."

"Oh." She shrugged inside his too-big jacket and twisted her head back and forth. She couldn't have looked any more thrilled if she'd been handed a rotten egg. "Well. Maybe once he's back—"

"I'll have it closed by then." Boy, he was just digging himself deeper. "What's this about, Paige? Did Willa and Nina tell you something we should know?" Like where he should start or why Jasper had hit the top of Butterfly Harbor's Most Wanted List?

"You mean am I going to give you a reason to go chasing after an innocent sixteen-year-old kid who was probably in the wrong place at the wrong time? No." Her eyes went ice cold. "I'm not."

Why did Fletch have the feeling she wouldn't have been so prickly if she'd talked to Luke about this? What was it about him that made her so…hostile? "Who says he's innocent? His family?"

"Who says he's guilty? Or what does? Why did Luke question him? What evidence is there against him?"

Had Fletch climbed onto some whirlwind roller coaster without realizing it? He knew Paige tended to jump in whenever anyone needed help, and he admired her for it. But picking up the sword to fight for a kid with Jasper O'Neill's reputation seemed a stretch even for her. "First, it's none of your business how we run an investigation, and second, this doesn't have anything to do with you. And unless you've taken up yet another job as a private investigator, there's nothing about the case I'm going to share with you."

"So you are going after him." She puffed up in defiance. "Are you looking at anything other than his record, anemic as that is? Fingerprints at the scenes? Witnesses who saw him loitering around those houses?"

"I'm not talking to a civilian about this." By the time this day was done he was going to be an expert in bluffing. "I can tell you, and you can assure Nina and Willa, that we'll take every proper step necessary where Jasper is concerned."

Her snort of derision had him taking a step back.

"So I was right. You aren't even considering anyone else."

He hadn't anticipated adding irritating as one of the missing pieces to the Paige Cooper puzzle. "It means Jasper is one avenue we're exploring. And he hasn't done himself any favors over the years by pushing legal boundaries. If you're done interrogating me, it looks as if you're needed for your bridesmaid pictures."

He motioned toward a frantically waving Abby Manning, blond curls bouncing, her maid-of-honor bouquet of yellow and white roses interspersed with eucalyptus leaves an odd kind of beacon.

"We aren't done talking about this." Paige removed his jacket and held it out to him. "I'm not letting you railroad him or his family."

"No one's railroading anyone, Paige. I'm a cop. I'm doing my job."

"Yeah, I've heard that before." She may as well have fired lasers at him given that look in her eye before she walked away.

The odd statement rang in his ears as he grabbed a new beer and rejoined his friends.

"That looked intense," Luke observed when Fletch twisted off the cap so hard he left marks on his fingers. "Everything okay?"

"Peachy." Fletch shook his head, dismissing his soured mood, and plastered on a congratulatory smile for his boss, the groom. "We can talk about it later. Today's about you and Holly." And he had the battle scars to prove it.

"You said it, Fletch." Burly Matt Knight slapped Luke on the back, but no amount of jostling, it seemed to Fletch, was going to erase that goofy smile off his friend's face. "Life as you know it is officially over, my friend."

"Life just got a million times better." Luke toasted his bride as Simon, Holly's nearly nine-year-old son by her first marriage, dived toward them and suctioned himself to Luke's side. "What's going on, bud?"

"When are we going to eat?" Simon whined. "I'm staaaarving and Jason said he's making burgers for all us kids."

"Two helpings of pancakes this morning and you're hungry." Luke laughed. "I might need to take a second job to keep the kitchen stocked. Fletch?"

"Yeah?" Fletch couldn't shake the feeling he'd inadvertently turned over an information-laden rock where Paige's past was concerned. What on earth had she meant with that parting comment? Why was she taking the situation with Jasper O'Neill so personally? "What did I miss?"

"I think it's more what we missed," Ozzy joked as he tugged at the snug cummerbund around his ample waist. "Did you have a nice talk with Paige?"

"You talked to my mom?" Charlie danced from where she'd been circling Simon over to Fletch. She grabbed his hand and twirled again. "Yay! I've been hoping you two would be friends. Spin me again, please, Deputy Fletch!"

"Again?" Who needed an upper-body workout when Charlie Cooper was around? The little girl looked like she belonged in his sister's childhood music box. He let out a dramatic sigh and let her grab hold of his hand. Before he could follow through, Simon leaped toward her and grabbed hold of her arm.

"Come on, Charlie! Let's go check out the buffet table."

"Later, Deputy Fletch!" Charlie called and let her best friend pull her away.

"Don't go far, please," Luke called after them. "You're not done with pictures."

"I'll keep an eye on them." Ozzy followed them inside.

"Tell me that woman put us out of our misery and asked you out," Matt said to Fletch, who couldn't tear his gaze away from Paige. "Since you haven't had the guts to ask her yourself."

"Far from it." If anyone else had accused him of using a troubled kid as a rung on the professional ladder, he'd have dismissed them in a heartbeat. But Paige Cooper? She'd only increased his fascination. What he knew about her could fill a bullet casing.

Clearly there was more beneath the surface than even he'd imagined.

"What you need, Deputy Bradley," Luke said, "is a plan of action where romance is concerned. Standing around mooning over her isn't getting you anywhere."

"*Sitting* around mooning isn't either." Matt choked on his beer when Fletch slugged him. "Oh, come on, man. I'm surprised you aren't doodling her name with little hearts or something."

"I don't doodle." He must have it bad if both Matt and Luke were both calling him on his unrequited…love? Fletch tried to dislodge that thought before it solidified. No. That wasn't possible. But whatever this… thing…was between them, Paige Cooper had just thrown down the gauntlet.

And Fletch was more than happy to pick it up.

CHAPTER THREE

STANDING ON THE bride's right listening to the *click, click, click* of the digital camera, Paige wondered just how big a mistake she'd made diving into the O'Neill situation without thinking things through. Story of her life. It didn't seem to matter her intentions, somehow she always ended up on the wrong end of things.

Only this time *things* included Deputy Fletcher Bradley.

What kind of luck did she have to have that he was in charge of the break-ins investigation? Of all people? Of all...

Paige blew out a slow, controlled breath. She'd have to be blind not to notice how appealing the deputy was in his khaki uniform, but that was nothing compared with how he looked in all his formal best-man finery.

Her gaze flicked over to him, reason battling against flights of fancy. He was tall enough for her to look up to, and those sea-green eyes of his had all but twinkled as he'd spun her daughter like a top in front of the inn. The genuine smile on his lips accentuated the lean features of his handsome face beneath a cap of wavy doe-brown hair. Boy, she needed to get some things under control. Beginning with her daughter's growing attachment to the Deputy and ending with Paige's own…attraction. Never in her life had she ever dealt with a man she couldn't seem to think straight around. If she was going to keep her promise to Willa and Nina, she'd have to interact with the good deputy in the coming days.

Wasn't that just a great big piece of terrific?

She recognized that look in Fletch's eyes when she mentioned Jasper O'Neill. She'd seen the expression on the face of the detective who had questioned her back in New York. The detective who had decided a kid was guilty simply because of his circumstances and history. The same young man whom Paige had gone out of her way to help.

Paige bit the inside of her cheek. Until now she'd thought Fletcher Bradley to be one of the most charming…and honorable men she'd ever met. Open, friendly, *honest*. Sticking her nose into a situation only to come up against him?

Paige clenched her fists around her bouquet.

Boy, she'd really stepped in it this time. She'd promised Willa and Nina. Following through meant dealing with Fletcher. Somehow she'd have to find a way to make that work and still stay under his speculative radar.

Did he have to sound so logical? She was an outsider. This really wasn't any of her business. But if she could make the days just a little easier on Jasper's mother and sister, how could she not jump into the fray? If Deputy Do-Gooder wasn't going to be forthcoming with more information, clearly she'd have to find out on her own.

"Take a break, ladies," the photographer called, motioning to his suddenly silent camera.

"Thank goodness." Holly Campbell, now Saxon, sagged a bit in her tea-length antique lace wedding gown and massaged her cheeks with her fingers. "I can't feel my face." The miniature roses and tiny fabric butterflies woven through her shoulder-length brown hair made the diner owner look like a fairy-tale princess come to life; all that was missing were cartoon birds flying around her head.

The just-married couple gazed at each other in a way that made Paige's stomach hurt.

She'd given up on happily-ever-after even before Charlie's father died; her one shot at happiness, and of course Paige had somehow found a way to ensure it completely misfired.

As if her eyes had a mind of their own, she found herself glancing at Fletcher before she ducked her head.

She couldn't let today be about lamenting the past or the choices she'd made. Today was about Holly and Luke's future. Listening to the roar of the ocean over the other side of the expansive Pacific cliffs, feeling the barest hint of sea spraying mist on her face, Paige had to admit, the day had been perfect.

"I thought maybe you were hiding in the kitchen with Jason a while ago." Maid of honor Abby swooped around the bride and wrapped an arm around Paige's waist. On the short side with tumbling blond curls and a generous, radiant smile, the hotel manager was considered Butterfly Harbor's personal pixie. "Imagine our surprise when we saw you up on the cliff with Deputy Studly."

"You did not just call him that." Paige couldn't help but consider the moniker appropriate.

"Hey, what's said between bridesmaids stays between bridesmaids, right, Holly?" Abby blinked wide-eyed innocent eyes at her.

"If you say so," Holly said before she wandered over to Luke, who slipped his arms around his new wife with as little effort as it took for him to breathe.

"Jason said something about needing a taste tester," Paige said against the rush of happy tears. "Just be careful you don't accidentally cook anything while you're in there." Abby stuck her tongue out at Paige. Paige chuckled. "Even today you couldn't drag him out of the kitchen, could you?"

"Jason's still working on the whole public-interaction side of things. We're lucky he came to the ceremony. But not to worry. I will acclimate him before our wedding day comes." Abby leaned her head on Paige's shoulder as they watched the bride and groom interact. "I'm so happy for her."

"Me, too."

"That could be you, you know." Abby squeezed her arm. "All you have to do is give Fletch the all clear—"

"I'm not interested, Abby." Even as she said it she found it difficult to pull her gaze away from the entertaining view of Fletch hamming it up with his friends. He always seemed to be having a good time. What it must be like to be so unencumbered. So carefree. "Even if I was—"

"Please." Abby rolled her eyes in the same irritated manner Charlie had a while ago.

"Even if I was," Paige repeated as her stomach gave an odd little jump, "he's not my type."

"He's a nice guy, he's got a steady job and he loves your kid." Abby looked at Paige as if she'd grown an extra head. "Plus he's quarterback handsome. How is that not any woman's type?"

"I don't date cops." There it was; she'd used her "don't talk to me about this anymore" tone. "Please stop pushing this, Abby. Yes, I agree. Fletcher is a great guy, but I'm not looking for anyone." Paige cleared her throat and eased her expression. She had to keep whatever happened between her and Fletcher completely professional. If she had to tick him off to ensure he kept his distance, so be it. "I've got Charlie and my jobs—"

"You work too hard." Holly joined them

while she kept an eagle eye on her son as he and Charlie reappeared in time to dance an awkward jig around the photographer's assistant. "I assume we're still talking about Fletcher?"

"How about you bask in your own joy right now and leave me alone?" Paige sighed. Never in her wildest dreams did she think that after a few months she'd feel as if she'd known these two women forever. Not that she was complaining. She'd spent most of her life wanting friends, needing them. Her welcome to Butterfly Harbor only proved what Paige had learned early on: life could indeed turn in the blink of an eye.

"Speaking of joy," she said to Holly. "When are you guys leaving on your honeymoon?"

"Well, we talked about going to San Francisco in a couple of days, but then we figured since Simon's got a school break in a few weeks—"

"You're taking Simon on your honeymoon?" Abby balked. "Honey, I love my godson to death, but he's a definite mood killer."

"We were thinking about Adventure-World." Holly looked between the two of them. "What? Bad idea?"

"Can't your dad watch him?" Paige asked before Abby could answer honestly.

"He's taking off on an RV trip with an old friend." Holly leaned back to where her father, the former sheriff, was helping Abby's grandmother up the porch steps into the inn. "He's really looking forward to his first vacation in years. I can't ask him to postpone."

"Leave Simon with me," Abby volunteered. "My hours are flexible enough now I can work around his school schedule. Besides, Jason would love to give Simon a lesson or two with the pressure cooker."

"Ten bucks says Simon turns the cooker into a space shuttle," Paige joked about Holly's wicked-smart son.

"A weeklong slumber party at your place?" Holly shook her head. "I love you, Abby. Why would I subject you to that?"

"Then I'll take him when she needs a break," Paige offered. "Charlie has a trundle bed in her room. I don't mind." Not a day went by those two weren't tied at the hip, anyway.

"It's settled," Abby said. "Unless Simon has his heart set on going."

"We hadn't told him yet," Holly admitted with a sly smile.

"Because you were hoping one of your best friends would offer another solution?" Abby nudged Holly with her shoulder. "You're a tricky one, Holly Saxon."

Holly's cheeks turned pink. "I'll talk to Luke tonight."

"Talk to him tomorrow," Paige corrected, her pulse giving a bit of a kick when she caught Fletch watching her. "Why does he do that to me?" She didn't realize she'd spoken out loud until she found Holly and Abby grinning at her. "What?"

"You only noticed he was looking at you because you were watching him." Holly touched a hand to one of the flowers in her hair. "I don't understand why you don't give him a chance."

"I'm not asking you to understand," Paige said as kindly as she could. "I'm just asking you to respect it."

Paige didn't take chances. Not anymore. Chances were what got her into trouble; taking a chance was what had her leaving her home in the middle of the night and high-tailing it across the country with her daughter. Charlie was already paying a price for Paige's lack of judgment. She wasn't about to add Fletcher Bradley to the mix. Any response she might have given her friends evaporated as the photographer waved them over.

Charlie's laugh eased the tension racing through Paige as the assistant arranged the hems of their dresses. Paige looked over to where Luke and his other deputy-ushers finally got to twist open their beers. But it was seeing Fletcher bend down to straighten Charlie's flower crown that made Paige's breath catch. Abby was right. He was great with her daughter and Charlie had a serious case of hero worship going on.

Fletch laughed as Charlie grabbed his hand and twirled herself like a ballerina.

"Yeah, guy like that, totally not your type." Abby leaned across Holly then frowned when the photographer ordered her to stand up straight. "But fine. I won't say another word."

Holly actually snorted.

Paige struggled to keep her smile in place, wishing she was wrong to keep Fletch at a distance. What she wouldn't give to trust herself, to confide. To believe…

But she couldn't. The secrets she held were too dangerous to share, when Charlie's future was at stake. She couldn't come clean. Not with her friends, not with anyone. Especially not with Fletcher Bradley.

PAIGE NEARLY STOMPED on the ragged bundle of flowers she found on the doorstep early the next morning. "What on earth?" She stooped down and scooped up the wilted daisies and sprigs of lavender that, despite their haggard appearance, gave off a subtle, relaxing aroma. No card, no note. Just flowers.

Picking up the anemic town newspaper, Paige leaned over the railing to peer around the corner toward Monarch Lane. No one around, just as expected. The stores and businesses were still closed, and there were no people wandering around town, nor friends meeting, groups organizing and kids racing between the bookstore to try to see past the still-boarded windows of the soon-to-reopen arcade. She loved this place. Especially this time of day, before anyone else was up.

Before the town came back to life.

The diner doors opened early, and it was near impossible to be late when Paige lived in the one-bedroom apartment above the Butterfly Diner. Not that that was why Holly had insisted she and Charlie take up residence here. Holly's offer had been exactly what Paige needed at the time: a new start. But the generous no-rent opportunity had instilled a definite sense of goodwill and obsessiveness when it came to Paige's friend and boss's business.

The longer she stayed here, the longer *they* stayed, the bigger the risk became. They should have left weeks ago and put some distance between them and Butterfly Harbor. Placing herself in jeopardy was one thing; if Charlie hadn't been part of the equation she never would have left New York in the first place. She'd have owned up to her mistake and taken her punishment. But that was before she'd been threatened with losing her daughter.

The banked fire of anger and resentment continued to burn. Why was hindsight always twenty/twenty? How many times did she wish she could go back and do...everything over again? But it was too late. She'd made her choices.

But no way was Charlie going to pay for them.

Two months. That's all she needed.

And with that, she pushed the fear and regret aside and settled into the day, beginning with a last glance down the street.

Butterfly Harbor wasn't exactly a hub of activity this time of year, but most residents didn't hold down three part-time jobs like

Paige. She'd gotten used to five hours of sleep back in school, and her internal clock had never reset. Not something she'd passed along to her daughter, who would sleep her life away if Paige didn't drag her out of bed every morning.

She closed the door, set the flowers on the table and bent down to pull her ready bag out for her morning check as was her habit ever since she'd been in care. The essentials were always packed to go: clothes, spare medications, a good chunk of cash—Paige didn't use credit cards or checks which made getting paid interesting—a framed photo of Charlie when she was a baby. Anything else, they could pick up on the way, like the odds and ends that decorated the small apartment her friend had cleaned up just for her.

Paige yelped when Charlie wandered into the doorway of her bedroom wiping the sleep from her heavy-lidded eyes. "What's going on, Mom?" She frowned at the bag before that familiar panic flashed. Darn it! "We're not leaving again, are we? Mom, you promised we could stay longer this time!"

"We aren't leaving." Paige popped up and kicked the bag back in place. She hated that alarm in Charlie's eyes—a look Paige was doing everything she could to avoid ever seeing again. "And we have stayed longer." Longer than any other place in the last year. "I promised to give you some warning next time, remember? Are you feeling okay?" She immediately pressed her hands against Charlie's freckled face. No fever. Paige breathed a sigh of relief. She didn't have time for either of them to be sick. "The sun's barely up."

"I couldn't sleep anymore." Charlie's gaze widened as she looked at the flowers. "Simon's coming to the diner for breakfast. We have stuff to talk about."

"Ah. Still thinking about the mysterious Butterfly Harbor treasure, are you?" Paige nodded and finished making her daybed that doubled as a sofa in the small living area. "I bet you miss Simon now that he's in school. Makes it hard to go cave searching." She'd worried how Charlie would adjust to Simon attending a charter school for gifted children just outside town. Thankfully Charlie's common sense had kicked in and she hadn't gone exploring on her own, while she waited for her school to start classes next week. All the more reason to keep her daughter occupied. A bored Charlie was never a good thing.

"Don't forget we have that meeting with your new teacher this week."

"I know. I even drew her a butterfly picture." Charlie's voice brightened. "Who gave you the flowers?"

"Who says they're for me?" Paige asked. "Maybe someone left them for you."

Charlie shook her head. "Flowers are things adults do. Do you think maybe they're from Deputy Fletch?"

"Fletch?" As much as the idea unsettled her, Paige had to admit the thought crossed her mind. Until she remembered how they'd left things yesterday at the wedding. She'd wanted to discourage him, to cut off his interest in her. Challenging his honor and reputation seemed to have done the trick.

She retrieved the flowers and put them in a glass of water on the small dining table by the window. No need for the flowers to suffer. One of the daisies drooped in exhaustion. "No, I don't think they're from Fletch. What makes you think they are?"

"'Cause he smiles when he looks at you. I heard Abby and Holly talking. They think he likes you." Charlie sat in her usual chair and watched Paige skim her schedule for the day. "I think he likes you, too, Mom. And that's what boys do when they like a girl. They give them flowers."

"Hmm." Paige typed notes onto her calendar app on her phone then set her reminder alarms. She needed to find some time to talk to Willa again and thought she might be able to pop by her house later this afternoon. Since Holly and Luke weren't leaving on their honeymoon until tomorrow morning, she wasn't due at the diner today until after ten, which gave her time to stop at Duskywing Farm and get Calliope's deliveries out of the way before heading to the Flutterby Inn for her second-floor housekeeping gig. "You want to come with me to Calliope's this morning before you meet Simon?"

"Moooooom, you're not listening to me. I said I think Deputy Fletch likes you."

"I heard you. There's just nothing to talk about." Paige set her phone on the table and tweaked Charlie's nose. "Deputy Fletch and I are friends. Nothing more." And maybe not even that.

"But I thought you liked him."

"I like him fine. There's nothing wrong with just being friends, Charlie." Paige tugged on her sneakers before heading into the bathroom to tie up her hair. When Charlie didn't respond, Paige looked over her shoulder. The frown on her daughter's face was part frustration, part confusion. "What's all this about?"

Charlie shrugged. "I've just been thinking about stuff. You know, how Simon has a dad now and he's really happy. They're like a real family."

"Hey." Paige tried to swallow the lump in her throat as she returned to the table to stoop down and take hold of Charlie's hands. On days that started like this, Paige had to wonder just how badly her mistakes had screwed up her kid. "We're a real family. We always have been, right? We do okay together, don't we?"

"I guess." Another shrug. "Sometimes I just wish I had a dad."

"I know you do, baby." Paige stroked a hand down Charlie's face. That Charlie had never known her real father was still a knife to the heart. Despite Doug's flaws, he would have made a great dad, but a freak accident at his construction job when Paige was six months pregnant destroyed Paige's hopes she'd finally found the family—and home— she'd always longed for. "But it's not as easy as wishing. We have to work for what we want, you know? Just like I have to work to make sure we can stay here. If I just stood back and waited for something to happen, nothing would. Life doesn't work that way." She leaned forward and kissed Charlie's forehead. "Now, how about you go get dressed. I bet Calliope will show you the butterflies if we're early enough. Five by five?"

The word *butterfly* worked its magic and erased the sadness from her little girl's eyes. "Five by five." Charlie confirmed everything was all right by using their secret code. "But I still think Deputy Fletch likes you."

"You can think that all you like, little Miss." Paige tapped her on the bottom to get her on her way. "But Fletch and I are friends. That's all. Now, scoot."

"Morning, Charlie!"

Charlie pushed open the glass door to the Butterfly Diner and waved at Holly. She took a deep breath and smelled fresh-baked pies, buttery pancakes and crispy bacon along with coffee, which made Charlie's nose wrinkle in distaste. Yuck. How did adults drink that stuff? "Good morning." Charlie shifted her new school backpack—an honest-to-goodness butterfly bag with wings and everything—higher onto her shoulder. She had a big day planned between going to the library and taking a computer class at the youth center, and maybe, just maybe, she could do some exploring and find those caves. She'd printed a map off the internet after doing a search for the treasure box, but none of that was going to matter if Simon came through for her.

She walked up and gripped the edge of the counter. "I'm meeting Simon before he goes to school."

"He's in your usual spot."

Charlie looked over to the two seats at the counter in the corner and found a sluggish-looking Simon slumping half-asleep, chin barely propped up on an unsteady hand, his other hand dangerously close to dropping into his bowl of uneaten oatmeal.

"I think the wedding wore him out." Holly chuckled. "Luke will be by to take him to school in a bit."

"M'kay," Charlie said and moved out of the way as the door opened and a bunch of customers walked inside. The noise in the diner picked up, much to Charlie's relief given what she needed to talk to Simon about. "Hey, Simon." She set her bag on the floor and hauled herself up on the bright orange high-backed stool as Holly set a mug of hot chocolate brimming over with whipped cream in front of her. "Thank you." Holly fixed the best hot chocolate ever.

"Simon, up and at 'em." Holly knocked her knuckles on the counter. "You've got company."

"Hmm?" Simon blinked sleepy eyes behind his thick-rimmed glasses. "Oh, hey." He smiled at Charlie. "Sorry."

"You want a waffle for breakfast, kiddo?" Holly asked her.

Charlie nodded. "Yes, please." She'd liked Holly from the instant she'd met her. Not only because she'd given them a place to live and her mom a job, even though that had been supercool of her. Knowing Holly was around reminded Charlie of New York, back when they had a bunch of neighbors around, people for her to talk to, stay with, play with. After New York and before Butterfly Harbor, Charlie had been afraid she'd never have friends again. And now she had a best, best friend. And his mom was superawesome.

"Simon?" Holly asked. "You want eggs?"

"Whatever." Simon shifted in his chair, his already askew tie going even more crooked.

Charlie frowned. She didn't like Simon's uniform or the changes that came with it. The light brown pants, white shirt, blue tie and matching button-down sweater reminded her of her teacher a few years ago, except Simon was way smarter than Mr. Abernathe had ever been. Simon was smarter than most people Charlie knew.

If anyone could figure out how to get her mom and Deputy Fletch to like each other, it was Simon Campbell. Charlie bit the inside of her cheek as Holly headed off to take care of her customers. "The flowers didn't work," Charlie leaned over and whispered in Simon's ear, her declaration knocking the exhaustion from his face.

"You mean I got up extra early to drop those off for nothing?" Simon covered a yawn and rolled his eyes in that dramatic, why-am-I-doing-this way he had. "And I almost got caught by Mrs. Ellison. I thought grown girls liked flowers."

"I didn't say she didn't like them, I said they didn't work." Charlie crossed her arms over her chest and huffed. She'd given up on finding the Butterfly Harbor treasure because Simon had ideas. But that was before he'd gotten so busy. "She still says they're just friends."

"Oh. Well, what do you think we can do about it?"

Charlie felt an odd tightening in her belly. This didn't sound like the Simon she knew, the Simon who had gone out of his way to make his now-stepfather's life miserable when Sheriff Saxon had first arrived in Butterfly Harbor. The Simon who was always plotting something.

"You told me you'd help," Charlie reminded him. "Just like I helped you try to get rid of the sheriff even though I didn't want to, remember?"

"I know." Simon's sigh made Charlie's nose twitch. "And I said I would, but I don't know—"

"That's because you haven't tried. You don't care anymore." Charlie did her best to stop the tears from filling her eyes. Her mom didn't cry when things got tough. She just pushed forward. "You got everything you want. A new school, a new dad, and now that you do you don't care what I want. If you did you'd be coming up with ideas in that stupid notebook of yours instead of falling asleep in your oatmeal. Don't you want me to stay?"

Simon frowned. "What are you talking about?"

Charlie pressed her lips together. She wasn't supposed to talk about it. Not to anyone other than her mom. "I think we're going to move again."

"What?" Simon shot up in his seat. "No, you can't. You're my best friend! Where will you go? I've never had a best friend before. You can't leave!"

Tears blurred her vision. She dropped her chin and shook her head. "I don't want to. But the way my mom is acting, it's like it always is before we leave. If we can find a way to make her and Deputy Fletch fall in love, maybe she'll change her mind. Unless you have another idea."

"I don't."

Her stomach gave that weird flip whenever she got upset. "Mom told me this morning that you have to work for what you want. If you aren't going to help me make Deputy Fletcher my dad, then I'll just do it myself." Charlie didn't want to leave this place. Ever. It was the best place in the whole world. But the only way she could make that happen was if her mom had a reason to stay. Charlie slid off the stool and picked up her bag.

"Charlie, wait."

Charlie felt a single tear drop onto her cheek.

"Charlie, don't cry. I'm sorry." Simon got up and bent down to stop her from putting her backpack on. "You're right. I promised I'd help, and best friends always keep promises."

"*Sorry* is just a word." Charlie repeated what her mother always said. "It doesn't mean anything. You need to *show* it."

"Then I will. I'll work during my lunch break at school, okay? I'll come up with a plan, a couple of plans to get your mom and Deputy Fletch together, and we'll figure out which one will work."

"You will?" Charlie wanted to believe him. "You promise?"

"I promise." Simon patted a hand on her shoulder and urged her to put her bag back down. "We'll find a way to make sure you stay. And for you to be happy again."

"Then help me make Deputy Fletch my dad." Charlie scrubbed a hand over her wet cheeks and let herself believe. "Then I'll be happy forever."

"RESERVATIONS ALL MADE?" Fletch knocked on Luke's office door Monday afternoon.

"Abby made them for us last night. Called in a few favors with a hotel in San Francisco." An easy smile broke across Luke's features as he dug out a file. The golden retriever sitting at attention beside the sheriff's desk let out a small whine. "I believe this is yours now."

"What?" Even as Fletch walked in and stretched out his hand, he knew. "Your report on the vandalisms and break-ins? You know?"

"That you're taking over the case? The mayor's email this morning confirming your meeting with him on Friday greased the wheels. That wasn't necessary, Fletch." Still, there was a glimmer of gratitude in his eyes. "You sure you want to take this on? It could get dicey."

"With the mayor?" Fletch shrugged. "Don't really care about that. You know he's just waiting for you to screw up."

"I had a feeling. These days we can barely agree if the sky is blue." Luke waved off any concern Fletch might have voiced. "It didn't help I've been more than vocal over his plans to empty out what's left of certain areas in town. That said, if people think my taking a break for my honeymoon is a dereliction of duty, then I don't want their vote anyway."

"Why didn't you tell any of us about Jasper?" Fletch asked.

"Because I was doing my best to eliminate him as a suspect before I had to. He wasn't as helpful as he could have been when I talked to him. Defensive. Secretive. Maybe you should take a crack at him. You've known him longer."

"Yeah." Fletch nodded. "Might be a good idea."

"Maybe we'll luck out and you can be his alibi the next time someone takes a sledge-hammer and spray paint to a newly abandoned property. I don't expect miracles in a week, though."

"Gil might."

"Yeah, well, Gil can shove his ideas—" Luke cut himself off. "You know what? I can't really blame Gil. These vandalisms couldn't come a worse time. We're getting a lot of business interest, not to mention a run on real estate. The planning commission is poised to approve the new construction project, which means we're going to have a lot of new residents around here, a lot of them renters. The last thing we need is visible evidence of town dissatisfaction. We need to put a stop to it."

"Then, Oz, Matt and I will get it done," Fletch said. "Before you get back."

"I appreciate the confidence, but I won't hold you to it. What was that yesterday with Paige about Jasper?"

"Nothing I can't handle." Not that the conversation hadn't replayed in his mind all night. She seemed to have taken Jasper's situation so personally. "You know Paige. She's a crusader. She doesn't like the idea of Jasper being set up for something he might not have done."

"Yeah, well." Luke gestured to the folder in Fletch's hand. "She's not the only one. You've got his entire history right there. He's made bad choices in the past, but rarely anything serious. I hate to pile on, but it's not looking good for him, not with having found his school ID at one of the scenes. Maybe you should show Paige that information. Get her off your back. If you want to."

Fletch ignored the twitch of a grin on the sheriff's face. "A, no, I'm not going to show her the file because that would be a violation of my sworn duties, and B, I'm not sure her seeing it would make any difference. She's practically got the kid wearing wings and a halo."

"She sees the good in people, Fletch. I thought that was one of the things you like about her."

"I did." Until that optimism got in his way. "I told you not to worry. I'll deal with Paige and Jasper and get this case closed up tight enough that the mayor won't have anything to complain about. Sound good?"

"I'm not going to argue with anything at this point." Luke grinned. "You're in charge, Interim Sheriff."

"I can't even tell you how not funny that is," Fletch grumbled.

"You good to take care of Cash while we're gone?" He scrubbed the dog's fur and earned a chuffed snort in return.

"Yeah, we'll be fine." It would be nice having some company in that big empty house of his on the outskirts of town. "Prime rib and French fries okay for dinner, Cash?"

Cash's ears perked. *"Woof."*

"If it comes in kibble form, absolutely. I told Charlie she could come by and take him for a walk. Matt's out of town visiting Kyle in detention for the next couple of days. Remember, you can always call on Sheriff Brodie over in Durante if you get into a bind."

"Uh-huh." Fletch bit his tongue. Sean Brodie would be his last call when it came to anything. "Come on, man. Stop worrying. You've earned this time off." About a gazillion times over. "Leave this place behind for a few days."

"Yeah, okay. You're right. I'm due to pick Simon up around four, then we want to take him out to dinner to celebrate."

"Yesterday's celebration wasn't enough?" It certainly had been for Fletch, who could still feel the vestiges of the hangover threading through his skull.

"Ah, well, Holly and I are filing the adoption papers this afternoon." Luke's eyes shifted. "How's that for timing? Looks like I'm officially going to be a father."

"Try not to look so terrified." Fletch laughed in an attempt to ease the tension in his friend's face. "It's what you wanted, right? To be Simon's dad?"

"It is, yeah. Just sometimes hard to keep those ghosts where they belong, you know?" Luke shook his head, stopping short when he caught sight of the band of gold on his finger and looked to fall into some kind of trance. "Never thought I'd ever be living in this town again, let alone married with a kid. And a job I love despite the politics."

Fletch never thought he'd be envious of the town's onetime bad boy. Until Paige had hit town he'd never really entertained the notion of settling down. Now, every time he saw her—or Charlie—he had to stop himself from daydreaming about just that. "You paid your dues." Luke's past wasn't something that needed voicing. Surviving an abusive childhood, nearly killing Holly's father in a car accident that technically wasn't his fault, doing everything he could to break the circle of violence that had encompassed his life, there wasn't anyone Fletch admired more than Luke Saxon. "Now take off and enjoy yourself. We won't burn the place down. At least not without you."

"I'll drop Cash off here in the morning on our way out."

"When you get back we need to talk about the youth center hours for when school's back in session." With Jake Campbell out of town for a bit and Luke heading out, aside from two or three scheduled classes, the center would be closed most days.

"Writing that down right now." Luke scribbled on his desk calendar. "You up for lunch at the diner later?"

"Ah, no, actually." Fletch glanced at his

watch. "I'm going to get a jump start on patrol. Change up the timing so we aren't predictable. Plus I told Mrs. Hastings I'd stop in and install some new security locks for her."

Luke's brows knitted. "I'd say let me know how things go with Gil on Friday, but you know what? Never mind. I'll hear about it when I get home."

"I'm sure you will." Fletch would lay odds that within minutes of walking out of the mayor's office, whatever they discussed would be flying around town faster than a monarch out of hibernation.

CHAPTER FOUR

PAIGE CLICKED OPEN the latch of Mrs. Hastings's garden gate and steered her bike to the side of the porch. Lifting the box of fresh-baked scones out of the handlebar basket, her contribution to the weekly tea she and the elderly woman shared, Paige turned toward the front door as it flew open.

"Fletch." Paige couldn't keep the surprise out of her voice at the sight of the uniformed deputy. "What are you doing—" The question died on her lips as she registered the concern on his angular face. "What's wrong?"

"Paige." She couldn't remember hearing her name said with such relief before. "Would you stay with her while I call for an ambulance? Her phone's not working and I forgot my cell in the—"

"Told you once, I have no need for an ambulance, Fletcher Bradley." The strained, familiar aged voice echoed from inside the house over the shrill whistle of the teakettle.

"If I'd known you'd go all busybody on me, I'd have told you to forget those new locks and send you on your way."

"I'm a deputy," Fletch called over his shoulder. "Busybody is in the job description."

"What's going on?" Paige planted her hand on Fletch's chest and pushed past him. She found eighty-four-year-old Celeste Hastings sitting in her antique rocking chair, a shaky hand pressed against her chest, eyes closed. She wore one of her usual floral high-neck dresses, her silver-threaded dark hair pulled back from her face in much the way Paige figured she'd worn it when she'd been the elementary and then high school principal.

"She said she feels dizzy," Fletch said from behind her as Paige set her box down on the wooden coffee table that had been made by Mrs. Hastings's late husband. "She was definitely wobbly."

"*She* can speak for herself." Mrs. Hastings dragged her eyes open wide enough for Paige to see the slight glaze. "I was getting our tea ready and felt a bit faint." She aimed to pat the back of Paige's hand but missed by inches. "The water's hot."

"So I hear." Paige motioned for Fletch to

turn off the stove before she focused on her neighbor. "Mrs. Hastings, have you been taking your medication?" Paige shifted to one knee and angled her fingers around so she could feel the old woman's pulse. Fast and thready. Her skin was clammy, but not overly so.

"I keep forgetting," Mrs. Hastings grumbled. "Darned pills are a nuisance. Too many of them. Makes me feel like one of those candy dispensers at the grocery store."

"We talked about this, remember?" Paige scanned the room looking for the container of medication bottles Mrs. Hastings had insisted on maintaining herself. "Taking them on and off only makes you feel worse. Now, I'm going to get your kit and we're going to test your blood. Then we'll decide if you're going to the hospital or not."

When Mrs. Hastings nodded and closed her eyes again, Paige hurried into the kitchen and pulled open the cabinet over the sink. "Do you know if she passed out?" she asked Fletch.

"Not while I've been here. She seemed fine when she answered the door, then started to sway. I helped her to her chair."

"Deputy Hero," Paige said with a smile as

she scanned the medication bottles. "A fall would have made matters worse. You probably got here just in time." She found the daily pill organizers she'd purchased last week still in their packaging.

"Looks like you know what you're doing," Fletch said. "What's wrong with her?"

"Diabetes," Paige murmured. "And she has some blood pressure issues." Neither of which were helped by missed dosages.

"I can hear every word you're saying!" Mrs. Hastings called weakly.

"I'm sure you can. Where's your testing kit, Mrs. Hastings?" Paige asked.

"By my bed," was the response after a long sigh. "Darn thing makes my fingers hurt, and I can't crochet with hurt fingers. I've got blankets to make for the holiday bazaar. No time for aches and pains."

"I'll get it." Fletch disappeared out the second kitchen door and into the back bedroom.

"Nice young man," Mrs. Hastings told Paige as she pulled up a chair beside the older woman. "Always been a good boy, that Fletcher Bradley. Took good care of his sister growing up. And his grandpa. He'll make some young woman a nice husband."

"I'm sure he will." Paige hoped Mrs. Hastings kept her eyes closed long enough so as not to see the blush in Paige's cheeks. The last thing she needed was for someone—especially this someone—playing matchmaker. "I thought we had a deal. I come for tea once a week and you take your medicine."

"I'm an old woman. I forget things."

"Old I'll give you, but your memory is just fine." Paige opened one of the bottles and dumped the pills into her palm. A quick count had her own heart jumping double time. Frustration bubbled in Paige's blood. Mrs. Hastings hadn't taken her pills in almost a week.

"Here." Fletch approached from behind, handing the black bag over. Paige quickly opened it, readied the apparatus and clicked the springed needle against the side of Mrs. Hastings's thumb.

"Ow." Mrs. Hastings jumped, her brows drawing together.

"You've been testing on the pads of your fingers again." Paige examined the faded black-and-blue marks. "You're supposed to test on the sides so it won't hurt after." She may as well have been talking to herself given the thinning of Mrs. Hastings's lips. When the readout blinked fifty, Paige's training kicked in. "Fletch, see if there's any orange juice in the fridge, please. If not, a soda or anything with high sugar in it."

"Yeah."

What Paige wouldn't give for a stethoscope or blood pressure cuff. She reached for the old woman's hand and took her pulse again, counting down the unending seconds until she felt a steadier beat.

"Here." Fletch handed her a glass of orange juice. "Should I call the ambulance?"

"That depends." Paige urged Mrs. Hastings to drink. "Let's give this a few minutes and see how she feels. Okay? Nice and slow. There you go." She smoothed Mrs. Hastings's hair back from her face.

Mrs. Hastings nodded, her trembling hands taking the glass from Paige as she did as she was told.

Paige set the medications out on the table and filled the organizer, something she should have done in the first place.

"Your hovering isn't going to make me feel any better, young man," Mrs. Hastings said in a stronger tone. "You go fix my locks like you said you would."

"Ma'am." Fletch nodded but stepped back to look at Paige, who added her own gesture of encouragement as the concern melted from his gaze.

"I'll call if we need you." Paige pulled Mrs. Hastings's free hand toward her and dropped today's pills into her wrinkled palm. "Take them, please."

"Don't need a babysitter."

"Apparently you do," Paige said with a forced lightness of tone. Dealing with elderly patients took care and patience. Fighting them did no good and often created more problems than solutions. "I think you did this just to get me back here more frequently."

Mrs. Hastings smirked, opened her now-clear eyes. "You have enough on your plate without worrying about an old woman."

"I'm not worrying about an old woman— I'm worrying about my friend. Besides, Charlie would never forgive me if something happened to you. She loves coming here. Now take them, please." She watched, satisfied when Mrs. Hastings followed instructions. "I'm going to go into the kitchen to finish fixing our tea. And if you're feeling better in a few minutes, I'll bring you one of the blueberry scones Charlie helped me bake yesterday."

"Would be nice to see your Charlie again.

You're a good girl, Paige." Mrs. Hastings caught hold of her hand as Paige got up. "I'm sorry to be such a bother."

"You're nothing of the sort. Now, you just rest and I'll be back in a bit." Paige returned to the kitchen and turned the kettle back on, sparing a glance over her shoulder to Fletch as he replaced the dead bolt on the back door. "It's a good thing you were here."

"Looks like." Fletch shook his head. "Reminds me of my grandfather. They can seem so…"

"Fragile." Paige nodded. "Yeah, I know."

"You were very good with her."

"I've had some experience with patie— um, situations like hers." Paige bit the inside of her cheek and reminded herself to choose her words more carefully. "An elderly neighbor, where we lived before, had similar issues. Charlie and I used to check on her." Had it really been over a year since she'd seen or spoken to Mrs. Brennan? Paige could only hope one of her grandchildren had stepped up to oversee her care.

"I think that's the first time I've heard you talk about your past." Fletch angled his screwdriver differently to pop the old lock off. "So much for my theory you and Charlie sprung out of someone's flower bed."

"I'm not one to dwell on what happened before." Paige's heart jumped in her chest. She spent most of her down hours doing just that. Could she be around the man for more than five minutes without lying? "How are you doing, Mrs. Hastings?" she called over her shoulder.

"I'm not feeling *fragile*, if that's what you're worrying about."

Paige chuckled. Yeah, Mrs. Hastings wouldn't be needing a ride to the hospital today.

"Fletch, I expect you to stay for tea once you're done with those locks," Mrs. Hastings called.

Fletch's cheeks went red. "Yes, ma'am."

"I'm not sure I've ever seen this side of you before." Nor had Paige ever seen him look so uncomfortable or out of his element. She found it more charming than she expected.

"Once my high school principal, always my high school principal." He bent down to retrieve the new lock and screw it into place. "I swear, I step foot inside this house and I'm a teenager again."

Paige poured the hot water into the teapot

to warm it before brewing—a lesson she'd received on her first visit a few months before. "It's a nice problem to have." She rose up on her toes to look out into the overgrown yard and spotted a collection of tools resting against the side of the house she didn't remember seeing before. "Mrs. Hastings, have you been doing yard work?"

"Isn't going to get done on its own. Stop snooping on me."

Fletch leaned out the back door for a quick look, then shook his head.

"I hate weeds!" Mrs. Hastings announced.

"Right. Weed hater. Adding that to the list." Paige pulled out her phone and tapped open her calendar, looking through for a spare few hours. "I get off from the diner early on Thursday, Mrs. Hastings. I can bring you an early dinner if you'd like." And while she was there she could tackle some of that yard work.

"I don't want to be a bother," Mrs. Hastings repeated after a long hesitation.

"If it were a bother, I wouldn't offer." Paige added it to her schedule, avoiding Fletch's curious look.

"I do like Ursula's club sandwich," came Mrs. Hastings's reply.

"Who doesn't?" Fletch said as he closed up, tested and locked the back door. "One down, two to go. Hold that tea for me, will you? I'll just do the shed and then the front door."

"Sure, yeah, okay." Paige watched him trudge through the overgrown grass and weeds on his way to the rusted-out storage shed in the backyard as she pulled out a third dainty flower-painted teacup and arranged it on the tray beside the other two. "Deputy Fletcher does tea. Who knew?"

"I APPRECIATE YOU not bringing up Jasper or the break-ins while we were in there," Fletch said a little over an hour later as he and Paige walked down Mrs. Hastings's front steps. "She's already worked up enough reading about them in the paper."

"A lot of people are." Paige retrieved her bike and walked beside him. "I hear plenty of them talking about it at the diner. I don't suppose you've changed your mind about Jasper."

"Contrary to what you might think, and the fact we did find evidence of his presence at one of the houses, I haven't declared him guilty, Paige. But I would like to find him and talk to him." Fletcher glanced at her. "Don't suppose you have any idea where he might be."

"No." She visibly swallowed and flinched. "Why would I know?"

Why would she, indeed? But it was clear she was hiding something. "I'm going to take another walk through the houses, check over the notes again. See if there might be something else we missed the first time."

"Well, that's something, I suppose. You made Mrs. Hastings happy, staying for tea."

"I try to make everyone happy." Fletch hid his disappointment at not being given more credit for taking her suggestion and looking for answers beyond Jasper. "You really were good with her. Put her at ease, got her numbers stable." With her blood sugar level, they'd gotten their charge settled in her room, an afternoon talk show on the TV, her latest crocheting project across her lap and a fresh-brewed pot of tea on the table beside her. "Am I wrong in thinking there's more to your story than an old neighbor with similar issues?"

"If I tell you will you let me help you with Jasper?"

He chuckled. "No."

Paige glared at him, and when he glanced

down, he saw her knuckles whiten around the handles of her bike. "Huh. Well, you're honest at least." She swung a leg over the bar, but Fletch darted out in front, grabbed hold of the bike and kept her in place. She arched a challenging brow at him. "Mind telling me what all this new determination about the case is about? Why can't it wait until Luke gets back?"

"Because it can't." Fletch clenched his jaw. He should just tell her the truth, that he needed to get his case closed if Luke was going to keep his job, but that would just open up a whole other avenue of questions…and probably send Paige down the warpath to City Hall.

Not even Mayor Gil Hamilton deserved to be on Paige Cooper's hit list.

"How about you tell me how you first started having tea with Mrs. Hastings?" If he couldn't get her to open up the direct way, he was happy to take the long way around.

Paige planted her backside on the seat, her feet on the ground, and looked at him. Before she turned to gaze at the house across from Mrs. Hastings. "She caught me daydreaming in the yard over there."

"I wouldn't have thought you left much

time for daydreaming. What do you dream about, exactly?"

"A lot of things. But mainly this house." Paige climbed off and tugged the bike from his grasp. She walked over to the sidewalk where a faded For Sale sign peeked out of a substantial growth of wildflowers blanketing the front yard of the bright yellow Tudor-style cottage. A weathered white trellis stretched up one side of the exterior and cascaded over with explosive red geranium blooms determined to see the end of summer in full glory.

"The day Charlie and I arrived, we took a walk up this way," Paige told him. "We were staying at the Chrysalis Motel at the time."

"I remember." Not the nicest motel in the area; but not the worst. "You made quite the impression helping Holly the way you did in the diner." There wasn't a lot Fletch didn't know about Paige's time in town since she and Charlie had arrived. But before? That was another story.

"Charlie fell in love with this house from the get-go." Paige tucked an imaginary loose strand of hair behind her ear and glanced up then down the street accented by an occasional parked car. "Once Holly hired me I started coming here on my lunch break. I'd just sit in the yard and listen to the silence."

"And the occasional seagull." Fletch glanced up as a pair of the feathered creatures squawked and circled overhead.

Paige smiled and followed his gaze. "I love that sound. Everything's so peaceful here. Like a sanctuary."

It wasn't often Fletch saw Paige in calm mode. She was always buzzing around town, doing something somewhere, never stopping long enough to take a substantial breath. But here? In front of this particular house she seemed to relax. And breathe. "So Butterfly Cottage caught your attention, did it?"

"Hmm." She pushed through the wooden gate and stood among the flora and fauna, looking as at home as a fairy in her garden. "That's what Mrs. Hastings called it, as well. I take it the name comes from the window over the front door?"

"It does indeed." Fletch had always loved the stained glass depicting a pair of brilliant monarch butterflies settling onto their eucalyptus branch. Almost as much as he liked the hand-carved door beneath it. His cell phone vibrated on his hip. He reached down, checked the message. Great. Another reported break-in. This time Everett White had called in to say his toolshed had been the target. Fletch mentally readjusted the next few hours of his day. "It's one of my favorite houses, too, actually," he admitted. "Is that what brings you back here? The window?"

"No. The For Sale sign." The second she said it he heard the regret, saw the way she bit her lip and looked away from him, closing her eyes against the sun. "I just like to know it's still available."

So much for him thinking Butterfly Harbor was a pit stop for her and Charlie. "You thinking of buying?"

"No." Her admission had the hope inflating inside him bursting like a bubble. "That would mean staying here permanently, and I'm not sure that's in the cards for us."

Paige confirming his suspicion only increased his disappointment. "But if you were to stay, this is the one you'd want."

"Yes." That she said it with a frown made him wonder if she'd thought about staying more than she was letting on.

"Because Charlie loves it?"

Ah, the frown vanished, replaced with that familiar heart-clenching smile of hers. "Because Charlie loves it. Speaking of Charlie, she said Luke gave her permission to walk Cash. I hope that's okay with you. I don't want her getting in the way of your…investigation."

"Charlie is welcome at the station anytime," Fletch told her. "If her mom doesn't mind."

"Even if I did I couldn't stop her. She's very fond of you, Deputy." And didn't Paige look positively thrilled at that idea.

"Fletch. And I'm pretty fond of her, too."

"We aren't staying," Paige said, and he could tell by her expression she hadn't meant to. "There will come a time we have to move on. So, I'd appreciate it if you didn't let her get too attached to…Cash."

Fletcher didn't miss a beat. "Consider… Cash…forewarned. Unless he can convince you otherwise. If it helps, I don't think you have a lot to worry about with this place being sold. The original owner's family has a say over who buys it. They want the right tenant, someone who will appreciate it as is. They won't sell it to just anyone."

"Why would anyone want to change it?" The wonder in her voice brought another smile to his face. "She's perfect."

"Yes, she is." But Fletch wasn't looking at the house. He was looking at her.

And closely enough to see the rise of pink in her cheeks before she locked down her face in that detached expression of hers that seemed specifically reserved for him. She returned to her bike, climbed on and looked at him over her shoulder. "I'm on my way to Nina and Willa's to look in on them. Is there anything you'd like me to ask them in particular?"

"Nice try." He recognized her baiting technique and refused to bite. "But give them my best. I know where to find them. And you, if I have any questions."

"I still think you're looking for something that isn't there."

"Maybe. Maybe not." Fletch could almost see the wall going up between them.

"As long as you're keeping an open mind." She offered that sarcastic closed-mouth smile and began to pedal her way down the hill. "We'll see who's right," she called. "Have a good day, Fletch."

CHAPTER FIVE

"Morning, sis." The next morning Fletch found his sister at her usual post behind the registration desk of the Flutterby Inn, tapping away on her desktop computer. "Everyone recovered from the wedding?" He didn't see a sign of the festivities hovering around the iconic three-story Victorian inn located on the highest hill in Butterfly Harbor. He'd worried as much as the rest of the town when a big hotel chain purchased the landmark property, but the new owners stayed true to their word—and the contract—that they would keep things as small-business minded and personal as possible. It didn't hurt they had a world-class chef heading up their state-of-the-art tourist-destination restaurant.

Lori held up her hand, tapped her ear and rolled her eyes. "Yes, Mrs. Flannigan. I can confirm we've adjusted your reservations back a day to accommodate your flight change. Your room will be ready as soon as you and Mr. Flannigan arrive." She nodded in that patient way she'd always had from when they were kids. "Yes, ma'am. Ocean-side tower room. I've made a special note. Yes, ma'am. We'll see you next week." When she disconnected she closed her eyes and took a long, deep breath. "You know you're ready for a break when you're anxious to get to a hotel manager conference."

"When do you leave?"

"Tomorrow afternoon. San Diego, here I come." Lori stood as one of the new front-of-house staff joined them. "I'm taking a coffee break, Alyssa. Mind the store?"

"Sure thing." The short dark-haired woman who looked as if she'd just leaped out of the pages of a storybook practically saluted. "Slow day today."

"It'll pick up once the school year gets into full swing. The mayor has booked a group of rooms for a few days. Some bigwigs having to do with the new construction contracts. Besides, we're running that September special, so we'll be plenty busy." Lori rounded the desk and motioned for Fletch to follow. "What brings you around here this time of day? Oh, wait. Let me guess." She gestured to the handwritten menu that changed daily and today boasted a Belgian waffle and poached egg special. "Flutterby Dreams breakfast?"

"How about you join me?"

Lori shook her head, her nutmeg-colored brown hair curling in waves around her shoulders. "I had my protein shake this morning. Only coffee and water until lunch."

Fletch refrained from commenting. His sister had battled her weight ever since…

He worked hard to stop himself from traveling down that depressing path. He could pinpoint the day her issues had begun; the same day his own childhood had ended. Given Lori's height, Fletch had always considered her a person with a larger physique, suggested it was something to embrace and accept, but her insecurities and self-deprecating humor kept her on one ridiculous diet after another. She was so pretty, her curves accentuated by her love of sweeping maxi-dresses, today's in shocking turquoise. No matter how Fletch approached the subject, he couldn't convince her she was perfect the way she was and that stressing over the weight only added to her struggle.

Then again, he'd never battled that particular demon, so what did he know? "Coffee it is, then." He followed her into the restaurant portion of the historic inn. Over the past month they'd done a major overhaul of both the exterior and interior of the Flutterby, modernizing where it made sense, letting the history shine through where it mattered most. The display of photographs showing the inn through its half-century-plus history was one of his favorite touches among the seafoam blues, greens and pristine whites that reminded him of the summer he and Lori had spent with their other grandparents back east. The summer before everything had changed.

Lori guided him through the smattering of guests enjoying their morning start and pointed to a small table by the window overlooking the ocean. "I'll check with Jason—"

"Are you taking my name in vain?" Jason slipped in behind her and set two cups of coffee on the table. "You're on a break, Lori. Take a full one. Fletch. How's it going?" They exchanged hearty handshakes.

"Can't complain." Much. He found himself smiling at the friendliness in the New York transplant's tone. Not so long ago Jason could have won an award for his less-than-amenable attitude. Amazing what falling in love with a terminal pixie like Abby Manning could do to a man. "You still working up your special today?"

"Waffles with fresh strawberries and a side of eggs from Calliope's farm," Jason said with an inordinate amount of pride. "If she had cows I'd be making my own whipped cream."

"Don't put ideas in Calliope's head." Duskywing Farm had enough going on with chickens, bees and more than the coast's fair share of butterflies, which always seemed to find someplace to nest on Calliope Jones's extensive and pesticide-free property. "I'm not up for taking mooing complaints."

Jason chuckled. "Lori, anything other than coffee?"

"No, thanks." Lori sighed and rested her chin in her hand. "I'm good."

"You taking up serving now as well as cooking?" Fletch asked.

"Necessary evil," Jason said with more than a cringe to his now-beardless face. "Matilda doesn't come on until nine, and Abby suggested I take more of an interest in those consuming my food. Keeps me on my toes."

Fletch laughed. "Sounds like Abby. You guys set a date for the wedding yet?"

"We need to recover from Holly and Luke's first. Depends on how Alice is doing," Jason added in reference to Abby's grandmother, who was in the early stages of Parkinson's. "We're hoping for spring, but we're keeping things fluid just to be safe. One breakfast special coming up."

Fletch found himself looking around the newly decorated restaurant, which was both elegant and welcoming at the same time. It was the perfect blend of modern and historic, continuing the homage to the past. This was one of the most picturesque spots in all of town, with the window seating booked out for special events and dinners far in advance.

He could appreciate the appeal, despite the hit his nerves took with the distant sound of crashing waves and rising tides. Fletch clenched his jaw and pushed through the unease and wished he could untie the knots in his stomach.

"So are you going to tell me what brought you by or do I get to guess?" Lori asked.

"Can't I just have breakfast with my sister?" At least conversation could be a distraction.

"Sure you can, you just don't very often." Lori's normally lively eyes turned serious. "What's going on? Have you heard from Mom or Dad?"

"No." A topic better avoided. "There's something I want to ask you, but I'm not sure how."

"Well, that doesn't sound suspicious at all. Go ahead."

Uncertain whether he was venturing into dangerous terrain, he took the plunge. "You and Matt have been seeing a lot of each other lately. How's that going?"

"Matt Knight?" She said his name as if he were a passing acquaintance, but the flush of color to her pale cheeks told a different story. "Yeah, I guess. It's not serious, if that's what you're wondering. We're…friends."

"That's all?" Those weren't the vibes he'd picked up from his fellow deputy, the army vet. "What's stopping you?"

The suspicion she rarely presented around him shot up like a force field. "What's stopping me from what? Who says there's anything to stop?"

"I was just wondering how you guys are doing as friends as opposed to…whatever else you might be." He really needed a personal Jiminy Cricket to tell him when to shut up.

"Whatever else…" She trailed off, inclined her head. "Please don't tell me this is the long-awaited big brother sex talk. I'm twenty-six years old, Fletch. Trust me, I'm well acquainted with the birds and bees."

Fletch gagged a little in his throat. He did not need to know that. "Yeah, great, no. That's not what this is about. Look, are you and Matt dating or not?"

"You're not allowed to have the *talk* with Matt either. We're friends, Fletch." She stirred a spoonful of chemical-laden sweetener into her coffee and nearly caused a tidal wave. "That's all."

"Exactly. But what does that entail? How do you become friends with someone you want more from?"

"Since when do you need help making friends with a…oh." Her attitude dropped and she smiled. Leaning her arms on the table, she grinned. "This is about Paige, isn't it? As Gramps would have said, you're smitten."

"Sometimes I swear you live in a 1950s sitcom. And yes, if you must know, this is about Paige. I'm interested, but the feeling isn't mutual." Especially now that she seemed to have declared war on him and his suspicions regarding Jasper O'Neill. Then again, maybe Paige had inadvertently given him the perfect excuse to keep bumping into her. "She acts differently around me than everyone else. I can't find anything to latch on to with her. I don't suppose you know much about her."

"You know." Lori looked at him as if she was trying not to laugh. "If you're really sneaky, you can pass a note to Holly in homeroom and she can ask Paige if she likes you, too."

"I'm serious, Lori." Although he couldn't help but chuckle. He did sound a bit…high school.

"I know what matters. She works hard, she's super-reliable and she's a great mom. Should be something there for you to, um, latch on to. Charlie especially. She's nuts about you."

The feeling was mutual. The kid was a spinning ball of positive energy that lit up his day with those crooked pigtails and wide-gapped smile of hers. "I'm not using Paige's daughter to get close to her. That's just wrong."

"Sometimes I think you're too good a guy, Fletcher Bradley. How about you stop trying so hard. Maybe then Paige will get over whatever it is she needs to get over and open up. If she wants to, that is."

So much for any answers from his sister.

"You women are really tricky, you know that? Tricky, frustrating and confusing."

"Yeah, I know." Lori smiled as Jason delivered Fletch's breakfast. "We all know."

"FOR THE LOVE of all that is right in this world, would the two of you leave already?"

Paige covered her mouth to stop from laughing at Ursula's frustrated order. The barely five-foot former navy cook who presided over the kitchen at the Butterfly Diner with an iron spatula waved a wooden spoon in Holly and Luke's direction as if landing a helicopter. "You're already a day behind on the honeymooning, so get your butts in the car and move it on out."

"Here." Paige handed over the padded picnic basket she and Charlie had put together earlier this morning. "Sandwiches, a thermos of soup, cookies and one of Charlie's special pies."

"Blackberry?" Luke reached out to pry open the lid only to have his wife slap his hand away. "I love blackberry pie."

"Which is why she made it for you. The, uh, crust might be a little overdone," Paige added in a whisper so Charlie wouldn't hear her. Not that her daughter was in earshot as she hovered over a spiral notebook that looked suspiciously like the ones Simon carried around as he plotted world domination. "But it was made with love."

"I kissed you for the first time after eating Charlie's blackberry pie." Luke wrapped his arm around Holly's waist and pulled her against him. "The kid helped change my life."

"She has the habit of doing that," Paige agreed. "But Ursula's right. You'd best get going. Abby and I have Simon covered. Cash all settled?"

"Already dropped him off at the station with Fletch," Luke said. "Feel free to call on him to get your canine fill. He's probably going to be whining a lot."

"Yeah, I'll do that." Paige shot a narrowed look at a suddenly innocent-looking Holly. "Twyla's cleared her schedule to be here every day, so all the shifts are covered. Go. Have fun. Relax."

"Okay, we're going. Bye, Charlie!" Holly called.

"Bye, Holly! Hey, Mom? Did you have any pets growing up?"

"Pets?" Paige almost got whiplash from the change of topic. When she was convinced Holly and Luke were actually on their way out of town, she approached her daughter. "No. I moved around too much. Why?" *Please, please don't tell me you want a puppy. Anything but a puppy.*

"No reason." Charlie shook her head before returning to her notebook. "Just wondering."

"What on earth are you doing?" Paige reached for the notebook, but Charlie snatched it against her chest. "This isn't more about those caves, is it? If you think a dog would help you, I'm sure Luke will loan you Cash." Thank goodness for surrogate pets.

"It's a quiz I found in a book. It's supposed to tell you who your perfect movie-star love match is. I wanted to see who yours is."

"I'm holding out for Clark Gable," Paige told her, longing for the nights she could spend curled up watching classic movies. "Mystery solved."

"Clark who?" Charlie's nose scrunched. "Is he related to Superman? I bet Simon knows who he is."

"Sure, yeah. Clark Gable is Superman's uncle," Paige fibbed. Ursula's order up bell clanged and shot Paige's attention back to work. "Just…keep doing what you're doing, okay? Are you planning to walk Cash today?"

"Uh-uh." Charlie shook her head. "Tomorrow."

Paige hesitated. She could feel them getting more entrenched in Butterfly Harbor with every day that passed. The nerves had returned, as they often did when Paige began to fear they'd stayed in one place too long, but school was about to start. She'd gone against her instincts and registered Charlie under her real name…and spent the next few days waiting, petrified, for law enforcement to come knocking on her door to haul her away in cuffs.

It had been weeks and still no knocks. Paige had just started breathing normally again.

Charlie had made so many connections here. Even with the two months looming over Paige's head, she couldn't help but take the chance that…maybe she was wrong when she told Fletch they wouldn't be staying. Maybe it was time, finally, for her to think about putting down some roots.

Besides, leaving would break her daughter's heart. What harm could crossing her fingers and hoping for the best do her for a change?

"Mama?" There it was. Charlie knew using

"mama" rather than "mom" tended to work magic on her. Also, spending time with the dog should stave off any vocal desire for her to get one of her own. "I can still walk Cash, right?"

"Definitely." She would have to find the time—and reason—to remind Charlie about what they could share with people about their past. "Just don't bother Fletch or Ozzy too much."

"'Kay. Oh, one more question. What is your perfect dinner date?" Charlie nibbled on the end of her pen like a determined reporter.

"My perfect—" Paige gave up. At least she'd stopped chattering about that hidden treasure and the ocean caves. "Lobster bisque and a midnight cruise on the ocean." Ha! As if that was ever going to happen. "Now, back into silent mode, Little Miss. I've got work to do."

"Okay. Thanks, Mom. You've been a big help."

Paige stumbled on the squeaky-clean tile floor on her way over to her latest customer. That statement probably shouldn't bother her as much as it did.

"Three mornings in a row." Paige poured coffee into the mug and offered a friendly smile to the amused-looking woman in the back booth. She had blunt-cut hair and stark porcelain skin, and she wore a beautiful tailored pantsuit in a shade of green that reminded Paige of Fletcher's all-too-knowing eyes. "That makes you a regular, which means introductions are in order. I'm Paige Cooper." She set the coffeepot down.

"Leah Ellis." The posh-looking woman held out her hand. "Attorney at law. That your little girl?" She looked pointedly at Charlie, who was back to scribbling in her notebook, so reminiscent of Simon Paige had to steady herself.

"Every precious inch of her." Paige smiled. "So you're a lawyer, huh? That's great news." Maybe this crossing-the-fingers thing had some merit after all.

"It is?"

"Well, I just learned our only other one moved out of town a while ago."

"Mmm-hmm. My uncle, actually. He's moving up in the world, so I'm taking over his practice." Leah sipped her coffee. "Okay, I don't know what blend this is, but I think I'm in love." She drank more deeply. "Definitely consider me a regular."

"So you're settling in, then? Same offices?"

"Just down the street from City Hall, yes." Leah's smile tightened. "I know that look. You're in need of a lawyer."

"Me? Oh, no, actually. I'm not." If Paige wasn't careful she was going to get struck by lightning any second. "I mean, I have a friend, no, really, I do." She laughed at Leah's smirk. "Her brother might be in a bit of trouble with the local sheriff, well, deputy, actually. I don't suppose you do any pro-bono work? They're going through a rough time financially."

"I do." Leah blinked. "But I'm afraid I'm not practicing criminal law any longer. If it's an emergency, please, feel free to give her my card. I'd be happy to make some recommendations." She dipped into her purse and handed a card to Paige. "Never too early to advertise. I'm specializing in family law from here on. Divorces, custody agreements, that kind of thing. Nothing exciting." And from her tone she hoped to keep it that way.

"Well, welcome to Butterfly Harbor, Leah. Would you like the same thing you've ordered before?"

"You remember?"

"Egg white omelet, two eggs, turkey sausage and side of wheat toast."

"Got it in one."

"Shouldn't take too long. And I'll keep that coffee coming." She moved off before she overstayed her welcome. Given Leah's thick briefcase on the seat beside her, she reckoned Leah had a few days' worth of work waiting for her. "Order up, Ursula!" She banged on the bell as she stuck the ticket on the counter.

"I hear ya, I hear ya." Ursula lumbered out of the walk-in deep freezer carrying a twenty-pound bag of flour. Why she kept it in the freezer Paige had yet to figure out. "Had to get my biscuit fixins."

"You get the butter already?" Paige knew her offer to help would get her a spatula across the back of her knuckles.

"In the back." Ursula grunted. "Get it if you want."

"I want, thanks." Paige unlatched the door and ducked inside, shivering as the cold hit her bare arms. It wasn't a large space, and Holly kept the freezer well organized. Since most of their produce came fresh from Duskywing Farm, they kept mostly perishable dairy and meat inside. Along with ice cream. Lots and lots of ice cream.

"Careful of the—"

Paige spun around at Ursula's warning just

as the door slammed shut behind her, leaving the buzzing of the solitary fluorescent bulb as her only companion. Darn it! Not again. Her breath fogged out in front of her. She located the block of butter and hightailed it back to the door just as Ursula pulled it open.

"How many times do I have to tell you to use this if you're going in?" Ursula kicked the rubber stop toward her. "It ain't there for decoration. One day I'm going to find your frozen bones in here."

"Yes, ma'am." She set the frozen butter on the metal counter where she knew Ursula would soon be making her famous buttermilk biscuits. "New lawyer in town. Leah Ellis." She joined Ursula at the grill top and stove and gestured to the back booth. "Taking over for her uncle."

"Heard some talk we'd be getting a fancy one from back east. Philadelphia, I think?" Ursula grinned. "Not that I pay much mind to gossip."

"Of course not." But Paige knew where to come for answers if she had questions. Ursula was as reliable as the Pony Express had been once upon a time. If what you needed was information. "Going to be a busy day. I have lunch orders for City Hall already coming in."

"Stack 'em and rack 'em. We'll get them taken care of. You get to hopping tables."

"On it." Paige had the sneaking suspicion Ursula wanted to be feared, but the truth was the old curmudgeon only inspired loyalty and amusement. Yes, indeed. It might just be time to start thinking about settling down once and for all.

CHAPTER SIX

"HEY, OZ?" FLETCH realized he wasn't going to find the file he'd been looking for the past five minutes. He waited for Oz to hang up the phone. "You have that list from Everett White about what he thinks was stolen from his shed while he was on vacation?"

"Right here." Oz riffled through the stack of files on his desk and brought it over to him. "That was Alice Manning. Said she saw something suspicious on her walk this morning over on Red Admiral Lane. Looks like we might have another break-in."

"Sure we do." Fletch glanced at the clock. Barely 10:00 a.m. Wednesday morning and he could already feel his day slipping deeper into a ditch. The week—and the time before Luke got back—was getting away from him. "Let's have the details."

Ozzy read off his notes. "Kyle Winters's parents' place. You want me to check it out?"

"No. I'll head over in a bit." Fletch sat back

in his chair, his chin resting on his fingers as he looked at the previous reports. "Not much damage that can be done. That makes four properties that we know of. All foreclosed on and abandoned."

Oz perched on the edge of Fletch's desk. "All these places were in pretty bad shape to start with. Seems odd to target them."

"Yeah. Tells me they must have something in common that we aren't seeing," Fletch said. "Let's pull up all the property records and check for any similar threads. And make a list of homes both here and in Durante that have been foreclosed on in the last year. Let's see what might be next."

"It'll take a call to City Hall to get everything you're looking for."

"That's fine. Feel free to tell whomever you speak with it's in reference to the break-ins. Might light a fire under the mayor's chair." Something Fletch might be able to use to his advantage at Friday's meeting.

Ozzy grinned. "Good idea. You know, it's weird. If it didn't affect him personally, I'd think Kyle Winters was up to his old tricks. But we both know that's not possible."

"True." But thinking about the troubled kid did give Fletch an idea. Kyle Winters, Butterfly Harbor's most recent notorious teenage delinquent, was in the middle of his sentence in juvenile detention fifty miles south. "But that doesn't mean he's completely out of the loop. Good thinking, Oz." Fletch picked up his phone and dialed Matt's cell.

Matt Knight answered in that typical devil-may-care tone of his. "Don't tell me you guys are lost without me. I go away for a few days—"

"We're doing just fine, thank you very much." Fletch rotated his half-filled coffee mug. "We had another break-in last night. Kyle's old place."

"Interesting. Moving closer to town." Matt's suddenly serious tone confirmed Fletch's suspicion. "You think whoever it is, is escalating things?"

"Maybe. I want to believe that it being Kyle's place is a coincidence, but he and Jasper used to hang out together." Fletch didn't believe in coincidences. "Look, this is going to sound bad, but do you think Kyle might have any idea who else other than Jasper might be behind this?" The silence that hung between them dragged. Fletch mentally kicked himself for letting Paige's voiced doubt seep into his head. "Maybe he can give us a place to start trying to track Jasper down. Or not. I know he's your foster kid and all."

"And for a minute there I thought you'd forgotten."

Being a foster parent was a role Matt—and Kyle—was still getting accustomed to. The last thing Fletch wanted to do was drive a wedge between them. But if Fletch was going to get this case closed and remove the target the mayor put on Luke's back, he had to use whatever he had at his disposal. "Kyle's the closest thing I've got to a lead at this point."

"He's only a kid, Fletch."

"He's a kid with a record for breaking and entering, vandalism, possession of a firearm—"

"And he's kept his nose clean ever since he went to JD," Matt snapped. "He hasn't had a lick of trouble while he's been serving his time."

"That doesn't mean the kids he used to hang out with aren't involved. It's an idea, Matt. Other than catching whoever this is red-handed, I don't have another thought, do you?"

After a long moment, Matt sighed. "Fine. I'll ask him what he thinks."

"Just feel him out about Jasper," Fletch

pushed. "Unless he throws some other names at you."

"I'm not asking him to snitch," Matt said. "Get that idea out of your head right now. I just got through talking to the administrator here, and Kyle's doing really well. So well they're talking about releasing him early. I'm not doing anything to jeopardize that. He needs to get back to his life, a good life, as soon as possible."

Fletch couldn't blame him. Given Kyle's seriously unstable upbringing—a violent, firearms-obsessed father whose illegal stash had gotten him—and nearly Luke—blown up a few months back, and an addict mother who disappeared soon after—Kyle Winters was pretty much all alone in the world. Or he had been until both Luke and Matt took him under their respective wings.

"You know what, never mind," Fletch said. "You're right. It's not worth bringing all that up with him. Forget I mentioned it."

"Yeah, like that'll happen. I'll play it by ear tonight when I see him," Matt said. "I've got some personal things to see to, but I'll be back in the office tomorrow morning. Maybe with some answers."

"Sounds good. Drive safe." Fletch hung up before he had any more regrets.

"You planted the seed," Ozzy said before Fletch could defend his actions. "Isn't anything wrong with that."

"Let's hope not," Fletch said. For being a sheriff's deputy, he detested conflict. He pushed to his feet as the door swung open and Paige strode inside. Speaking of conflict...

"Morning, Acting Sheriff." Paige's long ponytail swung with just as much attitude as she did. That she aimed that overly bright smile in his direction told him she wanted something. "I'm here to talk about Jasper O'Neill. You have a few minutes?"

"I was just on my way out, actually." Never had Fletch been so grateful to have to go to a potential crime scene. He grabbed his baseball cap and jacket. "We have a report of another break-in."

"Great. Charlie's at the community center, and I've got some time before I need to be back at the diner. I'll tag along." She jumped back as he approached the door.

"No, you won't." Irony of ironies, it hadn't been so long ago he'd looked for any excuse to spend time with Paige. With a new scene to look at, he wasn't about to take a chance with Paige's safety. Or his sanity. "I don't know how long it's going to take me, and I don't have time to schlep you around town."

"Good thing I have my bike." She followed him outside, picked up her bike from where it leaned against the side of the station and pushed it over to his SUV. "Put it in the back. I'll leave when I need to."

Fletch yanked open his door. "If you have information on Jasper, tell Ozzy. He'll write it down and leave it for me to look at when I get back."

"Or maybe you could use a second pair of eyes to look for something that might exonerate an innocent boy."

"This is a police matter, Paige. I don't care how concerned a citizen you are, you're not coming with me."

"Well, then you have a choice. You can either take me with you or I can follow you and we can continue this conversation at your destination. I seem to recall hearing Oscar talking about Red Admiral Lane while he had his breakfast."

"You taken to eavesdropping on your customers, Paige?" He should have known their elderly town barbecue master would already have the inside scoop on the goings-on before

Fletch had gotten word. That Cocoon Club Oscar belonged to—a collection of some of the town's more elderly and eccentric residents—seemed to be more active than usual these days. Just what they needed, a geriatric neighborhood watch.

"You're stalling, Deputy. We could be halfway there already. Now, help me put this bike in the back."

Because he suspected she'd figure a way to pop the lock if he didn't disengage it, he hit the button on his fob and followed her around the back of the SUV. When she bent down to lift it, he stopped her by placing his hands over hers. He shook his head. "What's this all about, Paige? Why do you care so much?"

"Because I do." She shrugged but avoided his gaze. "What does it matter why?"

"You've spent most of the time since you got to town avoiding me like the plague. Now I can't seem to shake you. But I'm onto you. You're hiding something."

"Everyone has secrets." Her hands went tight under his, and where he might have expected a different woman to pull back, to even shrink away, she straightened and faced him eye to eye, or rather eye to throat. "I don't think you're giving him a fair chance."

"And what business is that of yours? We aren't going to do anything to make this more difficult on Nina or Willa."

"Maybe I just need to be convinced."

"You really don't think much of me at all, do you?" Exactly what did she have against him? What had he ever done to her? "Don't you have enough going on in your life without taking on a lost cause?"

"No child is a lost cause," she snapped and made Fletch wish he'd rethought his choice of words. "And that attitude right there—" she poked a finger at his chest "—is why I'm going to see this through. Consider me your personal oversight committee."

"You know, not so long ago that would have been music to my ears." He inched down, just far enough to put them nose to nose. He could feel her breath, hot, determined, tinged with anger and frustration, brush against his face. "Tell you what. You want to tag along? Great. Tell me one thing about you I don't know, Paige. Trust me with one tiny tidbit of information about your life before you came to Butterfly Harbor." He'd never been prone to bribery, but then again, he'd never encountered a woman like Paige Cooper before.

Her eyes narrowed. Her brow furrowed. "What possible point—"

"It's called trust, Paige. I don't work with people I can't trust, and so far you've given me nothing to work with. Open the door, just a little, and let me in." He released her hands and took a step away. "Or you can climb on your bike and head on back to the diner." He could all but see her trembling with uncertainty. The longer the silence stretched, the harder she gnawed on her upper lip, the clearer the picture became, and for an instant he regretted pushing her. He'd been wrong. She wasn't only hiding from something. "You're running from something."

She jerked, hard enough that he knew he'd landed the answer in one guess. "Everyone has a past."

Now, that he couldn't argue with. "Have it your way." He reached up and grabbed the edge of the trunk to close it.

"Okay, you win." She hesitated and, for an instant when Fletch saw a flash of panic in her eyes, he wanted to apologize. "I married Charlie's father when I was eighteen. He died before she was born. There." She picked up her bike and slammed it in front of him, barely missing his toes. "I was a nineteen-year-old single mother. Is that enough sharing for one day? Did I pay your price of admission?"

"Today's price, yes. Thank you." But as he loaded her bike into his car, his heart twisted at the idea of Paige all alone in the world with a baby to care for. But she'd done it. On her own. With little help, he guessed. No wonder she had trust issues. "We'll talk about tomorrow's then. Hop in, Paige. Let's go."

BRADLEY FLETCHER MIGHT be considered many things in this town: deputy, good neighbor, reliable hometown boy. But as far as Paige was concerned, he was the quicksand of men. The more she struggled to stay away from him, the deeper she sank.

Paige climbed out of his car in front of Kyle Winters's house and followed Fletch up the overgrown, uneven brick walk to the front door. The air smelled stale, as if even it understood the trouble that had taken place inside these walls. The front door stood ajar thanks to a busted dead bolt and torn-up frame; the siding sagged and where the paint wasn't peeling, it was long gone. Fletch held out his hand as he placed his other palm against the hilt of his pistol.

"Hang back out here while I do a quick check, okay?"

She could tell by his stern expression he expected her to argue, but there were some chances even Paige wasn't willing to take. "Yeah, that's fine." She reached up and tightened her ponytail as he disappeared inside.

Judging by the front yard, from the broken wooden fence to the rough-and-tumble weeds, the Winters' property appeared as neglected as Kyle had been. She didn't know a lot about the family's history, but she'd gleaned enough over the last couple of months to know Kyle had been sent down a dangerous path. Her breath hitched in her chest. The same path Jasper O'Neill was walking? How was that possible when he had a family that loved him?

Guilty or not, her brief check-in with Willa yesterday afternoon hadn't done anything but convince Paige someone needed to be Jasper's voice. Paige didn't want to push his sister, not with Willa neck-deep in plans for transporting Nina to San Francisco in the coming days. They would be back in time for Maisey to begin school, but it wasn't a trip Paige would wish on anyone. How great would it be if, by the time Nina and Willa returned, Paige could tell them the situation with Jasper had been resolved? Now all she had to hope was that the most recent break-in would push Fletch in a different direction from Jasper O'Neill.

She could hear Fletch walking around inside the house. The floorboards creaked. Doors opened and closed. When he returned to the front door, she saw he'd pulled on a pair of black latex gloves. His face was tight as if he was struggling to hold on to his temper.

"It's okay. You can come in. But please don't touch anything."

"How bad is it?" The question echoed down the empty hall as she stepped inside.

"More sad than bad."

Paige had to agree. The bare furnishings that were left had definitely seen better days. The ripped, fabric-covered sofa sagged in the corner of the living room. A warped stand that at one time must have held a television looked as if it had been dragged out of a bomb shelter. Drapes hung in even tatters on each side of the large window. Huge splinters stuck out and up on the staircase leading up to the second floor. Everything looked so...dark.

A pair of green spray paint cans sat abandoned on the floor. Beside them lay a two-by-four, a pair of rusty nails sticking out of one end and a dark stain on the edge.

Her head spun, sending her back to those uneven days of her childhood when she didn't know whose home she'd end up in; what kind of people she'd be living with. Compared with some, this place was a monstrosity. Compared with others?

Paige shivered.

This would have been a palace.

"Poor kid." Paige swallowed around the lump of sympathy. "This couldn't have been fun for him to grow up in."

"It wasn't. Matt and Luke came in with Kyle before he began serving his sentence." Fletch flicked the light switch to no effect. "They took everything Kyle wanted and moved it all over to Matt's place. Not that there was much worth salvaging. Power's been out for a while. Matt gutted the place as far as perishables and anything that might be of value to anyone. The bank just started foreclosure proceedings."

"That seems to be what Hamilton Bank excels in." Even if she used a bank she wouldn't have chosen Hamilton. Paige wandered over to the mantel, where, if she'd been fortunate enough to live in a house like this, she'd have umpteen framed photographs of every stage of her daughter's life. What she wouldn't give to be able to do that and know they could stay there as long as she wanted. "Kyle's mom take off for good?"

"So it seems." Fletch kept his back to her. "Luke has a standing call in to all the surrounding sheriff's offices in case of any, well... In case she turns up. She's an addict. Chances are she will. In some capacity."

"I'm a big girl, Fletch," Paige said. "I've seen a lot, but this is...sad."

Fletch glanced over his shoulder at her. Even in the dim light, she saw him frown. "Even when Kyle was at his worst, I couldn't help but feel sorry for him. What chance does a kid have when he comes from this?"

"Whatever chance people will give him," Paige said. "Writing him off was one of the worst things any of you could have done. Luke knew that. He stood up for him. Got a bottle cracked over his skull because of it if memory serves, but what he did showed Kyle he had value to someone. He turned the corner."

"It's probably why this thing with Jasper pushes all my buttons. He's got it made by comparison. A family who loves him, someplace safe and secure to live—"

"A father who promised to be there and then walked out on all of them," Paige interrupted. "He's angry, Fletch. He was betrayed. It shapes a person. Doesn't mean he's responsible for all this."

"I wouldn't be so sure." Fletch crooked his finger at her and backed up toward the doorway behind him. "Come with me."

Paige followed, resisting the urge to hug her arms around her torso to keep the sudden chill off her skin as she entered the kitchen. Fletch bent down and picked up what looked like a thick marker off the floor. He looked up at her, held it out. "EpiPen for allergies." He turned it in his hand. "Jasper's name is on it. Dated a week ago." He shook it. "Empty. He's used it. He's been here. Recently."

"Willa said he has a peanut allergy." She reached out for it, but Fletch pulled out an evidence bag and dropped it inside. "I can call her and see how many he might have with him. He can't be without one, not when so many things can set off a reaction." She pulled out her cell phone and turned on her flashlight app, aimed it around the room. "Here we go." She found a knocked-over box of cereal bars on the back counter. "Processed in a facility with nuts. This could have caused him some problems."

"We'll check with the pharmacy, see if he's come in to have the prescription refilled."

"What would he have been doing here?" She looked around, and only then did she realize what she didn't see. "Wait a second. Didn't the break-ins include vandalism?"

"They took spray paint to the walls and floors. Ripped off cabinets, doors, hammer holes in the walls. Pretty destructive."

"Well, I saw cans of paint." Paige wandered back into the living room. "But not that they were used." And there wasn't a sign of any other damage like Fletch described. She headed upstairs. The bedrooms sat as bare and vacant as the lower level. The rusted and stained bathroom almost made her gag. The door at the end of the hall, however, caught her attention. With the stickers and signs, she knew it was Kyle's room. "Fletch?" She turned the knob and began to push open the door.

"What are you doing?" Fletch grabbed her arm and spun her back, his hand back on his gun. "You shouldn't be opening doors when you don't know what's behind them."

She tried to breathe, but Fletch was so close, his body pressed almost against hers as he stretched out a protective arm between her and whatever might be inside.

She licked her suddenly dry lips, pushed up her chin to look at him and collided with those solid, penetrating green eyes of his. If she tried, she could feel his heart beating against hers. "I think what's behind this door is Jasper's sanctuary. Or was. He's not here, Fletch. He's gone."

Fletch finished pushing open the door, released her and moved inside.

Paige stayed back, not because he'd have ordered her to, but because being so close to Fletch unsettled her. Unnerved her. Okay, Fletch flat out scared her. Not because he was a cop. Not because he could upend her life with the wrong question at the wrong time. No, he scared her because, for those few seconds, she didn't care how much of a threat he was.

She hadn't wanted to move away.

"You're right," Fletch called. "He's not here, but I think he might be hurt."

"Hurt how?" Paige shot through to the other room, taking brief notice of the huddled blanket on the mattress on the floor, the ripped posters and pictures on the wall. Around the corner she found Fletch in a small bathroom, red-stained towels hanging over the edge of the rusted sink and dumped in the trash can. Her heart skipped a beat. At no time did she actually consider Jasper might be in danger. Trouble, yes, but… "That piece of wood downstairs, by the cans of paint. There was something on it. Blood, maybe?"

She yanked a pen out of Fletch's front shirt pocket and moved one of the blood-soaked towels around. "Here. Looks like the bleeding stopped. Or he got it patched up well enough to move." She leaned over and saw a bunch of small bandage wrappers in the wastepaper basket. "Something else to check with the pharmacy about. He might have had to buy bandages and antiseptic. Whatever is going on with Jasper, I don't think it's what you've been thinking, Fletch. He's running. Going where he thinks he'll be safe. Maybe…" She trailed off.

"Maybe what?"

"Willa told me in confidence Jasper hasn't been home since Luke spoke with him. Before now, it's been a couple of days, no more. For the last week, there's been no sign of him. No calls. Nothing. Not to mention Willa and

Nina live all the way across town. Why would he come here of all places? This isn't about him being guilty of something, Fletch. This is someone who's running scared." Seriously scared. And for a kid like Jasper O'Neill, with few places to go and even fewer people to count on, he'd be running out of options.

"How do you know all this?" Fletch bent down beside her, took back his pen before he reached out and grabbed hold of her hand. "Paige?" He gripped her tight, urging her to look at him as she fought back the shadows of her past. "How do you know?"

"Because." For once in her life, she couldn't hide the truth. She knew it was written all over her face. If she didn't confide something, it would only pique Fletcher's curiosity, and that she couldn't have. She cleared her throat and…trusted. "Because it's what I would have done." She pushed to her feet and backed out of the room. "We need to find him, Fletch. We have to help him. Before this goes very, very wrong."

CHAPTER SEVEN

BY THE TIME Fletch followed Paige outside, she'd reclaimed her bike from the back of his SUV and was pedaling down the street.

He stood there, evidence bags in hand, feeling as if he'd missed whatever train she'd jumped on. Should he go after her? For the second time in as many days, she'd uttered some cryptic declaration that lodged like cement in his thoughts. "She really needs to stop saying things like that."

Fletch watched her disappear around the corner and, listening to the better angel of his nature, let her go. She'd open up if and when she was ready. He'd gotten two admissions out of her, meager as they were, in a relatively short amount of time. It wouldn't take more than another bit of a push to open the door further.

She had managed to convince him of one thing: Jasper wasn't the only one in trouble in Butterfly Harbor.

"One problem at a time." Mumbling to himself, he retrieved his camera from the car and returned to the house to take pictures and close up as best he could. When he was driving away, he called Ozzy back at the station. "Hey, Oz. I've got another stop I want to make before I head in. You want to check with Brad Naylor over at the pharmacy and see if he's filled any prescriptions for Jasper O'Neill in the last couple of days? And let's put out the call to all the local businesses, see if anyone's seen him in town lately. Also check with Harvey and get a list of everyone who's bought spray paint since Luke instituted the mandatory ID check."

"Sure thing. You onto something?"

"Maybe. I want to go back and check the other houses again." Something about the fact those full paint cans hadn't been used bothered him. "Call my cell if you need anything."

"Will do."

By the time Fletch pulled his SUV into the cul-de-sac on Bud Spring Way, he'd replayed those moments with Paige in the bathroom more than a dozen times. In so many ways she was one of the most open people he'd ever met; when it came to helping others at least. But for those few moments, watching her fall into something that she clearly hadn't completely set aside from her past, all he'd wanted to do was reach out, hold her and tell her everything was going to be all right.

Whatever was going on, she had to trust someone sometime. Fletch was going to make sure it was him.

He eyed the house on the left that had been the vandal's second target. The small one-story structure didn't look any worse than the other abandoned homes in the area, only two of which were still occupied. It was hard to say whether the broken windows, plywood door and scarred stucco were the result of wanton destruction or neglect. Just like the property now being considered for the new butterfly sanctuary, this section of town was barely hanging on.

That some residents had survived the economic freefall of Butterfly Harbor was the only reason the break-in had been reported. This part of town had been hardest hit as it tended to be occupied by lower-income families. Families that had lived on hope for loan forgiveness or, at the very least, understanding or compassion.

Neither of which Hamilton Bank or its

CFO—Gil's late father—had extended to its property owners. Having to issue eviction notices on behalf of the financial institution had been one of those life-defining moments for Fletch. He'd come within minutes of resigning only to be pulled back from the edge by Jake Campbell, the then sheriff, who ended up issuing the notices himself.

Fletch had wanted to be a cop in Butterfly Harbor from the minute he'd arrived in town. He'd been determined to save people, help people wherever he could. He'd become a cop to do good. What he didn't want was to be the one responsible for ending people's lives as they knew it.

Yes, Fletch had taken an oath to uphold the law. But there was the law and then there was the right thing to do. It wasn't that Fletch hadn't understood the tenants weren't making their payments. What he'd been unable to fathom was, when there was no one waiting to move in and pick up the financial shortfall, people were being forced out.

His doubts had been proved right after it was revealed the bank in question had been ready to fold. By the time the smoke cleared, all the tenants had left, the properties became part of the bank's assets and Gil Hamilton's father was six feet under in Butterfly Harbor cemetery. Cause of death? Undetermined.

Not so long ago the entirety of Butterfly Harbor had been brimming with families, homes filled with laughter and busy lives. It would be again; slowly. Fletch couldn't wait to see it come all the way back to life.

For now, it was as if this portion of town was stuck three years in the past; nothing had changed except for the weathering of siding and shutters. As far as Fletch knew, the bank had few if any plans to fix up the homes, which left the owners who did still live here to deal with plummeting property values and safety issues. No wonder Fletch was hearing new rumblings about another round of exoduses even as the public campaign to bring in new residents got under way.

Fletch flipped through the photographs Luke had taken over the last couple of weeks. Trash cluttered the front walk and weed-infested overgrown lawn. No one could say when the green and red spray-painted accents had made an appearance, but whoever had tagged the property certainly needed some grammar and spelling lessons.

Feeling closed in, Fletch left the SUV. He compared the pictures with what he saw now.

By the side of the house a rusted gate swung in the gentle sea breeze. The jagged glass that remained in window frames was clearly a hazard. Fletch made a mental note to come back out and board them up. Not that that would stop anyone from venturing inside should the desire arise.

He pushed a finger against the side door. His boots crunched in glass. The stained linoleum and dank smell told him this property wasn't anywhere near salvageable. Better to knock the whole building down and start again. He'd bet half a year's salary that's exactly what Gil Hamilton had in mind.

He stepped into the kitchen and ignored the rat droppings and filth-caked counters. A worn kitchen table and mismatched chairs were situated as if the owners had left mid-meal. Cabinet doors sagged, the ancient refrigerator listed. How many other houses had suffered this same fate?

How many other homes had given up hope of being saved?

Fletch set the photos on the table and checked out the two small bedrooms in the back of the house. The living room had a nice stone fireplace, but the wood-paneled walls were warped. When he turned toward the kitchen again, he spotted the giant dollar sign, an odd quirk at the end of the lines before a thick red X sliced through it. He tapped his finger against the paint. Dry. No after-fumes. No one had been back.

Fletch returned to the pictures, checked the first house. There. First floor, living room wall. Smaller this time, almost timid as if whoever had painted them had almost been afraid they'd be seen. He squinted. Yeah. Same dollar signs. And he'd bet the same paint. It was a pattern. A small one, but a pattern nonetheless. With the same line quirk.

He tapped open his phone, checked on the pictures he'd taken at Kyle's house. No paint. Only the cans.

Fletch frowned. "Did you interrupt them, kid? Or did someone stop you?" He straightened, an entirely new scenario playing out in his head. Is that who Jasper was hiding from? The people who really were responsible for the vandalism?

"But why these homes?" Fletch gathered up the photos and headed back outside. He stood on the edge of the property line, scanned the other half dozen houses. Phone out, camera on, he dropped the pictures back in the truck and followed his gut. He headed in to check the rest of the homes.

Twenty minutes later he was walking back into the station. He hung up his jacket and hat, tossed his keys on his desk. "Any word on those property records, Oz?"

"Records clerk is out sick." Oz set his soda can down and coughed. "The mayor's assistant told me she'd let me know as soon as I could pick them up. Might be a few days."

"Great." Just as it seemed he was making some kind of progress. "How about Jasper's prescriptions? Anything there?"

"Last time they were filled was six days ago. Willa picked them up."

"Willa?" But Paige told him just a while ago that Willa hadn't seen or spoken to Jasper in over a week. How would she have known to refill his medication? "I've got some items we need to send to the lab for prints. You good to take them tomorrow?"

"You bet." As much as Ozzy liked his computer work, he was always anxious for something different to do. "I've got this." He grabbed at the phone when it rang.

Fletch pointed to the evidence bags to let Ozzy know he'd be stashing them in the gun safe in Luke's office. As soon as he returned to his desk, the door swung open and shut again. Until he saw the bounce of high red pigtails he hadn't realized who'd entered. "Charlie? That you?"

"Yep!" Charlie jumped up high enough for her big eyes to shine at him. "I came to walk Cash."

At the sound of his name, Cash shot to attention and let out his typical "that's me" whine.

"Thanks." Fletch waved. "Stay close to the station, okay? There's a ball he likes to chase by the door."

"'Kay. Come on, Cash." She bent down so Fletch could see her under the counter and patted her legs. "Let's go for a walk."

"Woof." Cash stopped long enough to shoot a questioning look at Fletch, who gave the golden retriever a quick nod. The sound of dog nails clacking against the wood floor echoed in the sheriff's station.

"Stay within eyesight, please," Fletch called before the door slammed. "You got something, Oz?" he asked when the deputy hung up.

"Not sure. Harvey's sending us copies of his paperwork on the spray paint. They had a run a few weeks back where he couldn't keep it in stock, but at least it's something to go through."

He picked up the list of missing items from Everett White's shed. "Or maybe someone got spooked and found a different way to get what they wanted." He set the paper down, tapped on the line. "How much you want to bet Haskins had red and green paint stored in there?"

"Elliot does a lot of woodworking around the holidays," Ozzy said.

Fletch fixed himself a cup of coffee. He loved the noise of a fresh-brewing cup even though he did prefer the special blend Holly served at the diner. The diner.

Fletch picked up his mug, sipped, considered. Went over to the window to look out on the parking lot. Thanks to Paige they had a solid lead on what was going on with Jasper. Maybe he needed to fill her in on their progress. Or maybe he was just looking for an excuse to see her again. "I don't see Charlie."

"I'm sure she's around," Ozzy mumbled.

"Yeah, but where?" He set his mug down on Ozzy's desk and headed to the door. "You up for some extra patrolling tonight? You take the beach stretch and I'll head inland?"

Maybe if they were lucky one of them would come across Jasper.

"Will do." Oz shrugged in his movie-sidekick kind of way. Ozzy had always been one of those blending-in kind of guys, not the sort you'd ever expect to go into law enforcement. "Not much else to do. Not like Butterfly Harbor is brimming with excitement in the off-season."

"True. And I'd like to keep it that way." Speaking of excitement. "I'm going to see where Charlie's gotten to."

The second he stepped outside, he knew she wasn't close by. He circled the lot, checked under his SUV, around Ozzy's rickety used sedan. He even looked up into the old cypress tree that was older than he was. "Charlie! Cash!" He lifted his fingers to his lips to whistle, but when all he heard was the breeze in his ears, he stopped. "Charlie!" He raised his voice, not liking the uneven pounding of his heart. "Charlie Cooper!"

His entire body went cold when he heard a distinctive squeal come from down the path to the beach.

The beach.

"Charlie!" He ran to the fence line and gripped the rough wood in his hands as he looked down. He spotted Charlie and Cash racing around each other in the sand at the bottom of the steep path, heading toward the sheer outcropping of rocks. Only feet away from the shoreline. "Charlie!" His voice cracked through the air but was carried away on the breeze. Heart jackhammering against his ribs, he took a shaky step down. His knees wobbled as he forced himself to descend the plank stairs. He stopped short of the sand. Try as he might, he couldn't make his feet move another inch. The idea of sinking into that sand, feeling it slip into his shoes and weigh him down…the blood drained from his face. His hands went cold. "Charlie!"

Her head snapped around and she sent a large stick soaring off into the water. Cash barked. Charlie giggled. Her backpack jostled back and forth as she raced after the stick and the dog.

The past roared louder in Fletch's ears than the crashing tide during a storm. He swayed and gripped the railing so hard his fingers went numb.

He couldn't move; he couldn't think. The sight of a jean-clad, neon-sneakered little girl transformed into a boy with missing front teeth, a too-big swimsuit and dark curls tight around his head. The image broke through the haze, through the fear, through the anger. "Charlie! Get over here. Now!"

Charlie darted into the water to retrieve Cash's stick before she raced back to him. She dropped her backpack on the sand as she stood in front of him.

"Sorry, Deputy Fletch." She panted, her feet and jeans soaked and picking up every granule of sand like a magnet. "I threw it too far and it landed down here and I think I found the caves where the treasure box..." She stopped, blinked up at him. "I was coming right back."

Fletch dropped down and grabbed hold of Charlie's arms, went nose to nose with her. "I told you to stay in sight. You should never come down to the beach alone. Never, ever, do you hear me, Caleb?" He didn't mean to scare her, but he leaned back as tears exploded into her big blue eyes.

"I'm sorry," she whispered. Cash moved in and nudged his head under her arm. "I didn't mean anything by it, I promise. I was just playing—who's Caleb?"

"What?" The name struck him like a slap.

Charlie took a step back. "You called me Caleb. I'm Charlie."

"I know who you are." Even as he said it, he felt the blood drain all the way to his toes. "Charlie. You should always, always pay attention around water." His tone harsh enough to scrub his throat raw. "Don't ever turn your back on the ocean, Charlie. Don't ever play around it. Promise me, you won't come down here by yourself again."

"But Mom—"

"Your mom isn't here, I am. You are in my care at this moment, and you will not come down here without an adult, do you hear me?"

"Y-yes." Her nod was accompanied by more tears. "Can I go home now? I want my mom." She gripped her fingers hard in Cash's coat.

"I'll take you back. Go on." He pushed to his feet and backed up so she could race up the stairs. Fletch ignored the scathing look he received from the dog as Cash trotted behind Charlie. That the little girl ran away from him hurt more than he expected, but he couldn't let it. She could have gotten hurt. She could have fallen or… Fletch tried to take a deep breath. Or she could have been pulled out with the tide.

But she hadn't been. She was okay. She was safe. He hammered his fists against his thighs, trying to knock himself back into the present as he grabbed her backpack and climbed the stairs.

He watched her scramble back to the station. That she was perfectly fine kept him breathing. He bent down and brushed off his shoes, taking an extra moment to get himself under control. Before he turned his back on the ocean and the haunting memory of the day he'd been too late.

"WHAT ON EARTH happened to you?" Paige's laugh died as Charlie launched herself through the door of the diner and dived into Paige's arms. "Hey, now. What's this?" She hauled Charlie up, unnerved by her daughter clinging to her, shaking. Crying. Charlie didn't cry. And she didn't scare easily. "Are you hurt? What's wrong?" Damp sand fell in clumps off Charlie's pants and shoes.

Paige glanced around the nearly packed diner, at the concerned expressions aimed in her direction. She caught Twyla's eye and gestured for her to take over her tables as she carried Charlie into the kitchen, past Ursula and to the back prep area near the deep freezer.

"I thought you went to walk Cash," Paige said to her daughter.

"I did." Charlie mumbled into her shoulder as Fletch entered. "Deputy Fletch got mad and yelled at me."

Paige's entire body went hot. "He did?"

"Yes, he did." Fletch set Charlie's backpack on the floor. "I asked her to stay in eyesight and she went down to the beach on her own. She was headed for the rocks."

"Last I heard that wasn't a criminal offense." Paige glared over her daughter's head, only to feel her anger fade at the shell-shocked expression on Fletch's face. "You scared her, Fletch." She pressed a kiss on the top of her daughter's head.

"Not as bad as she scared me. She shouldn't have been down there alone."

"Okay, I think you've made your point," Paige said. "I'm sure there was a reason—"

"I threw Cash's ball too far," Charlie mumbled. "And then I saw the rocks and thought about the treasure-box caves Mrs. Hastings told me about. I came back when he called me. I said I was sorry."

Paige heard the tinge of anger in her daughter's voice and knew she was going to be all right. She pulled back so she could look into Charlie's eyes. "And what do we say about saying sorry?"

Charlie silently buried her face in Paige's shoulder.

"I grabbed her by the arms." Fletch cringed at Ursula's tsk of disapproval. "I was wrong. I apologize, Charlie."

Charlie hiccupped.

Paige set Charlie on the floor and pushed the little girl behind her. Charlie grabbed hold of her waistband and held on, peered around her mother at Fletch. "I apologize to you as well, Paige. It won't happen again."

"Charlie, go up to the apartment and get changed. We have that appointment with your teacher this afternoon, remember? And then I want to stop in and see Mrs. Hastings." Paige shoved her hands in her pockets to keep from clenching her fists. "Ursula, would you please give us a minute?"

"Come on, little one." Ursula held out her gnarled hand in an uncharacteristic gesture of protectiveness. "We'll let these two talk. So you get to go to your school today, do you?"

"Yes, ma'am." Charlie stopped next to

Fletch, tilted her tear-stained face up to his and blinked. "I am sorry, Deputy Fletch. I won't ever do it again."

Fletch nodded, his jaw pulsing as if he was trying to control his temper, which only fueled Paige's.

"The least you could have done was accept her apology."

"Catch me in a few hours when my heart starts beating again," Fletch said. "What I did was wrong. I never should have put hands on Charlie. But when I saw her running toward the water…" For an instant his expression went blank, as if he was lost in some dream. He cleared his throat, ducked his head. "There's no excuse."

"Charlie will be fine." Paige wasn't so sure about Fletch. "She learned a lesson. Maybe the hard way. I bet she won't look at the beach the same again."

"You're making a joke out of this?"

"You got a fifteen-minute dose of being a parent, Fletch, and learned your own lesson." Like how not to deal with a situation. "It's all fun and games until…" She stopped and realized she needed to change tactics. "I do appreciate your telling me the truth about what happened."

"I always tell the truth."

"Don't I know it." He still looked as if he'd been caught kicking a puppy. "Fletch, you're overreacting. She'll be fine."

"She has you. I'm sure she will." He gave a short nod, narrowed his eyes and backed out of the kitchen. "I'll see you around, Paige."

But for the first time since she'd met him, she wasn't so sure she would.

And that she didn't like.

"Mom, do you think Deputy Fletch is going to be mad at me forever?" Charlie looked up as her mom swung their linked hands during the five-block walk from the school to Mrs. Hastings's house. She loved afternoons like this, when they weren't rushed, when her mom wasn't looking at the clock. Especially when they were going to visit one of her favorite people.

"He's not mad at you, Charlie. You scared him and he's not sure how to deal with it."

"He sure seemed mad." Charlie frowned and wished that squishy feeling in her tummy would go away. "I didn't think grown-ups, especially police officers, got scared of anything."

Her mom was quiet for a long while, her

hand tightening around Charlie's. "Do you remember a couple of years ago when you got really sick and I had to take you to the emergency room?"

"Uh-huh." She'd never felt so bad in her entire life. She'd hurt all over, especially her head and stomach. The bed had been really weird, thin and squeaky, and they'd stuck her with a bunch of needles. "You cried and everything."

"And you told me that you didn't think moms could cry."

"You mean you were scared?" Charlie was confused. "You cry when you're scared?"

"Sometimes. Just like you cried today when Deputy Fletch yelled at you. You know something else?" At the corner of Chrysalis Lane, Paige stopped and bent down, tugged on Charlie's crooked pigtail and made her smile. "People only get scared like that when they really care about someone."

"So the angrier someone gets, the more they like someone?" That didn't seem right.

"Not exactly. When some people get scared they overreact and do and say things that maybe they shouldn't."

"So Deputy Fletch shouldn't have yelled at me?"

"I didn't say that."

"But you don't yell at me."

"No. Because I didn't like being yelled at when I was a little girl. It made me feel sick. Right here." Her mom pressed her hand against the same place Charlie's tummy hurt. "Is that where you hurt?"

Charlie nodded. "Did it go away?"

"Mostly."

Charlie knew her mom hadn't had a mom of her own. Or a dad. She'd heard her mom talking to Mrs. Brennan one night after they thought she was asleep, talking about some "system" and how Paige was determined that Charlie would never be put into it.

Charlie didn't know what this system was, but it was only a couple of days later that they'd left New York. She agreed with her mom. She didn't want to have anything to do with it. Not if it meant having to leave their home, especially now that their home was Butterfly Harbor. But what if she'd ruined things between her mom and Deputy Fletch? What if they weren't friends anymore? "Were you lonely when you were a little girl, Mom?"

"I was very lonely. But I haven't been lonely in a very, very long time." She leaned over and pressed a kiss on Charlie's forehead.

"Because I have you and you are the best thing I've ever done."

Charlie grinned. "Even when I make you mad or scared?"

"Especially when you make me mad or scared."

"I didn't mean to scare Deputy Fletch," Charlie said. "Do you think we can be friends again?"

"I think he's still your friend." Her mom took hold of both Charlie's hands and squeezed before they resumed their walk. "Remember when you got angry at Simon when he broke into Sheriff Luke's computer and you stopped talking to him?"

"Because he did something I didn't like. Something he shouldn't have been doing." Oh. Charlie bit her lip. "It's kinda the same thing, isn't it? I shouldn't have gone to the beach by myself."

"Kinda."

"Maybe if I made him something he'd stop being angry and scared?"

"I don't know. What did you have in mind?"

"Cupcakes!" Charlie bounced on her toes.

"I think that sounds like something you'd like. Try again."

"Hmm." Charlie squeezed her eyes shut and looked up at the sky. "Maybe we can make him a big cake. Your special recipe? You promised me you'd teach me."

"I think that sounds like a good idea." Her mom pressed her lips to Charlie's forehead, and just like that, Charlie's stomach stopped hurting. "We'll stop at the store on the way home. Now, how about you help me figure out a way to make sure Mrs. Hastings takes her medication every day."

"Why doesn't she want to take her medicine?" Adults were strange. They were always telling kids what to do, but they didn't do what they were supposed to. How was that fair? "Don't they make her feel better? Doesn't she *want* to feel better?"

"That's a good question."

"I know why she doesn't take them. It's because she's lonely and doesn't have anyone to remind her. Like Mrs. Brennan back in New York, remember, Mom? I used to remind her to take her pills all the time."

Her mom got that funny look on her face again, the same look she had whenever Charlie mentioned New York. "Charlie—"

"I know, I know." Charlie stomped her feet and rolled her eyes. "I'm not supposed to talk about you-know-where, but that's when no one else is around. It's okay when it's just you and me, right? We can talk about it. I miss New York. And our friends. And our apartment. Even though I love it here. I can still miss it, can't I?"

"You can."

"Does it make you sad when I talk about it? About…before?" Charlie was never sure what was okay to talk about. She didn't like to see her mom upset, and talking about before always made her mom really quiet.

"I'm sad we had to leave."

"Because you helped Mrs. Brennan's grandson and you got in trouble for it?"

"Yes."

"But you always told me we should help people, Mom. How did helping Robbie get you into trouble?" If helping people had gotten her mom into trouble, then why was she still doing it?

"It was what happened after, Charlie. Helping him was the right thing to do. I thought we were talking about Mrs. Hastings. We need a plan of action, don't you think?"

"I guess." Charlie skipped then hopped to stand in front of her mom. "How come you don't like to talk about what happened with Robbie, Mom?"

"Because I don't. Now put your thinking cap on."

Charlie sighed. Sometimes her thinking cap made her head hurt. "Why can't we just ask her how we can help?"

Her mom stopped walking again, this time in front of Mrs. Hastings's yard. "You know what? You're absolutely right. We should just ask her. Or how about you ask her, Charlie?"

"Me?" Charlie asked. "But this is something important, isn't it?"

"Yes, it is." Her mom nodded, dropped a hand on the top of her head. "Which is why I think you're the perfect person for the job. You can start by ringing the doorbell. I'll be up in a minute."

"Okay!" Charlie's entire body buzzed like she had a hive full of bees swarming inside her. Her first real job helping someone. Just like her mom! But she had to be careful. She couldn't risk messing this up. Bad things happened when helping people went wrong. And Charlie wasn't about to do anything to make them have to leave Butterfly Harbor.

Ever.

LIKE MOTHER, LIKE DAUGHTER. Paige watched Charlie scramble through the gate and run up the stairs to Mrs. Hastings's front door. Her little girl's heart was so big, her attitude so positive, she couldn't conceive of the wrongs that were possible to commit. It wasn't as if Paige didn't want Charlie to learn from the mistakes she made; she just wanted to do her best to mitigate the pain those mistakes could cause.

Then again, Charlie wouldn't do anything that might force them to leave their home and spend months on the road. It wasn't Charlie's lapse in judgment that had Paige constantly looking over her shoulder waiting for her world to blow up.

How she wished hindsight clarified what she'd done, but it wouldn't change anything. Even now, knowing treating Robbie Brennan for that gunshot wound had started Paige down a path that would throw the trajectory of her life and Charlie's into chaos, she would have made the same decision.

No. Paige had to be honest with herself. It wasn't treating Robbie that had gotten her into trouble.

It was not reporting the gunshot wound to the police, something every nurse and nurse-in-training was obligated to do. But Mrs. Brennan had been desperate to save her grandson, and Paige couldn't bring herself to turn him in to a system she didn't trust. But, as usual, her good intentions had backfired. Whether Robbie was innocent or not hadn't mattered: she'd broken the law. And she'd gotten caught.

Last she'd heard the case was still pending, which only made things worse. It didn't surprise her, not when Robbie hadn't hesitated to throw her to the wolves when asked who had treated him, which, as far as the investigating detective was concerned, made her an accessory after the fact. That accusation combined with the material witness warrant, and Paige didn't feel as if she'd had a choice but to run. Charlie didn't understand what had happened in the weeks that followed and, if Paige was honest with herself, she should be open with her daughter and let her talk about her feelings. It wouldn't do Paige any harm either. Instead, Paige chose to push all that down to where she could try to ignore it, try to forget. At least until the statute of limitations on that warrant ran out. Sixteen months down. Two to go.

In the meantime, making a big deal out of

talking about New York would only be a sign to Charlie that what had happened was even worse than Paige had let on, and she wouldn't have her child living in fear.

Paige had done enough of that for the both of them.

All the more reason she should be relieved at the thought of Fletch keeping more of a distance from them now. The last thing she needed was for him to be even more curious about her past. She didn't need a by-the-book cop breathing down her neck; however appealing that idea might be.

Paige embraced the extra few minutes it took for Charlie and Mrs. Hastings to greet each other, and she found herself smiling at their easy banter and friendship. Without even trying, somehow Paige had found Charlie the grandmother she'd always wanted and never had.

That was what she needed to focus on. The here and now and not linger in the past she couldn't change.

That said, Paige couldn't risk getting too comfortable. Yet the very idea of leaving made her sick to her stomach.

The more excited Charlie became about her new school, her new teachers, new friends…

how could Paige even think about ripping her away from all this? And yet that's exactly what she'd have to do if she wasn't very, very careful.

At least helping people like Mrs. Hastings felt as if Paige was putting her nurse's training to good use. All her hard work and study hadn't gone to waste after all. As she was only half a semester shy of earning her license, there wasn't a lot she'd had left to learn. She loved helping people; she didn't have to limit it to medical care. Sometimes, like with Mrs. Hastings, just being around to lend a helping hand was enough to make a difference.

"I wasn't expecting you until tomorrow." Mrs. Hastings waved Paige through the gate with a bright, healthy smile on her face. Her pallor was worlds better, and whatever wobble she'd had on Monday was gone. "Two days in a row. And look at you, Miss Charlie." Mrs. Hastings cupped Charlie's chin in her palm and tilted it up. "Have you grown since I last saw you?"

"Uh-huh. A whole half an inch." Charlie waggled her hand over her head. "Mom said I'm going to be taller than her in no time!"

"Well, I just bet that's true. Do you have

time for a cup of tea and some cookies, or do you need to get back to the diner?"

"We have a few minutes," Paige said. "We just had our before-school meeting with Charlie's new teacher."

"One of the better decisions I made when I was principal." Mrs. Hastings closed the door behind them and led them into the living room she called her parlor. "Always thought it made sense to have the students and teachers meet one-on-one to take some of those first-day jitters out of the equation."

"Mrs. Thompson was so nice!" Charlie announced as she slipped out of her sweater and draped it neatly over the arm of the flowered sofa. "She showed us the new art room. You should see all the paints and crayons and paper, and we're going to have a show around Christmas. And you know what? I get to ride my bike to school like a real big girl! Except when it rains. I don't think I want to ride my bike in the rain."

"Nobody likes a soggy bike ride," Mrs. Hastings agreed.

"Would you like me to fix the tea?" Paige asked and earned a stern look from Mrs. Hastings.

"You mean can you go snooping through

my kitchen to see if I took my medication this morning."

Paige grinned. "That, too."

Mrs. Hastings harrumphed. "Well, you're honest, I'll give you that. I took my pills. Don't want you and that nosy deputy of yours poking around my business."

"Fletch is not my deputy." Even as she said it, her cheeks went hot. She avoided her daughter's curious expression. "He was concerned about you and rightly so, given you almost passed out in front of him. Keeping up with your regimen is the best way to make sure you're around for a while. I feel pretty secure speaking for most people I know, we'd miss you, Mrs. Hastings."

"I would," Charlie announced. "And you know what else? I think you're right, Mrs. Hastings. I think Deputy Fletcher likes my mom."

"Do you, now?" Mrs. Hastings turned amused eyes on Paige. "That boy always did have good taste." Mrs. Hastings cackled at Paige's mortified expression. "How about you come and help me fix the tea, Miss Charlie. Teach your mom a thing or two. Paige, you take a seat and relax. If you know how to, that is."

"Yes, ma'am." Paige reminded herself of Fletch and she did as she was instructed, watching with a slightly heavy heart as Charlie took hold of Mrs. Hastings's hand and slowed her pace to walk beside her.

Their lowered voices spoke of conspiracies and secrets and, knowing her daughter, treasure boxes, but Paige didn't mind. She loved the idea of Charlie becoming acquainted with as many different people as possible. The sound of running water and the clacking gas flame lulled Paige into a daze as she admired the bookshelves filled with books and memories, photographs and mementos of a well-lived life.

"Hey, Mom, guess what!" Charlie ran into the living room and set a plate of cookies down on the table. "I talked to Mrs. Hastings about her medicine and she wants to give me a job!"

"A job?" Paige pushed herself up in her chair. How long had she been out of things? "What kind of job?"

"Seeing as you all clearly think I need a keeper—" Mrs. Hastings stood in the doorway, a stern albeit understanding expression on her face "—Charlie could stop by here in the morning on her way to school, then again on her way home. That's about the time I take my pills. That way she can report back to you and Deputy Fussy Pants that all is well. She could also help me with some little chores around the house. Child could use some spare pocket money, I'm betting."

"Please, Mom, can I? Now that Simon's not around that much, I get so bored and I love it here."

The last thing Paige should be encouraging is a connection that would be difficult to break, but how could she resist both Charlie and Mrs. Hastings ganging up on her? "If you're sure she won't be a bother." Paige reached out and drew Charlie to her side; pride that Mrs. Hastings would offer Charlie a job warmed her from the inside. She might have screwed up a lot of things over the years, but she'd exceeded all expectations when it came to her daughter.

"And she has more books than the bookstore," Charlie said. "She said I could borrow some. And maybe we could plant some flowers in her backyard."

"Well, didn't you two have a long talk in the kitchen." Paige patted Charlie on the hip. "You up for all that, kiddo?"

"Yes. It's like what you do all the time. I'm

so glad we came here, Mom." Charlie looped her arms around Paige's neck and squeezed. "I don't ever want to leave."

CHAPTER EIGHT

"YOU LOOK LIKE you could use this." Abby slid a slice of triple chocolate cheesecake in front of Paige and dropped into the chair across from her.

Paige glanced up from the list she'd made of where Jasper O'Neill might be hiding. She'd already crossed off more than a dozen places Willa thought he might go. If Paige timed things out properly, she could check the rest by the weekend. All she wanted was a chance to talk to him, to get a feel for what was really going on before Fletch managed to track him down. If Jasper was in trouble as Paige suspected, maybe she could convince him to go with her to talk to Fletch… and ask for his help.

"Cheesecake?" Paige's sigh stopped halfway in her throat. "Ah, you didn't make this, did you, Abby?" Paige asked with what she hoped was a teasing lilt in her voice.

"Just for that, you lose the first bite."

Abby forked off a chunk and popped it in her mouth. "Boy, that man of mine really knows what he's doing in the kitchen." She sat back in her chair with a contented smile on her face.

Paige followed her gaze out the window of Flutterby Dreams and wished she could lose herself in the sound of the waves crashing over the rocks far below. After making a colossal cake mess in their own kitchen, Charlie had insisted she needed to see Simon tonight. They had something serious to discuss that could not wait one more second. One phone call later, Paige found herself at the Flutterby Inn for an early, quiet dinner. Simon and Charlie sat nestled at a corner table eating butternut-squash-infused macaroni and cheese and working on some secret project that made Paige's chest constrict.

"You have any idea what those two are up to?" Paige had lost track of the number of times she'd asked that particular question. Normally she would be asking Holly.

"Not a clue," Abby said. "Simon's had his nose glued to that notebook of his for the past day and a half. And I don't think it has anything to do with school."

"Doesn't he have homework to do?" Paige

was beginning to think the busier Simon was, the easier her own life would be.

"His new school doesn't believe in homework." Abby smirked. "Yeah, something Holly sprang on me after we agreed to keep a hold of him. Funny how that worked out."

"Trust me, fighting the homework battle is not fun. Count yourself lucky."

"What's going on, Paige?" Abby reached across the table and nudged the plate closer. "Something's bugging you. I can tell because you tend to run silent when your mind's racing. I thought about putting truth serum in the chocolate sauce, but Jason said that was overkill."

"Smart man, your Jason." Unable to resist any longer, Paige scooped up her own bite and dived in. "Something odd happened with Fletch today."

"Define *odd*."

"He yelled at Charlie." Part of her still couldn't quite believe it.

"Fletch?" Abby's eyebrows shot up and disappeared under her blond waves. "That doesn't sound like him. Did she tell you what happened? Why he yelled at her?"

"Mmm-hmm." Paige nodded. "Something about the water and the beach and her going down there unsupervised. He owned up to it, by the way. Didn't try to hide it, which I give him credit for. But he just seemed really upset by it." Way more than he should have been.

And that bothered her more than it should.

"Yeah, well, our neighborhood deputy isn't exactly known for confrontation. That said he's definitely a ride-to-the-rescue kind of guy. I've never known anyone so willing to do whatever it takes to protect his family and friends."

Paige agreed. Fletch was attentive when it came to trying to make other people's lives easier, hers included. Not that she made it easy for him. How was he to know doing so could do more damage than good? "I don't know. With Charlie, it felt like more than that." She'd never seen that particular look in his eyes before. Sad. And sad simply didn't suit him. "I almost felt as if he's punishing himself for what happened."

"I'm curious as to why you care." Abby folded her hands on her stomach and stretched out her legs, the bright peach floral dress she wore settling around her knees. "I thought you weren't interested in him."

"So that means I shouldn't care when

something's bothering him?" Paige closed her book.

"Pretty much." Abby grinned. "I knew you were protesting a little too loudly. You do like him."

"Everyone likes Fletch," Paige countered. "I just don't like to think of anyone in pain."

"Then might I suggest you have this conversation with him instead of me?"

But that would mean having to have an actual conversation. It would mean expanding on what was already too friendly a relationship. And because...because... "That might have been an option before. Now, I'm not so sure. It's like he closed some kind of door in my face." And she didn't like the feeling at all.

"That definitely doesn't sound like Fletch." Abby frowned. "But it does sound as if you got what you wanted. Except now you have me curious. Too bad Lori's out of town. Otherwise we could pick her brain about this. Want me to talk to her the next time she calls?"

"No." Paige shook her head. "No. I think you're right. If I'm this concerned I should just ask him directly." As if that wasn't going to open a whole new can of worms. No good would come from prying. She needed to let it go. "I'm probably making more out of this than I need to."

"I'm not so sure. I've known Fletch more than half my life, Paige. In all that time I've never seen him go all googly-eyed like he does when you and Charlie are around. If he's pushing you away, there's got to be a pretty big reason. And I, for one, would be very interested to know what that reason might be."

"WHAT'S THE MATTER with you?" Simon sighed and rested his cheek in his hand. "I thought you wanted to get your mom and Deputy Fletcher out on a real date."

"I did. I do." Charlie couldn't sit still. She tried to keep her voice down. Her mom and Abby were watching both of them as if they knew she and Simon were planning something. Which of course they were.

Even though her mom had tried to make her feel better about what had happened at the beach, she couldn't stop thinking about how Deputy Fletcher had yelled at her. He'd scared her. And… Charlie rubbed a hand against her chest. He'd hurt her heart. "Does Luke ever get mad at you? Does he yell?"

"Luke? No." Simon shook his head. "My

mom does, though. But that's because I'd try the patience of a saint." He puffed out his chest as if his statement was something to be proud of.

"So he never got angry with you? Not even when you broke his computer?"

"Sure he did." But Simon shrugged it off. "He got real mad, but we talked it all out and he said it was okay to be angry with him for all the stuff I'd heard he'd done. We worked it out like men."

Charlie's nose wrinkled. What did that mean? "But he didn't stay mad at you, right? He still likes you?"

"He must. He's adopting me." Simon frowned and looked at her. "Did Fletch get mad at you for something?"

"Yeah. But my mom says it's because I scared him and he overreacted." She still wasn't completely convinced she hadn't broken something between them. She looked out the window into the dark, wondering yet again how close those ocean caves were. If their plan to get her mom and Deputy Fletch together didn't work, she'd have only one thing left to try.

But that she'd have to do on her own.

"Moms and dads yell," Simon said. "Well,

except for Luke, but Mom says that's because his dad was really, really mean. Yelling is part of the job. Trust me, I've been yelled at a lot. It doesn't mean they don't love you anymore."

"I don't think he liked doing it," Charlie thought out loud. "I made him a cake, so maybe he'll like me again."

"Why wouldn't he like you anymore?"

Charlie sighed. "I told you. He yelled at me."

"Yelling at a person and not liking someone are two different things. Look." Simon closed his notebook and brought his head in real close. "Once we do what we're going to do, there's no going back. I promised you I'd help, but you have to be really, really sure. I can't get into any more trouble."

"It's not trouble if you're helping a friend," Charlie said.

"Doesn't mean what we're doing is right. We can use one of the other ideas."

"I'm not going to run away and scare my mom so she asks Deputy Fletcher for help." Charlie had her limits. "And I'm not going to lock them in the freezer at the diner." Where did he come up with this stuff? From those stupid comic books of his, probably.

That new school of his wasn't doing him any good as far as she was concerned. Simon was becoming…boring.

"Then this is what we're left with. We just need to find a way to pay for it. So." Simon tapped his pen on his notebook. "Does your mom have a credit card we can use or not?"

Charlie's heart sank. "I thought you said we could use your mom's."

"The one I memorized expired and I can't find the replacement one." Simon's face twisted in disgust. "She must have taken it with her. It's like she doesn't trust me to leave it lying around."

Charlie didn't answer. She didn't like lying, especially to her best friend. But not answering him turned out to be just as bad.

"Charlie?" Simon narrowed his eyes. "Does she have one we can use?"

"I'm not supposed to know about it." Charlie sat back and scratched her finger into the paper of her own notebook. "It's only for big emergencies."

"This is an emergency." Simon looked like he was getting angry with her. Charlie tightly shut her jaw. She was tired of people getting upset when all she wanted was to have a real family like Simon did. "Do you want Deputy Fletch as your dad or not?"

"Fine." Charlie ducked her head. "I'll get it." But she didn't have to like it.

"And I'll need to use your mom's computer. What?" His eyes went wide when she glared at him. "Abby won't let me use hers without her watching, and I can't do this at school. As important as this is to you, I'm not going to risk getting kicked out."

"I'll figure it out." This getting-adults-to-like-each-other thing was more work than she expected. She was tired of trying to be sneaky. She didn't like keeping secrets or lying.

But if it was the only way for her to get a dad of her own, if it meant she'd never have to leave Butterfly Harbor again, she didn't have a choice.

FLETCH SAT UP behind his desk, stifled a yawn and stretched as he finished sorting the property information he and Oz had gathered yesterday. With Oz currently out on morning patrol, Fletch was manning the station and trying not to let the lack of sleep get to him.

As if he needed confirmation four and a half hours of driving around Butterfly Harbor in the dead of night was not conducive to productivity. He hadn't come across a hint of a disturbance, and as near as he could tell, Jasper O'Neill had vanished. The entire case felt like a waste of time, and he had less than twenty-four hours before he needed to report in to his highness the mayor and convince him he was close to stopping the mini-crime wave for good.

Matt's truck rumbled in the parking lot. Fletch gave a silent prayer of thanks for the reprieve. So far his big property-connection idea had turned up zilch, at least not with the limited information they'd gleaned to date. Oz was doing his bit keeping the mayor's assistant abreast of things; that Oz had mentioned the cute redhead on more than one occasion told Fletch he didn't have to worry about that task falling through the cracks.

Fletch wasn't giving up. In fact he'd reached out to the county assessor's office, but as he was in meetings for the rest of the day, once again, they were in hover mode. Whatever was going on with these break-ins and vandalisms, Fletch was more convinced than ever there was more to the crimes than mere delinquency.

Fletch fixed himself a cup of coffee, adding a second pod to the machine as the door opened.

"Miss me?" Matt's bellow rang through the station.

Cash sat up. *"Woof."*

"Ah, thanks, Fuzz Face. I missed you, too." Matt grabbed one of the treats they kept on the counter and gave it to the dog. The quiet, distinctive click of Matt's prosthesis served as the only physical reminder of his service in the army. The loss of his leg, near as Fletch could tell, hadn't slowed the former soldier down. As Matt was fond of saying, he'd made it home. A lot of his fellow grunts hadn't; reason enough to be grateful. "What's going on around here? You find Jasper yet?"

"Not a sign of him," Fletch said. "I think we've hit a wall, so we're going to let you take a crack at it. Fresh eyes and all. Unless you have something to share?"

"Didn't take you long to ask." Matt headed to the coffee machine and set a piece of paper on Fletch's desk. "Kyle gave me a couple of names for you to check out. Some of the places they used to hang. He says he hasn't been in touch with any of his friends. I checked with the officers in charge and they back that up. Kyle didn't seem that torn up over someone trashing his house, so I'm going to give him the benefit of the doubt and believe him, especially since he didn't give me any grief for asking."

"Kyle was never destructive for destruction's sake," Fletch said. "What he did was out of self-preservation." No doubt it was making a difference to have someone actually interested in his well-being. Given Kyle had managed to squat in one of the Flutterby Inn's on-site cottages for a few weeks before anyone—anyone being Luke—caught on, he was probably the best source they had. "We all get that."

"We do, indeed. Anything exciting happen while I was away?" Matt made his way to his desk against the far wall, unloaded his stuff and slipped his sidearm into the locked file cabinet.

"Nothing of note," Fletch said. "Oz should be back in a bit. We both went on extra patrol last night, trying to stave off any new break-ins."

"Sounds like fun to me. Any place in particular you're looking at for tonight?"

"You want to take one?"

"Someplace else I should be?" Matt

frowned, his dark eyebrows veeing over his equally dark eyes.

It was on the tip of Fletch's tongue to ask how Matt felt about Lori being out of town, but best he actually be awake for the conversation. Whatever response Fletch might have offered was cut short by the office door opening.

"Knock, knock." Paige poked her head in, caught his gaze, then looked down. "It's okay. He's here."

Fletch shot to his feet. He scrubbed his palms down the side of his pants as Paige and Charlie rounded the corner. "Um, hi." He focused in on a timid-looking Charlie carrying an oversize bakery box in her arms. "Paige, I didn't expect—"

"I know." Paige pushed her daughter forward. "We thought we'd surprise you. Charlie has something she'd like to say."

Charlie took an uncharacteristically shy step toward him. "Deputy Fletch, I'm very sorry I scared you yesterday. Mom says *sorry* doesn't mean anything without proving it, so…" She leaned forward and set the box on the corner of his desk. Fletch reached out and caught it before it tumbled to the floor.

"I baked this for you. I hope you can forgive me and we can be friends again."

She clasped her hands behind her back. The buckles of her bright pink overalls shimmered in the late-morning sun.

Shame crashed through him. His overreaction with what had happened on the beach yesterday had been the main reason he hadn't been able to sleep last night. All he could envision were Charlie's round eyes filling with betrayed tears…when he wasn't thinking about the damage those waves could have done to her. "You didn't have to make me anything, Charlie." Until this moment he didn't realize just how much he'd missed seeing her around. He sat on the edge of his chair and pried the corner of the box up. "Mmm. Chocolate. My favorite."

Charlie beamed. "Really? I hoped so. Everyone likes chocolate, right, Deputy Matt?"

"Right, kid." Matt sat back in his chair, folded his hands behind his head and cast an amused look in Fletch's direction. "I was just asking the deputy here if anything exciting had happened while I was gone. Sounds like I missed something."

"Nothing worth getting into," Paige said.

"What's done is done. All is forgiven. On everyone's part. Okay, Fletcher?"

Fletch's heart constricted as he met her pleading gaze. This wasn't about him or his issues or a past he couldn't change; it wasn't about what he needed at all. This was about Charlie and her desire to fix what she thought she'd broken. "Agreed." He held out his hand and waited for Charlie to take it. "Now, are you going to tell me how your meeting went with your teacher?"

"Oh, we don't want to interrupt—" Paige said, but Fletch shook his head.

"You're not. And besides, I think Deputy Matt and I need a piece of this cake."

"I heard that." Matt jumped to his feet and headed for the makeshift kitchen they kept on the side table.

"I'm afraid Charlie and I have to get back to the diner. I'm up for the lunch rush."

"I can bring her back if that's okay," Fletch said. "After she has some cake. That okay with you, Charlie?"

"Uh-huh." Charlie nodded so hard she rocked back on her heels. "We can take Cash for a w-a-l-k, too. But I won't go anywhere alone. Especially the beach. I promise."

"It's fine with me, if it's all right with

Fletch." Paige looked more than halfway convinced. "I'll see you a bit later, then. Matt, glad you're back. Everything okay with Kyle?"

"What is it you and Charlie say?" Matt asked. "Five by five? Boy's doing well."

"Nice to hear. Charlie, behave please."

"I will, Mom." Fletch smiled as the little girl's eyes landed on the cake. "May I have a small piece?"

"I think that sounds like a good idea." Fletch took the knife from Matt and cut a chunk of lopsided cake. He cut a larger piece for Matt, then felt like a heel when he couldn't give any to Cash, who looked more than offended. "Chocolate isn't good for dogs," he told Charlie when she leaned against his leg.

"I know. Poor Cash. Maybe we can give him a treat later."

Cash's ears perked.

"This looks amazing, Charlie." Fletch took a healthy forkful, the unusual biting flavor exploding in his mouth. He glanced over at Matt, who gobbled his piece appreciatively.

"Um, Charlie?" Fletch reached for his coffee after swallowing hard. "What flavor cake is this?"

"Banana. Mom has a special recipe." Charlie shot him a chocolate-coated grin. "You like it? Did I do a good job? Someday I want to bake as good as she does."

He nodded, feeling the prickly heat work its way down his neck. "It's great. Good job." He took another bite, forced himself to chew as the itching erupted under his shirt.

"Oh, before I forget. Simon's doing this project for school." Charlie dug out a folded set of papers and placed them on his desk. "Would you mind answering some questions for us?"

"Us? You're helping him?" Thankful for an excuse to set the cake aside, Fletch focused on the questions. He tugged at the collar, swallowed again. "What kind of pet did I have growing up? What's my favorite dinner? What's my ideal night out? Seems like strange questions for school."

Charlie shrugged. "They're weird, but very important. I'm done." She dumped her plate in the trash, wiped her face and turned her attention to Cash. "May I take him outside? I promise I'll stay in the parking lot where you can see me."

"Yeah, good," Fletch choked, his eyes watering. "Go ahead." The heat was moving its way up the sides of his neck.

The second Charlie and Cash were gone, Fletch dived for the bathroom.

"What on earth is the matter with you?" Matt stood in the doorway as Fletch frantically searched the medicine cabinet for the antihistamine.

"Bananas," Fletch gasped as he looked in the mirror. The hives were taking over, working their way up his face, under his hairline. He felt as if a hill of fire ants were eating him alive. "I'm allergic." He downed two pills and gripped the sink.

"Oh, man." Matt's laughter might have pulled a smile out of Fletch if he'd had the ability. "You're allergic to bananas and you still ate the cake? You have it bad for those two."

No doubt about it, Fletch agreed with a painful nod.

He certainly had it bad.

CHAPTER NINE

"Ah, Paige. I was just thinking about you." Mrs. Hastings opened her door and stood back to let her in. For the first time in a while, Paige was grateful to leave the dinner rush, such as it was, to Ursula and Twyla and have an evening to herself. Given she'd have both Simon and Charlie over the weekend after their secret-mission-sleepover Friday at Abby's, she'd take what downtime she could get.

"As promised." Paige hefted up the cardboard take-out box from the diner and carried it into the kitchen. "Club sandwich made especially by Ursula for you. She added extra tomatoes just the way you like."

"Lovely, just lovely." Mrs. Hastings trailed behind and got a plate out of the cabinet. "Goodness." She flipped open the box and gasped. "This will take me days to eat. I'd forgotten how big these are."

"Then we'll know you're eating well." Paige shrugged out of her jacket and bent down to retie her sneakers. "I wore my grubbiest clothes so I can make the biggest dent in those weeds of yours. Do you have the key to your garden shed?"

"Oh, well." Mrs. Hastings sounded more sheepish than she looked. "I'm afraid I have a confession to make, my dear. I have someone already working in the backyard."

Paige was surprised at how disappointed she was. She'd been looking forward to the mind-cleansing activity of attacking a runaway yard. "I hope they aren't charging you very much. I was happy to do it for you."

"I know, dear, but it's such a big job. And I misspoke. I asked someone to come and help you. I didn't think you'd mind."

"Of course not. It's your yard." Paige eyed the bottles of medications on the counter.

"It's getting so I can read your mind, young lady. I have my pills already by my chair in the parlor. My game show is about to start, so you run on and weed away. I'll bring out a pitcher of lemonade in a bit."

"You're the best, Mrs. Hastings." Because she felt like it, she walked over and kissed the old woman's cheek. "Thank you for giving my baby her first job."

"If that girl's anything like you, she'll be

running the world in no time. Now, off you go. Don't keep your helper waiting." Mrs. Hastings went back to puttering around the kitchen, her orthopedic shoes squeaking against the aged, yellowing linoleum.

Paige could just imagine which unsuspecting teen Mrs. Hastings had roped into being her yard assistant for the afternoon. She exited the back door with more than a hop in her step. If she was lucky, she'd be out of here in a few hours and she could take a care package over to Willa before heading out to mark a few of Jasper's potential hiding places. Perfect night-biking weather if the last couple of days had been any indication. The more she'd mapped out her plan of exploration, the more confident she became that she'd find Jasper—and talk to him—before Fletch got his cuffs on him.

"Hello!" Paige called as she crunched through the thigh-high weeds. At this level of decay, they should be easier to pull out and get rid of than she expected. She could hear the hack-hack-hacking of a hoe chopping through debris, or was that a shovel? Well, whatever tools might be waiting for her, she'd make the best use of them. "I'll be over to help in just a…" She peered around the back of the house and stopped. "Fletch!"

"Hey, Paige." He stood up, leaned a filthy arm over the top of the shovel and grinned at her. Sweat glistened on his face. Mud and dirt stained his dark T-shirt, and browned thistle-like spheres clung to his jeans. He was huffing a bit, but he looked…happy. "Mrs. Hastings called me this morning. She thought you could use a hand."

"She called, did she?" Paige kicked out a hip and crossed her arms. "And you just came running?"

"I'm the interim sheriff." His grin grew wider. "It's my job to help where I can. I'm not one to ignore a damsel in distress's call."

"Is that what I am?"

"No, dear, I'm the damsel," Mrs. Hastings called from the back porch. "And I'm more than happy to lay claim to the title. I've put the lemonade out here so it's nice and cold. Now stop gabbing and get to work."

"Yes, ma'am." Fletch blinked innocently at Paige. "See? And for the record—" Paige stopped with her back to him "—the last thing I'd ever consider you is a damsel in distress. Now, how about you grab that rake and get to helping?"

Grumbling, Paige whacked her way to the toolshed and retrieved the metal-pronged rake, along with a pair of clippers and garden gloves. For as much effort as she'd put into keeping her distance and doing her best not to like him, she was failing miserably. And Paige did not like to fail. She tugged on the gloves. At anything.

By the time they'd cleared more than half the space, Paige dropped the rake, pressed her hands against the base of her spine and arched her back. "Okay, I need to take a few minutes." She groaned. "When did I get old?"

"About ten minutes after I did." Fletch leaned his shovel against the wall and motioned her around the house to the back stairs. She dropped onto the bottom one as he poured them each a glass of lemonade. "Here you go."

"Mmm. Thanks." She rolled the glass across her forehead before drinking. "I can't remember the last time I did yard work."

"Not many yards where you're from?" Fletch took a seat above her, turned and leaned his back against the railing. Because he'd closed his eyes, she knew he couldn't see the flash of panic she knew crossed her face.

"Um, no. Not many." Aside from a rooftop garden Mrs. Brennan and some of her neighbors had maintained during the summer. "It's one of those things where the idea of it is more appealing than the actual doing."

"Copy that. My grandfather turned his yard over to me once we moved here." He drank down half the glass's contents before resting it on his thigh. "He called it good mental therapy."

"It is that." Cleared the mind, opened the pores and definitely made her want to dive headfirst into the ocean. "Holly said you moved here in high school."

"Mmm-hmm. Just before freshman year."

"Where did you live before that?" Paige could have bitten her tongue. Her brain must be fried to venture into a conversation that in all likelihood would require a reciprocal response.

"Florida. Orlando area."

"Ah. Hot in the summer." Small talk. Paige cringed. She was actually talking with him about the weather.

"Humid and hot." He rolled his head against the railing, opened his eyes and looked at her. "What about you? Where did you grow up?"

"Back east." It was as close to the truth

as he was going to get. "Different area from you." She ducked her head, but not before noticing the angry splotches on his bare arms and running up the sides of his neck and face. Poor guy must be having an allergic reaction to some of the plants. "You don't think there's poison oak or ivy in here, do you?" She set her glass down and jumped to her feet to examine the plants around them. As if she knew what to look for.

"Nope, we're good."

She reached up and pulled her ponytail tighter on the top of her head. "Are you sure? It looks like you've got some kind of rash—"

"It's nothing." He pushed to his feet, refilled his glass and drank, giving Paige the chance to move closer and look at his skin.

"It's not nothing—it's an allergic reaction." She grabbed his arm and pulled herself up beside him, pressed her fingers against the side of his neck. "It looks miserable."

"Paige, I told you—"

"Quiet." She'd seen this on her training rotations. Clearly allergies. And a mean one. Not serious enough to warrant an EpiPen, but awful just the same. "You're as bad as Mrs. Hastings. Where's your medication?"

He sighed, set his glass down and pushed her hands away. "I took it already."

"You did not. I've been with you the last couple of hours and you haven't stopped long enough to go inside." Although now that she could see the blotches up close, they did look less red than she would have expected.

"Let's get back to work, okay?" He tried to slip past her, but she stepped in front of him, stretched out her hands and gripped both railings, blocking him in. "Paige, has anyone ever told you you're incredibly exasperating?"

"More people than either of us can count." She narrowed her eyes, tried to lock onto his, but he was a master at avoidance. "How long ago did this start?"

"It started this morning." He grabbed hold of her arms and set her back so he could pass. "It'll be clear by tomorrow, Nurse Cooper."

Her heart skipped a beat at the title she'd come so close to earning. The dream career she'd had to abandon. "Why are you making such a big deal out of this?" Darn it, she hated mysteries and secrets. The irony, funny enough, was not lost on her.

"I'm not the one making a big deal out of this, you are." He yanked the rake up and glared at her. "And if you must know, I'm allergic to bananas."

"Bananas?" He couldn't have surprised her any more than if he'd smacked her in the face with a banana peel. "Oh, Fletch." She covered her mouth with dirt-caked hands, uncertain whether to laugh or cry. "And Charlie insisted on making you my famous banana cake. Wait." One bite wouldn't have done this much damage. "You ate it? Even after you knew what it was?"

"Of course I ate it." He looked at her as if she'd tried to shoot him. "Charlie made it for me."

Something shifted inside Paige. In that instant, she didn't see a cop who could blow apart her life; she didn't see a man she needed to avoid at all costs. What she did see was a man who was so crazy about her kid he was willing to poison himself to avoid hurting Charlie's feelings. Tears burned the back of her throat.

She couldn't remember the last time someone had done something so…kind. Stupid, but kind. "You really are a nice guy, aren't you?"

Before she could stop herself, Paige walked

across the yard and grabbed hold of his arms; solid, muscular arms that tensed at her touch. Looking up at him, memorizing every inch of his handsome face, from that slight twitch as he fought a grin to the amused glint in his sea-green eyes, she stopped thinking. Without breathing, without worrying, Paige stretched up on her toes and very softly, very carefully, pressed her lips to his.

What she'd thought was an expression of gratitude shifted in the blink of an eye, in the flex of his fingers. She held on to him even as his hands moved and settled lightly on her hips. He didn't take, he didn't demand. He let her lead wherever she wanted to take them.

Until she realized she couldn't go where she wanted.

She gasped, the sound catching in her throat as she dropped down and broke contact.

Fletch looked at her, his hands still where they were, the tension in his fingers evidence that he wasn't sure what to do next. "Well." He cleared his throat as she stared up at him, wide-eyed. "If I knew that's what it would take to get to kiss you, I'd have bought my own banana tree."

She laughed.

"If you two are done canoodling out there, it's time to get back to work. Fletcher!"

"Ma'am?" Fletcher called over Paige's head without breaking eye contact.

"You heard me, young man. You, too, Paige. Plenty of time for socializing once you've finished."

"Yes, ma'am." Paige stepped back. "Um, so, you want to keep raking or should—"

"Paige—"

"Don't." Paige shook her head. "You made a little girl over-the-moon happy, and for that I thank you. But that's all that was." Even as she said the words, she wanted things to be different. "Gratitude."

In that moment she realized the mistakes she'd made in New York hadn't only destroyed the life she'd struggled to build for herself and put her child at risk. She'd managed to destroy any future she might have had with a man like Fletch.

Any future with Fletch himself.

"Let's get this finished, okay?" She held up her hand and stopped the question she suspected lay poised behind his lips. Lips she'd only just kissed. Lips that carried a hint of happiness mingled with disappointment. But she couldn't think about that.

And she wouldn't. Think about it. Ever again.

"WE MAKE A pretty good team." Fletch pushed open the front gate and waited for Paige to wheel her bike out of Mrs. Hastings's front yard. The good kind of exhaustion began to creep over him, but along with that came a good dose of exhilaration, no doubt caused by that surprising and—most welcome—kiss. "Have to admit I didn't think we could get it all cleared out in one evening."

"Determination breeds success?" She hiked her leg over the seat. "You heading back to the station?"

Fletch rolled his shoulders to stave off sore muscles. "Going to go home first to shower and change." He hesitated. "I thought I'd drop in and see Willa and Nina in a bit. Maybe you'd like to come along? Make sure I don't browbeat them or anything."

Her lips twitched. "I never said you were browbeating anyone."

"That's not the way I heard it. Look, Paige." He moved in front of her to stop her from pedaling off. "When it comes down to it, we both want the same thing. We want to stop whoever is behind these break-ins before someone gets hurt."

"Someone's already hurt," Paige argued. "Jasper."

"Yeah, well, we won't know that for sure until we actually find him." They could agree to disagree on the level of the boy's involvement. For him, an easy solution meant his meeting with the mayor in the morning would go more smoothly. He wanted Luke— and the sheriff's office—out of the political line of fire. "Doesn't it make sense for us to work together?"

"Yes." She glanced around as if she was afraid of being seen with him. "Yeah, I guess it does. As long as you agree to hear him out before you go arresting him."

Fletch sighed. "You know nothing is black-and-white, right? Did it ever occur to you there's more going on with this situation than one person's involvement?"

Paige's eyes went wide and her brows knitted. "Should it have? All you've talked about since this whole thing started was catching up to Jasper and closing the case. What else could there be?"

All this time he'd been pushing Paige to

trust him, to confide in him. How could he do that without having offered to do the same? He was right on one account: Paige had become one of the town's warrior women, ready to fight for a cause, or anyone she decided needed her help. Why shouldn't he throw his hat in the ring? "What if I told you the longer this case drags on the bigger the chance Luke will lose his job?"

Paige blinked. "What are you talking about?"

"I'm talking about the mayor looking for someone to blame when these vandalisms continue. The only reason Gil hired Luke in the first place was to appease people like Jake Campbell, people whose support he needs if he's going to remain mayor."

"Holly's father was pushed out of the sheriff's job," Paige said. "That's how Luke…" She stopped, her mouth pressing into a thin line. "You're telling me this whole thing with Jasper is some political juggernaut Gil Hamilton is trying to manipulate?"

"It wouldn't be the first time he's tried to twist things to his benefit. I saw him talking to Sheriff Brodie from over in Durante at the wedding. It's not a secret he'd have preferred to bring in his former best friend from high school to help him run this place. Luke doesn't exactly bend to Gil's will."

"Luke doesn't bend to anyone's will other than Holly's." Paige smirked. "So you did lie. This isn't about going after Jasper necessarily. This is about you trying to protect your friend."

Fletch felt his cheeks warm. Well, if she was going to put it like that… "I don't like anyone getting a raw deal," he said instead. "And maybe I was wrong to try to handle this myself, or keep it among the deputies. You're smart and cagey, in a good way," he added when her frown deepened. "And I'm betting you don't like the idea of Luke being forced out of a job he's really good at."

"I don't like anyone I know getting a raw deal either. Not to mention Luke isn't the type to want to cause any trouble that could backfire on the entire community. He'd throw himself on the sacrificial pyre if it meant it was best for the town."

That she understood Luke so well told him his faith had not been misplaced. "So what do you say? Can we stop working against each other and see what we can accomplish together?" And maybe…just maybe he'd finally slip around those defenses she had boarded up tighter than a military installation.

"You mean should we join forces to defeat the evil mayor? Oh, you bet your sweet—" She broke off, her frown disappearing behind a glint of determination. "I mean, yes, absolutely. Beginning with seeing if there's anything Nina and Willa neglected to tell us."

Fletch let out a breath he hadn't realized he'd been holding. "I was going to grab some dinner first. How about I pick you up in about an hour?"

"For dinner?" Did she have to look as if he'd just offered her a plate of salmonella?

"You did plan to eat, didn't you?" She'd opened the door. He wasn't about to not nudge it a bit further when he had the opportunity.

"Um." She cringed, ducked her chin. "Yeah, of course." She seemed to shake herself out of whatever internal conversation she was having with herself. "Dinner sounds good. Can we make it someplace other than the diner, though?"

"How about Zane's? I can call ahead, cut down on some time. What do you like on your pizza?"

"Anything other than pineapple." She shuddered. "See you in about an hour?"

"Perfect." Fletch tapped his hand on the handlebar of her bike and headed for his car. "Oh, hey, is Charlie—"

"She's having dinner at Abby's. I'm picking her up around eight."

"Don't worry, Cinderella, I'll have you back in plenty of time to get your pumpkin." Feeling lighter than he had in days, Fletch hopped into his car before she could change her mind. And she was thinking about it; he could tell.

Progress, he told himself, however slow, was still progress. He drove away and kept his eye on the rearview mirror as Paige began her ride to her apartment. Fletch grinned. Mrs. Hastings's matchmaking intentions hadn't been lost on him. He knew his former principal still had enough of her faculties to remember he'd heard Paige offer to come and weed her yard.

He appreciated the unsolicited support.

But never in his wildest dreams did he expect Paige to make the first move.

She'd kissed him.

Fletch found himself humming as his smile widened. All the discomfort of the allergic reaction, all the aches and pains he'd have in the morning, had paid off sooner than he could have hoped for.

Gratitude or not, he wasn't going to quibble. No way she didn't feel that spark between them. Spark? He let out a whoosh of air. More like she'd set off a forest fire inside him. He hadn't been imagining it all these months.

His sister had been right. He'd just needed to find the right path to take with Paige. He'd gambled on Charlie's cake, on Mrs. Hastings's good intentions, and won big. A pizza dinner with Paige felt like he'd just won the World Series of dates.

And he wasn't going to take any of what was to come for granted.

CHAPTER TEN

OH, BOY.

Wrapped in a bath towel, skin clammy from the hot after-yard-work shower, Paige leaned against the bathroom counter and stared blankly into the fogged mirror.

She'd accepted a date with Fletcher Bradley.

She took a deep breath and leaned over, her insides twisted in knots. It was dinner. That was all. And yes, maybe she could have—should have—said no. Except she hadn't wanted to. She liked spending time with him even if doing so kept her on the edge of panic. He'd extended an olive branch by telling her the truth about Luke's situation; how could she fight for Jasper O'Neill and not her best friend's husband? Besides, going with Fletch to speak to Nina and Willa just made sense. All she had to do was take things a minute at a time, a word at a time and do whatever she could not to raise any suspicions about herself. Easy, right?

She straightened, gave herself a good mental shake and exhaled.

Yeah. It might have been if she hadn't been dumb enough to kiss the deputy. All her life she'd made the mistake of jumping first and worrying later, except this leap might just have thrown her off one of those cliffs near the Flutterby Inn.

And Paige wasn't the strongest of swimmers.

What she wouldn't give to not have the memory of his touch emblazoned in her mind; to not feel the sweet memory of his fingers brushing over the curve of her hips or the unending longing that her life was different enough that she could explore further what that kiss could lead to.

"Yeah, dwelling on that's definitely going to help." She started to hum to herself, the only way to make the thoughts stop swarming, and pulled open the bathroom door. The cool air rushed over her, cleansing and invigorating. She retrieved clean jeans and a shirt from the closet in the short hall. She'd installed a second bar in the center for Charlie to use. The space was small, but she didn't mind. Their apartment in New York hadn't been much bigger, but at least here Charlie could have her own room. Paige had definitely added her own touches. The thrift and vintage stores in town had been a godsend, and she'd even managed to get a decent collection of cookware and dishes in the kitchen. Pictures of faraway places lay scattered on the walls, small vases with gerbera daisies— Paige loved daisies—brought fun pops of color throughout.

Home. Paige hugged her clothes against her chest and smiled. At some point in the last few weeks, Butterfly Harbor—and this apartment—had come to feel like home. As she turned back to the bathroom, her gaze skittered across the oversize duffel bag beneath the table by the door.

The familiar pang of uneasiness struck, with more force and louder than it had in a while. "Don't get too comfortable," she whispered to herself, willing her heart to return to its normal beat. "You're not safe yet."

She'd just finished drying her hair when a knock sounded on the door. She glanced at the clock as she padded barefoot to the door, knowing whom she'd find on the other side. "You're early, Fletch."

And that was as far as she got. Seeing him, lounging against her door frame, snug jeans and an even snugger navy T-shirt, a large pizza box in his hand and that pulse-kicking grin of his, erased any thought her brain might have held. Those shimmering green eyes of his…how did women breathe when those were pinned on them?

"Given all the hours you spend at a busy diner and then in Mrs. Hastings's yard, I thought maybe you'd like a quiet dinner in."

"Oh." Her hand tightened on the doorknob. She glanced over her shoulder, wishing she was more of a slob so she could use a messy apartment as an excuse. Instead, the space seemed to glitter back at her as if mocking her attempt at avoidance. "Absolutely. Come on in." She took a step back and tried not to notice the spicy heat of his aftershave as he walked into her home. "Kitchen's around the corner, just there. I have some soft drinks in the fridge. I'm afraid I'm not much of a drinker so—"

"Soda's fine."

She watched him disappear before she remembered to close the door. When she joined him in the small galley kitchen, she found him rummaging in her cabinets for plates and cups.

"Cute place." He grinned at her and sent her belly to flopping. "I remember Holly's grandmother using it as a storage area a while back."

Now who was making small talk? "Holly, Abby and Ursula were nice enough to fix it up for me and Charlie."

"Yes, I know." He arched a brow in her direction. "Who do you think lugged the old stuff out and did the new paint job?"

"You?" How did she not know that?

"Me and Ozzy. We got a free dinner out of it from Ursula." His voice dropped. "And I finagled a month's worth of mocha shakes out of Holly." He leaned back, fingers skimming the edge of the pizza box. "Turned out pretty good if I do say so myself."

"Thank you."

He turned around, braced his hands on the edge of the counter and looked at her. "Does that mean more gratitude? Because I'm up for as much as you want to give me."

Her cheeks went volcano hot. She moved toward him, took an inordinate amount of pleasure in watching him watch her as she stepped closer. Her hands came up. His hands tightened on the tile.

She ducked around him and flipped open the box. "What did you get?" The aromatic steam rose up and slapped her in the face with promises of oregano, garlic and…sausage and mushrooms. "My favorite." She leaned over, breathed deep. "I can smell the fennel."

"I smell roses." He turned and locked a hand on the counter on each side of her. He dipped his head, brushed his lips feather light against the side of her neck. "Hothouse roses and summer."

Paige closed her eyes and leaned back. Okay, maybe he could read minds. If she moved just a touch more, another inch, it was all it would take, she was certain, to have him wrap those amazing and protective arms around her.

The front door slammed open. "Mom! Hey, Mom, are you home?" Charlie's voice exploded through the apartment and Paige jumped, turned and, in one move, pushed Fletch far from arm's distance.

"I'm here." She dived away from Fletch and darted into the sitting area, where her bed and makeshift sofa sat. "I thought you were having dinner at Abby's."

"I am. I forgot my notebook and…" Charlie's eyes narrowed. She leaned over, way over until her backpack slipped off her shoulders. "Fletch! You're here!"

Paige crossed her arms, brushed uneasy fingers against her throat as her daughter's face brightened at the sight of the deputy.

"Hey, Charlie." He caught her as she leaped at him, swinging her into his arms as if she weighed no more than a bag of feathers. "Word around the community center is you're getting as whip smart as Simon with the computer. You going to be up for a job with the sheriff's department soon?"

"I already have a job with Mrs. Hastings." Charlie played with the collar of his shirt. "I don't think I can manage two, can I, Mom?"

"I think your mom is the wrong person to ask about how many jobs you can handle."

The teasing glint in his eyes made Paige's heart ache. He was so good with Charlie. Even when he thought he wasn't.

"I like keeping busy," was all Paige said as she walked over and retrieved her daughter. "Go get your notebook. Did Abby drive you over?"

"I rode my bike. Simon's waiting for me downstairs." She sniffed the air as Paige maneuvered her toward her room. "I smell pizza. Is that from Zane's?"

"It is."

"We're having fried chicken," Charlie called. A few loud bangs, some tossed items and the crash of her closet door later, she emerged, notebook in hand, before she stuffed it back in her bag. "And mashed potatoes and something Jason called kale surprise. What do you think that is, Mom?"

"I bet the surprise will be if Simon eats it," Fletch muttered. "Hey, Charlie, it's okay that I'm having dinner with your mom, right?"

"That depends." Charlie tilted her head just enough so her pigtails evened out. "Is this a date?"

"No."

"Maybe." Fletch grinned at Paige's emphatic response. "What? It qualifies. That okay with you, Charlie?"

"Uh-huh. Wait until I tell Simon it's working!" She squealed and raced for the door. "Bye, Mom."

"I'll see you around eight!" Paige raced after her and called, but all she got in response was a dismissive wave as her daughter disappeared down the street. "Well, that's just great. Why did you tell her that?"

"What? That we're maybe on a date? Because maybe we are. You just don't know it yet."

"You can't do this to her, Fletcher. She's already got notions of the two of us being more than friends. I don't want her getting her hopes up."

Fletch rolled his eyes and returned to the kitchen, leaving Paige to follow. Again. "You sure it's Charlie's hopes you're worried about? Come get your pizza before it gets cold, Paige."

"I don't care if it's cold. Fletch—"

"You like cold pizza, too?" He flipped two healthy slices onto a plate and handed it over. "See? We have something in common after all."

"Fletch—"

"If you keep saying my name like that I'm going to kiss you."

Paige opened her mouth, reconsidered and closed it again. She glared at him.

"Huh. Kissing as a threat. Noted for future reference." When she didn't laugh at the joke, he sighed, and after retrieving two cans of orange soda from the refrigerator, he carried them and his plate to the table by the window. "I'm not going to do anything to hurt Charlie, Paige. Not intentionally anyway."

For an instant, she could see the same shadows that had hovered in his eyes after what had happened at the beach.

"For the record, I'm not going to push you or Charlie into anything you're not ready for. If pizza is as far as this goes, fine. You know me well enough by now to recognize when I'm telling the truth about something."

"Yeah, I do." And that's what worried her. There weren't a lot of people who wore honesty and integrity like a badge of honor. She'd wager she could see Fletch's from outer space.

"Whatever issues you have, whatever is holding you back, I'm willing to work through them with you, Paige. I promise you can trust me. I like you. But then I guess you figured that, too."

She smiled as he sat in what was normally Charlie's chair. "I had a feeling."

"And I'm betting, quite a bit actually, that you like me a little, too." He circled a finger in her direction.

Her lips twitched. "Maybe."

"Yeah, see, your kissing me the way you did kinda gave you away. But hey. I'm not greedy. Most of the time." He pointed to her plate. "Now, let's eat. The sooner we get over to Willa and Nina's, the sooner we can put this whole Jasper thing behind us."

She dropped into her chair, swallowed around the lump in her throat. "And then what?"

"Then we see what else we can find to argue about."

"Evening, Willa." Fletch wished the sight of him didn't put fear in the young woman's eyes. All the more reason he wanted to make this visit as unofficial as possible. Not coming in uniform seemed to be the best way to convey his intention that he was only looking to help.

Standing on the O'Neills' front porch, listening to the boards creak under his feet, he was ashamed to admit he hadn't realized just how much work needed doing to their home. So many houses needed to be repaired, and while a lot of the properties were gaining interest from potential new owners or renters, those providing shelter seemed to have fallen by the wayside. "Paige and I wondered if you and your mom have a few minutes to talk."

"About what?" Willa hugged the door against her.

"It's about Jasper, Willa. Please." Paige stepped forward and pulled open the screen door. "We're both here as friends. Friends who want to help put an end to all this."

"Willa, don't you let our guests stand out there. That's rude. You let them in, you hear?"

Willa's eyes narrowed. "We're packing for San Francisco." Her voice was soft, as if afraid that speaking too loudly would scare any good vibes away. "Please don't upset my mom," Willa whispered as he stepped inside. "Not now."

"It's not my intention at all, I promise." He dropped a reassuring hand on Willa's frail shoulders. "Or you either. I know you're all dealing with a lot. If anything, I want to help."

Willa nodded, but he could see she didn't trust. Not entirely. "Come on in. Would you like tea or coffee?"

"No, thanks." Paige answered for both of them with a spring in her step and a gleam in her eye, no doubt from the two sodas she'd guzzled at dinner. He'd bet she'd be flying off the caffeine buzz for hours to come. "Nina, how are you doing? You all ready for your big trip?"

Nina's strained smile stretched her gaunt face. "As ready as I'm going to be." She motioned Paige and Fletch toward the overstuffed sofa and held out her hand for little Maisey, as fair-haired and blue-eyed as Willa was dark. Made sense given they had different fathers. Willa's had died serving in the first Gulf War. Maisey and Jasper's...well. Not all men were as honorable.

As decrepit as the house appeared on the outside, Fletch was relieved to see the inside had been well taken care of. Comfortable, cozy and warm, exactly what was needed to help Nina get through whatever treatment she needed to save her life.

"You must be Maisey." Paige smiled at the young girl, who blinked her overly wide eyes in their direction. "You're a bit older than my Charlie. Do you know each other?"

Maisey shook her head. "I don't go out much."

"We've been trying to convince her to go to some of the events at the community center," Willa said, pulling Maisey onto her lap as the older sister settled into the easy chair by the fireplace. Nina, from her seat on the other end of the sofa, beamed at her daughters with as much pride and love as Fletch had seen Paige bestow on Charlie.

Powerhouse single mothers. Fletch shook his head. Was there anything stronger on this earth?

"You know Jason Corwin has been talking about starting up some children's cooking classes at the Flutterby in a few weeks." Paige leaned her arms on her knees. "Maybe you'd be interested in those."

Maisey's eyes brightened a bit. "Maybe. I'll have to see how Mom is."

"Doesn't make any difference how I am, young lady." Nina tugged the afghan tighter around her legs. "That sounds like a wonderful idea. In fact, I'm going to insist you take part."

"Mom." Maisey shook her head and looked far older than her ten years. "I don't like making plans that far ahead."

Fletch's chest constricted as he saw Willa's arm tighten around her little sister's.

"Then we'll play it by ear. Tell you what. I'd like some hot chocolate. Do you think you can fix some for me?" Willa brushed Maisey's blond hair back from her face and kissed her cheek.

"Sure." She stood, bent down to pull up the white kneesocks that disappeared under her long flowered skirt. "I'll be right back, Mom."

"Thanks, honey."

Fletch watched Maisey vanish into the kitchen down the hall. "Quite the little adult." He made sure to keep his voice low.

"She's had to grow up faster than I would have liked," Nina said. "Now, what brings you two by? Can't be good news if you've decided to team up."

"On the contrary," Fletch said before Paige could answer. "We decided it would save time and make it easier on everyone if we worked together. The more information we have, the sooner we can get this case closed and everyone back to where they belong."

"Exactly." Paige shot him an uncertain look. "I actually saw one of the buildings that has been vandalized. Kyle Winters's old house. Do you know it?"

"Certainly." Nina nodded. "And I know Kyle, too. He's had a rough go of things over the years, but I always thought there was more to him."

"He's a tough kid," Willa agreed. "But I

always liked him. Never heard a young man say thank you quite so much."

"So Kyle and Jasper were friends?"

"Definitely. Kyle sort of looked on Jasper as a big brother. Until things changed."

"What changed?"

"Well, Fletch knows this already, but Jasper was a pretty good kid up until his father left. That's when the trouble started. He became very solitary. Stopped hanging out with Kyle and his buddies."

"He was always a help around here, though," Willa added. "I still think he's just had a really bad string of luck."

"You honestly don't believe he's responsible for the break-ins, do you, Willa?" Fletch kept his tone even and kind. Now wasn't the time for accusations.

Willa sighed. "Like Mom told Paige the other day, I don't want to believe it. But he's just so angry. And I'm not even sure what he's angry about anymore. Everything seems to set him off. But I can't let myself believe he'd go so far off the rails he'd resort to something like this."

"Is that why you've been helping him hide?" Fletch ignored Paige as her head shot up. "I know you had his prescription refilled a few days ago, Willa. Even though you'd told Paige you hadn't seen him in over a week."

"Willa?" Nina asked. "Is this true?"

Willa's eyes filled. "I couldn't let him think we didn't care about him, Mom. Yes, I did. I'm sorry I lied about it. But I'm not sorry I did it."

"Of course you aren't." Paige held out her hand across the narrow coffee table and waited for Willa to take hold. "He's your brother. You care about him."

"Where did you meet to give him his medication, Willa?" Fletch asked.

"Far end of Skipper Park. You know, over where they had that cooking competition this summer? On the other side of the playground."

"So he's all right." Nina's sigh of relief punctured a hole in Fletch's determination for more answers. "Thank goodness."

"He was as of a few days ago." Willa sighed. "I took him some food, too. And gave him what money I could. He looked a little pale and he was limping when he left. I told him we were taking you for treatment soon. That seemed to upset him."

"He hasn't done well with all this," Nina

explained. "He can't fix it, you see, and Jasper's always been a fixer."

"No, I understand." Fletch nodded as he recalled an energetic boy who'd always been willing to help. "Willa, do you have any idea where he's staying? Any friends he might call?"

"I'm sorry, no." Willa shook her head. "I swear, I'm telling the truth this time. He made me promise not to tell anyone I'd seen him. He said he'd be in touch when he could. Almost as if…" She trailed off, bit her lip, as if uncertain whether she should share what she'd been about to.

"Willa, he needs help. You're not going to be here, and neither is your mom. Please trust us." Paige squeezed her hand so hard Fletch almost felt it himself.

"You're going to be fair with him, aren't you, Fletcher?" Willa asked him point-blank. "You aren't just going to lock him up without evidence."

"With Paige watching my every move? Absolutely not." Fletch attempted some humor to lighten the mood. "But I can't promise it's going to be easy. Finding him is the first step. Beyond that, all I can promise is I'll get to the truth."

"Okay." Willa took a long deep breath. "Okay, I wasn't sure at the time, but when I spoke to him, it was almost as if he was on some kind of mission. Like he was investigating something. I thought maybe he knew who was behind the break-ins, but when I asked, he took it to mean I was accusing him and I wasn't. It's probably why he hasn't been in touch since."

"That's something to consider." If the kid didn't think he had anyone to rely on…he could be even more difficult to locate.

"Would it be possible for us to look at Jasper's room?" Paige asked as she pulled her hand free from Willa's trembling one. "It's asking a lot, but I promise we'll be respectful."

"If it will help." Nina nodded, and it was then Fletch noticed she'd lost even more color in her face since they'd arrived. No wonder Paige was so protective. "Since the two of you have put yourself on this case, I'm going to state this here and now. I'm trusting you with my boy. Whatever the truth might be, I know you'll find it. This treatment I'm going to start will likely throw me for a loop, and I need to know I can trust someone to watch over this. Keep my head in the game, so to speak." Nina patted Paige's hand.

"This treatment they're giving you is very promising, Nina," Paige said. "I've seen it do wonders for late-stage cancer patients. And you're right. A positive attitude going in is absolutely your best weapon."

Fletch didn't know how Paige could talk about something as serious as Nina's diagnosis with such empathy and understanding. She slipped into the conversation as easily as if he was talking about the latest fingerprint results. Speaking of fingerprints...

"I'm going to head on up to Jasper's room. Which door is it?" He pushed to his feet.

"I'll show you," Maisey said as she carried a mug of hot cocoa to her sister. "Is that all right?"

"That's more than all right, Maise. Thanks." Willa accepted the mug with a smile and nodded her encouragement.

"After you." Fletcher waited for her to climb the stairs, and before he followed, he looked back at Paige, who continued to surprise him with her utter and complete dedication to making anyone—and everyone—feel better.

CHAPTER ELEVEN

"WAS THERE ANY particular reason you didn't tell me Willa lied about the last time she saw Jasper?" Paige closed and leaned against the door, her eyes following Fletcher around Jasper's bedroom like a laser beam. "I don't appreciate being blindsided, Fletch. I thought we were working together."

"We are. I needed to see her honest reaction." If Fletch picked up on the irritation in her voice, he didn't show it. He was more methodical than she expected, wearing another pair of latex gloves and examining everything from the stack of books on Jasper's desk to under his mattress. "No offense, but I couldn't be sure you wouldn't give her a heads-up."

Paige started to argue, but one skeptical glance from Fletch had her snapping her mouth shut. Yeah, okay, she had to give him that one. "Is there anything else you aren't telling me?"

His hand froze on the edge of the mattress. He sat back on his heels. "Does this room surprise you as much as it does me?"

"What?" Paige stepped farther inside, turned in a circle and scanned the contents. Giant posters of space and machinery were meticulously lined up on the wall. An over-size version of the periodic table had notes scribbled around various elements. His bed was made, his clothes put away. She walked forward and peered into the highly organized closet. The entire top shelf was filled with DVDs of crime shows, forensic documentaries and true crime books. "It's certainly not your average teenage boy's room."

"I'll attest to that. It's neat. Compulsively so." Fletch frowned. "Why is it every time I think I get a handle on this kid, he surprises me? This isn't anything like what I expected." He pushed to his feet and returned to the desk, shuffled through the stack of receipts peeking out from under a stack of reference books. "Closest Brayden's Book Store is over in Durante. These are from a couple months back. What's Jasper doing with textbooks on crime scene investigations and forensics?" Not to mention the microscope and box of lab strips on the desk.

"Matches what's in his closet. Willa and Nina said he's a fixer." Paige joined him and flipped open the largest of the texts. "Well, they aren't for show. He's made notes here in the margin." She drew her finger down the side column. "What-ifs and reminders about other books and authors. Okay, everything I've heard about Jasper, none of this fits. Look. This one's on survivalist techniques." How to live out in the wilderness with limited supplies.

"Willa said Jasper was talking as if he was investigating a mystery." Fletch reached for the remote control and turned on the TV. He checked the DVD player, closed it again and hit Play. "Well, I think we know why we found his ID at one of the scenes." They watched as a video of someone wandering through a darkened, vandalized house appeared on screen. The calm, clear voice of a teenage boy dictated exactly what he was seeing…from the damage to the structure to speculating over the type of paint that was used. "He's playing crime scene investigator."

"And somehow managed to get himself incriminated." Paige let out a relieved breath. "Thank goodness."

"Hardly," Fletch said. "Why on earth

wouldn't he have come to us with his suspicions about the break-ins? Me or Luke or Ozzy or Matt? Why let us continue to believe he was responsible when he had evidence to the contrary?"

"Gee, I don't know." Paige raised both eyebrows. "It isn't as if he'd be judged on his past behavior or record or anything, would he? Trust isn't an easy thing to have in people, Fletcher. It's also one of the easiest things to break. We need to find him, Fletcher. And the sooner the better."

Fletch nodded, and she had to give him credit. He seemed to be fully embracing the idea he'd completely underestimated the young man. "Yeah. And you know what?" His mood seemed to lift as he met her gaze. "This gives me a better idea of where we can start looking for him. I've got a list Matt brought back from when he saw Kyle." He snapped off his gloves and headed to the door.

Paige cleared her throat. "We can compare it to this one I've already made up. With Willa's help. The other day." She reached into her back pocket and pulled out the sheet of paper. "I was planning on checking them out when I had time, but since we're working together now, we can either divide and conquer or whittle down our choices."

He looked down at her list. She braced herself for a less-than-positive reaction, but seeing the smile spread across his face eased any trepidation she might have felt in offering her first sign of trust. "These are great. And I can mark a few of them off already. I checked these here." He dug out a pen and drew a line through some of the abandoned stores just off Monarch Lane. He frowned briefly. "The caves? You think he'd hide out there?"

"Willa said he loved them when he was a boy. Something about the mystery of them. That they're not the easiest to find."

"Not to mention one of the more dangerous areas of town." Did Paige imagine it or were his hands shaking? "Let's say we keep that idea in reserve for now." He glanced at his watch. "It's after seven. You have to pick Charlie up at eight, right?"

That he'd remembered felt like the brush of a feather against her heart.

"We can knock a couple of these off the list on our way to Abby's. Then we can pick up where we left off tomorrow."

We can? She wasn't about to let that opportunity slip out of her grasp. "I start at the diner at nine and I'm off at four. Charlie's spending tomorrow evening at the inn with Simon. You can have me the rest of the night."

The second the words were out of her mouth, she realized what she'd implied.

"That might be the best offer I've ever gotten in my life." There it was again. That grin of his that could charm the wings off a butterfly. "And I'm going to say deal before you change your mind."

"ANYONE WHO'S THIS good at hiding out deserves a medal." Fletcher turned onto the gravel driveway that led to Luke's onetime and Abby's current home. He'd been part of the group that had done a serious makeover on the property when it looked as if Abby and her grandmother were going to need a new place to live. Instead Alice Manning had moved in with a group of her fellow Cocoon Club members and Abby had taken up residence in the brightly painted, single-story home that had, not so long ago, clung to Luke's dark past like a leech. "Maybe I should have taken some of those books Jasper's been reading with me. Might give us a better idea of his mind-set."

So far they'd ruled out at least two more abandoned houses in Butterfly Harbor, along with the campground scheduled for refurbishment, three businesses on the main stretch and the property behind the high school. Tomorrow they'd hit up some of his friends—if they were friends—from school.

"I'm just glad we were able to ease Willa and Nina's minds a little before they head out tomorrow." Paige unbuckled her belt. "And I think you were right not telling them about what we found at Kyle's house. Worrying about him being hurt wouldn't have helped anyone."

"Good night's sleep and we can come at this again tomorrow." He climbed out of the car and came around to open her door. The surprised smile that spread across her lips made his heart beat faster. If this was how their dates were going to go for the foreseeable future, so be it. At least until he managed to knock down some more of those walls she'd built around herself.

Night hadn't completely descended. The sun continued to hover and cast its last rays across the sky, bathing it in the fiery colors of twilight. He wasn't in any rush for the evening to end, despite the odd outing. Then again, Paige Cooper was anything but predictable.

There was something to be said for adding a bit of excitement to his life.

"You were awfully good with Nina," he said as they walked down the curving path to the front door. "Same as you are with Mrs. Hastings. I wish you'd been around to give me some advice with my grandfather. I never knew how to feel when I was around him, if I was doing or saying the wrong thing. All those medications and doctors' visits. It all felt so…"

"Overwhelming?" Paige hugged her arms around herself. "It can be. I've spent enough time around patients to develop a pretty thick skin. I just try to remember to focus on who they are beyond whatever's wrong with them. You treat the full patient, not just the disease."

Fletch's admiration mounted. "You'd have made a great doctor."

She looked away from him, her feet dragging among the rocks. "I wouldn't have, actually. I had one teacher tell me I had too much empathy for patients. She was right. I couldn't leave it at the door. I brought every one of them home…" She trailed off, ducked

her head in that way she had when she realized she'd said too much.

"So you were what? A nurse?" He didn't
want to push, but this bit of information
wasn't enough to satisfy his mounting curiosity. What was stopping her? What could
she be hiding that she couldn't be open about
her education and training?

"No." She shook her head and stopped
walking. She lifted her chin and looked at
him. For an instant, he could almost see the
battle going on behind those beautiful eyes of
hers. Dare she trust him? she appeared to ask,
and it was all he could do not to reach out,
take her in his arms and whisper, *Yes, dare*.

"It must be difficult," he said instead. "Not
feeling as if you can be yourself. Not share
your life with people. With friends." Friends
who longed to be more. And he did long for
more. The time he was spending with her felt
like precious gems being doled out by some
omniscient power: just enough to keep him
interested; not enough to bring him peace of
mind. "No one is going to judge you, Paige.
Whatever it is you're hiding, it doesn't have
to haunt you the way it does."

"You think that's what I am? Haunted?"

Haunted, hunted. What a difference one

letter could make. He wanted to make her understand that he could help, that he could maybe fix whatever it was she believed was wrong with her life. But he'd also learned enough in the last few days to understand Paige wasn't the type of woman who wanted or needed anyone to fix anything for her.

At least…she would never ask anyone to.

"Seems to me you're tired of running from whatever you think is chasing you." He gave in to the impulse that had struck hours before and stroked a finger down the side of her face. "You look around here and see a home you want, but one you're afraid of fully committing to. Your heart might be here in Butterfly Harbor, but your head?" He inclined his to the side, wishing he could erase the sadness he saw creep into her eyes. "Your head in a sense might be on its way out of town already."

"I don't know how to live any other way, Fletch." She surprised him by taking a hold of his hand and squeezing. "It's all I've ever known. I appreciate what you're trying to do. But believe me when I say I need to live in the here and now."

"Then why don't you?" He took a step closer, could feel the way her breath trembled as she released it. "I hear you saying the words, but everything about you tells me you're stuck back there. Wherever it was. In whatever happened. Maybe if you told me, told someone—"

"I can't." She closed her eyes and leaned into his hand. "As much as I want to, there's too much at stake. I won't take the chance and risk Charlie's future. She's all that matters to me, Fletch. She's all that's ever mattered."

The idea that she'd turn her life upside down for her child was one of the things he loved most about her. That she may have sacrificed her own future…if only there was something he could do to fix the situation. Convince her the only way through whatever it was that had driven her to Butterfly Harbor was to ask for help.

The only thing he wanted, at this moment, was for her to be safe. And happy. To stop looking over her shoulder…

If lightning had cracked through the sky and struck him in the heart it wouldn't have had the same effect her words did. He realized what he'd been struggling with ever since he saw her step onto the porch of the Flutterby Inn at Holly's wedding.

He was in love with her.

"What about your future, Paige?" How he squeaked out the words he didn't know. There was no admitting his feelings to her, not now. Not when that might be the final shot that would send her racing out of town. He needed to gain her trust, to be there for her if and when she was ready. "What are you teaching Charlie if you don't do what it takes to make yourself happy?"

"Please don't do this, Fletch." She attempted to back away, but he tightened his hold, ever so gently. Enough to keep her in front of him with nothing more than the pressure of his fingers and the longing in his eyes. "Please understand that this is the only way I know to keep my daughter safe. Can't we just…be…friends?"

Friends? He'd passed the point of friendship days, weeks, maybe months ago. He leaned down and brushed his mouth against hers. The way her breath caught in her chest, the way her hand clenched around his, he knew this wasn't what she wanted, but that she believed it was all she could have. "For now." He stroked his thumb across her lower lip. "But if and when you're ready for someone to share the burden with, you let me know, okay? Now, how about we get Charlie home?"

IN THE DARKNESS, Paige reached onto the shelf over her head and grabbed her phone to check the time. Again. It was 3:00 a.m.

She threw her arm over her eyes. Her stomach kept dropping as if she was on an unending loop of a roller coaster. One she'd been trying to jump off ever since they'd gotten home.

What was it about the early hours that made the world press in on her? Pushing the air and life out of her as the universe struggled to right itself. It didn't help she was chastising herself for tumbling into the exact situation she'd sworn to avoid.

As if Fletcher Bradley was a situation. A complication, sure. A distraction, certainly. A man who could make her smile by simply looking at her.

She'd heard people lament about the right guy at the wrong time, but never in her life did she expect to experience it firsthand.

And did he have to be so...*right* all the time? She was stuck in the past. But it was a past she couldn't ignore or forget. Not when it was nipping at her heels. She couldn't very well ask him to wait two months without triggering every alert the man possessed. Leave it to her to need to get beyond a statute of limitations before she could attempt the one thing she'd assumed she'd never get another shot at.

Paige rolled onto her side and stared at the wall. Nope. No answers found there. Some people had nightmares keeping them up at night. By all rights she should have them. But no, her brain spun in the complete opposite direction and refused to stop running the unending film loop of Fletch carrying Charlie up the stairs and tucking her into bed.

It was all Paige could do to breathe around the memory. He took such care with her little girl, this tall, lanky deputy who pulled a pink lace-topped bedspread over her child as if it had been made of spun gold. He'd left in silence, but not before he'd stopped to press his lips to the top of Paige's head.

He didn't need to say anything. Because he'd said it all in Abby's front yard. Everything she wanted…

Everything she couldn't have.

"Okay, that's it." She sat up, threw the covers back and sighed. Sleep was officially out of reach. She needed to put this useless stretch of time to better work.

She fixed herself a pot of coffee, clicked on her laptop and settled in at the kitchen table with what remained of the list of places Jasper O'Neill might be hiding. She'd made note of the books in the teen's room, including something she'd bet had slipped Fletch's notice. Clicking over to the search engine, she typed in the different titles, found some of the entire texts online and skimmed through them to confirm her suspicions. She wasn't sure what options might be available to a young man with a criminal record like his, but maybe his record wasn't as set in cement as Fletch would have her believe.

Paige chewed on her lip, sipped her coffee, curled up in her chair. He'd probably be more open to any information requests she might make of him now. There had been a distinctive shift in their…relationship or whatever she might call it. The ball was entirely in her court. But it wasn't a game she was willing to start playing unless she had some rules in place.

Rules and protection.

The edge of the duffel bag peeked out from under the table, a visible reminder of the past she lugged behind her. What she wouldn't give to unload, as Fletcher suggested. Maybe…

Paige reached over and pulled the thin lace curtain over the window to the side so she could look down the backstreet into the darkened depths of Butterfly Harbor.

Maybe…if he knew what was at stake, if he knew why she'd done what she had…maybe she could trust him?

From Charlie's room she heard her daughter let out one of her night sighs, as if she was working through her own frustrations in her sleep.

Whatever softening Paige might have been feeling where it came to Fletch solidified. She couldn't take the chance. That police detective back in New York had promised to make her life impossible if she didn't cooperate with the investigation; if she didn't testify against the young man whose life she'd risked her entire career to save. She might have agreed if he hadn't taken things a step too far and threatened to have Charlie removed from her custody, which sent Paige spiraling into the awful memories of her years in the foster care system. Possible or not, it didn't matter. The threat had been enough.

The thought of losing Charlie…

Paige tasted bile in the back of her throat. There was nothing Paige wasn't willing to do to prevent that from happening. She wasn't losing her daughter.

It didn't matter how much she wanted to believe Fletcher—and by extension, Luke, Matt and Ozzy—would understand her situation. When all was said and done, she'd aided a young man suspected of trying to murder a police officer. Cops bled blue for each other. It was a bond that couldn't be breached.

And as much as Paige wanted to believe Fletch might understand, she wasn't willing to risk her daughter's future on the off chance he would. If that meant setting her own feelings aside, so be it.

Charlie was all that mattered.

Making sure she could stay in Butterfly Harbor was all that mattered.

And in that, Fletcher was right. She had to stop running from the past. It was time to have faith, to believe that this would work out in the right way. Maybe, at some point, she could reevaluate and confide. In Holly, in Abby. In Fletch.

But for now… Paige gave herself a good mental shake and started a new search that

brought up a map of the entirety of Butterfly Harbor. For now, she had another young
man, another family to protect.

And this time, she wasn't going to make
any mistakes.

CHAPTER TWELVE

CHARLIE TIPTOED OUT of her room, rubbing her eyes as she approached the table where her mom was sleeping. "Mom?" Notes and papers lay on top of each other, an empty mug by her hand. Everything was a mess. That wasn't normal. Charlie frowned, looked at the clock. "Hey, Mom. It's almost seven." She reached out and shook her mom's arm. "Mom, wake up."

"What?" Paige jerked up in her chair, her hair mussed around her head. "Oh, hey, baby." She reached out and patted Charlie's shoulder. "What are you doing up so early?"

"You're going to be late for Calliope's deliveries." Charlie didn't like this. Her mom was never late. For anything.

"Oh. Jeez." She shoved her hands into her hair and jumped to her feet. "I must have fallen back asleep. Coffee." Her mom turned in circles, as if she couldn't remember where she was going.

"I'll fix you some."

"You know how?" Paige frowned.

"Of course. I've watched you enough." Charlie beamed. She loved impressing her mom.

"You are an angel. Thanks." She grabbed Charlie's face in her hands and gave her a smack of a kiss on her forehead. "I won't be long."

"Okay." Charlie hurried into the kitchen, opened up the coffeemaker, measured out the coffee the same way she'd seen her mom do most mornings and added the water. When the pipes groaned and Charlie knew the shower was running, she crept to the door, waited to hear the rumble of the sliding shower door and her mom's usual yelp at the cold water.

Charlie bit her lip so hard it hurt. She returned to the table and ducked down. She dragged the duffel bag free. Her mom was so careful with how everything was arranged. Charlie stuck her hands inside and gently pried open the sides. The plastic bags of clothes, the extra shoes, a small stack of cash. Charlie slipped her fingers inside and felt around for the thin wallet her mom stashed their credit cards in.

When she had it in her hands, she stopped. Her heart pounded. Her stomach rolled. Credit cards were a no-no. Her mom had told her that on more than one occasion. Charlie wasn't entirely sure why, except they were for use only in an extreme emergency.

Charlie unsnapped the wallet and pulled out the bright red card. This was an emergency. That her mom had yet to unpack this bag told Charlie all she needed to know. She wasn't planning to stay in Butterfly Harbor. She was ready to leave again.

Seeing Deputy Fletch in their apartment last night was proof Charlie was right. He'd been super nice to her again, and seemed to have forgotten about what had happened at the beach, just like Simon told her he would. Simon also had said she'd know when the time was right.

They had the perfect plan. All they needed was to pay for the tickets to be waiting for them at the restaurant. An email invitation would be sent…as if Deputy Fletch had won a contest. She'd even helped Simon create it on his tablet computer.

Charlie stuck the card in her teeth, put the wallet back in the spot where she'd found it and zipped the bag back up. She grunted as she pushed it under the table again, then ran to her room and hid the card in her underwear drawer with her treasure-hunting notebook. She and Simon had been working on this for the last two days. Now all she had to do was get Simon to a computer before he went to school and they could finish it.

The bathroom went quiet.

Charlie gasped as the bathroom door swung open. "Coffee's ready!" She carried her mom's mug into the kitchen and poured a new cup, added a little of that weird nut milk she liked and a tiny spoonful of sugar. She held it out as Paige came out, her hair dripping, her anxious eyes flitting around the room.

"Thank you?" Paige looked at her over the rim of her mug as she drank. "You're up to something. This isn't going to be another conversation about how you need a cell phone, is it?"

"Maybe." Charlie fibbed. She grabbed hold of the blankets and sheets and pulled them up toward the top of the bed. "What if I need you? How will I find you?"

"Look to your right. It's where I always am."

Charlie laughed at the familiar joke.

"Maybe in a couple of months we can talk about it again. But for now, you do not need a cell phone." She walked over and caught Charlie's chin in her hand. "Everything okay with you? I know we haven't seen each other a lot lately."

"Everything's great! Did he tell you? Deputy Fletcher loved the cake I made. He ate a huge slice!"

"I think I heard something about it." Paige nodded. "You definitely left an impression, kiddo. Now, how about you go get dressed and we'll head over to Calliope's?"

"Sorry we're late!" The car door creaked as Paige climbed out, her feet hitting the gravel drive of Duskywing Farm with enough force to send a plume of dust up over her sneakers. The days that began with her delivering fresh produce purchased from Calliope's farm to homes and businesses always seemed to hold the most promise. "Calliope? Oh." She stumbled. "Fletch. What are you doing here?" It was too early to deal with Fletcher. Especially with him in that eye-catching uniform.

"Good morning to you, too." If he took offense to her abrupt question, he didn't show it. Seeing him back in uniform might just be the reminder she needed. Law enforcement. Danger. "Calliope called. Said she thought maybe someone had gotten into her supply shed overnight."

"Oh." Paige reached out and tugged Charlie close. "I hope there wasn't any damage."

Calliope Jones popped up out of her extensive vegetable patch, her turquoise-and-lavender flowing skirt and blouse swirling against her and the morning breeze. Long red hair tipped with braids, beads and an occasional tiny bell whipped around her shoulders as she waved. She retrieved her full basket and walked out to greet them, stopping at the edge of the gravel path.

Bare feet and gravel definitely did not mix. "I should be able to get all the deliveries in before I head to the diner." Paige took Charlie's hand as they walked toward one of the more mysterious and intriguing characters Butterfly Harbor had to offer. Being around Calliope Jones was a bit like reading an ancient mystery: informative, interesting and completely unpredictable. Those filters most people had? Yeah, Calliope didn't seem to possess any of those.

"I only have three customers on the list

for today," Calliope said in that musical lilt of hers. "I'm not worried."

Paige wasn't sure what a worried Calliope would look like. "If you have the boxes ready to go, I can load them in the car…" Paige stopped short when she saw the unfamiliar expression of uncertainty on Calliope's pale, freckled face. "Is something wrong?"

"Wrong? No." Calliope shook her head and set her hair to jingling. "I understand you've been working with Deputy Fletcher recently. Something to do with Jasper O'Neill?"

"Um." Paige glanced down at Charlie, who was tugging her arm out of Paige's socket as she reached her hand out for one of the hundreds of monarch butterflies flitting about the property. It didn't seem to matter the season, the butterflies could always be found at Duskywing Farm.

Calliope, never one who needed a spelled-out explanation, pulled Charlie's hand free and pointed far into the distance. "There are some friends waiting for you out there." She bent down, kept her voice low and, after she reached into her pocket, withdrew a small silver locket. "Give me your hand, little one."

Charlie's eyes went wide as she did as she was asked.

"It contains a mixture of mineral oil and milkweed," Calliope said as if to ease Paige's mind. Not that Paige was ever worried about Charlie around the woman. She had one of the most soothing, calming effects on people; it almost felt like a meditation session to come to the farm. "You just sit or stand very, very still and hold this out in your hand." She closed Charlie's fingers around the amulet. "They'll come to you. Go on." Calliope patted her on the back and pressed her forward. "It's not everyone whose connection I can feel, Charlie. But yours is a strong spirit. The butterflies will always lead you where you're meant to go. Now go on. Your mom will call for you when she's ready to leave."

"You don't need my help?" Charlie asked even as excitement twinkled in her eyes.

The last thing Paige was about to do was wipe that happiness off her daughter's face. "Calliope and I can manage. Go play for a few minutes."

"Ah, Stella," Calliope said without turning around. "Perfect timing as always."

Calliope's sister, only a few years older than Charlie, emerged from the house, her own bright red hair tied back at her neck, the green of her dress making the emerald of her eyes sparkle like clover in the Irish mountains.

"Hi, Paige." The young girl's face broke into a wide smile as she walked over, as barefoot as her sister.

"Would you mind keeping an eye on Charlie, poppet?" Calliope smoothed a hand down her sister's hair. "I need to show her mom and Fletcher something."

"Sure. Hey, Charlie!" Stella called as she raced down the narrow path dividing exploding bundles of kale and spinach.

"I thought you had your meeting with the mayor this morning," Paige said to Fletch as they followed Calliope through the narrow rows of the garden.

"Not until ten." Fletch glanced at his watch. "Still trying to figure out exactly what I'm going to tell him."

"How about the truth? That there's no evidence to support the idea Jasper O'Neill is in any way responsible for the vandalism and that we believe he's actually been investigating the crime."

"Might be hard to sell without actually having spoken to Jasper." Fletch shook his head, lowered his voice. "I'll come up with something. Don't worry. I'm not going to throw the kid under the bus."

Paige's jean-encased legs brushed through the greenery of the garden—not an accurate description given the expansive acreage billowing over with everything from broccoli to turnips to...well, if it grew in the ground, Calliope worked her magic on it. If Paige took the time to listen, she was sure she could hear Mother Nature herself carefully tilling and tending the soil.

"I don't believe whoever was here meant any harm," Calliope said as they joined her at the sizable wooden shed. "I don't keep it locked, and everyone knows I'm happy to share what I have. But I was a bit concerned when I came in this morning and found this." She pulled open the slat door and stepped back. "Fletcher."

Fletch stepped inside, followed by Paige, who felt as if she was getting a glimpse behind the scenes at an amusement park. Baskets and bushels of containers were filled with various garden offerings, the vibrant colors exploding in the dim light of the storage shed. The gardening tools—simple as they were—hung organized and stored on hooks on the far wall. Other than a push-and-cut lawn mower, there was nothing resembling machinery here. Everything Calliope did was by hand, from planting to tending to cultivating. She even used homemade baskets for storage and collecting.

Fletch stooped down in the center of the shed, picked up the bloodied bandage and held it toward a beam of light streaming through a knothole. "What did he take?"

"I don't believe that matters," Calliope said. "But I'm certain Jasper thought himself desperate. Clearly he is injured."

"Why do you say it was Jasper?" Paige asked before Fletcher could.

Calliope inclined her head. "I might not venture into town often, but word gets around. People were talking at the wedding. It's not in him to be destructive," she said with more candor than Paige might have expected. "He has a calm mind. A curious one. And a generous heart. Despite what others might think."

"You sound like Willa." Fletch circled the shed, but Paige couldn't figure what he was looking for.

"I speak from experience. He's helped me at planting season the last few years," Calliope offered. "And while I don't like the idea of getting him into trouble, I don't want him ignoring whatever injury he might have." She turned to Paige with that knowing expression that had Paige squirming in her sneakers. "He needs a healer. And an advocate." Her attention turned back to Fletcher. "You don't need to sacrifice one person for another, Fletcher. And you, Paige, have neglected your gifts long enough. It's time to trust your heart. Something for both of you to keep in mind as you follow the trail. If you'll excuse me, I'll go finish getting the orders ready. I'll see you back at your car, Paige."

"Um, sure, yeah, okay." Paige stepped out of the shed as Calliope all but glided away through her garden. "You ever get the feeling she's not exactly…"

"Living on the same plane of existence as the rest of us?" Fletcher finished for her. "Every time I have a conversation with her. But she's not wrong about him being hurt. Or about the path. He's bleeding again." He handed her the fabric, and sure enough, she saw the darkening red splotches on the makeshift bandage. "How many days can he go like this before it's bad?"

"Honestly?" Paige's pulse hammered in her throat. "I'd say it's already bad." She looked down at the ground and saw dark splotches. "Do you think she's right? Can we follow that to him?"

"Only one way to find out. Two pairs of eyes should help. This way."

"Wait." Paige held up her hand. "I'll be right back." She ran back to her car, careful not to trample anything in the garden—a feat unto itself. She dug around for the first aid kit she kept in the trunk of her car. "Just in case."

"Always prepared." Fletch gave a nod of approval. "Good thinking."

She followed Fletch to the fence line. The path Paige saw on the other side was one that had been worn in, not one that had been carved out. Made for an easier—if not camouflaged—getaway. "There." Fletch pointed to a spot of red on a glistening leaf as they passed. "Yeah, this way." He reached back for her hand, and only after a moment of hesitation did Paige take it. "Careful where you step. The light's not great."

"I'm good." Not that she'd spent any time in the great outdoors. One of the activities she and Charlie had embraced on their cross-country drive had been exploring various national parks and hiking trails. She lost track of time as the trees and shrubbery swallowed them up. Whatever noise might have accompanied Paige to the farm dispersed among the rustling of branches and the utter, calming silence. She smelled damp earth, molting leaves, oddly fresh and thrilling as she focused on every breath she took. The occasional broken limb caught Fletch's attention, his hand tightening around hers as they rounded a large redwood and stopped.

"What?" Paige didn't know why she was whispering. "What is it?"

"Do you smell that?" Fletch tilted his head back, sniffed the air. "Burning wood."

"I love that smell." She inhaled deeply, caught something else. "Is that onions?"

"Our smarty-pants fugitive knows how to cook outdoors. He put those books to good use. Come on. Quiet. We don't want to spook him."

The deeper they went, the stronger the aroma of fire and roasting food became. When they broke into the small clearing, the first thing that crossed Paige's mind was thank goodness Jasper was a smart kid. The campfire he'd built was in a cleared area, surrounded by rocks, as if he'd realized how dangerous it could be given the current drought in most areas of California.

But whatever fire he'd started, he wasn't tending to it now. As Fletcher dropped his hand, Paige looked past him and saw that Jasper was lying on top of a worn sleeping bag, his body shaking and trembling to the point of convulsing. "Jasper," Paige whispered.

Fletch reached him first. Jasper's dark eyes opened as Fletch rolled him onto his back, but as Paige dropped down beside them she could see the teen's eyes were glassy. She pressed her hand against Jasper's forehead, sucked in a sharp breath between clenched teeth. "He's burning up." She looked down at Jasper's blood-soaked leg, setting the first aid kit on the boy's stomach. She dug her fingers into the torn fabric and ripped it apart, exposing his attempt at trying to stop the bleeding. The soaked bandage was stuck to his skin.

She spotted a bottle of water by his head and reached for it, emptying it over the bandage so she could ease it off. She bent over to examine his leg that looked angry, raw. Infected. "Those nails on the two-by-four must have caught him. Hold him down, Fletch. By his shoulders," she ordered as she cracked open the kit she'd made for herself and pulled out the travel bottle of alcohol. When she poured it over the wound, Jasper jerked, let out a cry that she'd heard all too often on her ER training rotations. "I'm sorry, Jasper. That was just the start. The wound's infected. See how it's turning dark purple here?" She ran her fingers down his leg, shoved off his shoe and sock to feel for a pulse in his foot. "We need to get him to a hospital. He's developed a blood clot."

"An ambulance isn't going to be able to—"

"No, it's not. You'll have to take him when I'm done. You have a knife or something on that deputy tool belt of yours?"

"I was a Boy Scout." Fletcher released Jasper long enough to pull out a Swiss army knife. "Surprised?"

"Not even a little." She appreciated him trying to keep his sense of humor, especially as this next bout wasn't going to be remotely funny. She pulled open the largest blade, set it on the edge of the rocks to heat up as she arranged the padded gauze and medical tape so she could get a hold of it quickly when she needed it. "He's going to buck." She waved the blade deep into the flame until she felt her fingers singe. "I need you to keep him as still as you can. Use all your weight if you need to. You understand?"

"Yep." Fletch braced his hands on the boy's

shoulders, planted his knee on Jasper's unin-jured thigh. "Do what you need to. I've got you covered."

Paige took a deep breath, held the knife in her palm securely, but not too tightly. "Here we go." She sliced the wound open, increas-ing the pressure around the blackening skin. Blood poured out, sprayed over her jeans and shirt. Jasper groaned and tried to jerk away from her. Fletch held on, kept him still.

Paige eased the heated blade against the raw edges in an effort to cauterize as much as possible. Even as the blood continued to pool under his leg, she could see the purple skin begin to ease and relax. She held the bandage tight and secured it by tape, then added a second layer to be safe.

"Okay, that's as good as I can do for now. You need to get him to the hospital." She leaned back and scrubbed her hands into the dirt to get as much blood off as she could, tossing handfuls into the fire to douse the flames. "Now, Fletch. He could lose the leg."

"How long do you think he's been like this?" Fletch sat Jasper up and hefted him up and over his shoulder.

"Twelve, maybe twenty-four hours. He had to have been in a lot of pain to make it to Calliope's, but he could have done it last night if he was determined enough."

"Good to know. You coming?"

"I'm going to get his stuff together. You go. You don't need me muddying the waters when you talk to the doctors. Just tell them about the rusty nails from the wood and what we think happened. He'll need a tetanus shot and they'll have to watch for sepsis." She closed his knife, stuck it in her back pocket as he situated Jasper over his shoulder. "Call me at the diner when you know something."

"Yeah. You did good, Paige. And you were wrong last night." He headed into the trees. "You might not have made a great doctor, but you make one hell of a nurse."

"YOU PICKED A darned good day to be late, Missy." Ursula zoomed out from behind the counter looking as frazzled and haggard as Paige had ever seen her. "We've got ourselves a full house and…" She stopped, her tiny eyes going wide as she took in Paige covered in blood, dirt and sweat. "What on earth happened to you? You're not hurt, are you? You're covered in blood! Land's sake girl, you better sit down—"

"I'm fine." Paige glanced around the diner

as the place went silent. So many familiar faces painted with vivid curiosity, including Gil Hamilton as he got to his feet, abandoning the trio of middle-aged men he was meeting with. "It's not my blood!" She looked down at her hands, then at her daughter, who looked so proud she could burst. Whatever energy had propelled her into cleaning up Jasper's campsite before making the drive back to town drained. "I just stopped in to tell you I'd be late. I could do with some coffee, though, before I clean up."

"Of course you can."

"Paige, what's going on?" The concern in Gil's voice caught her completely off guard. "Are you really all right?"

"Mom just saved Jasper O'Neill's life!" Charlie announced. "Deputy Fletcher told me before he took him to the hospital."

"I need to go upstairs," Paige said. "Please, let's not make a big deal out of this. I hate being late. I didn't realize just how bad…" She waved a hand down the front of herself. "I must look a fright."

"You look like an extra from that zombie TV show all the kids love," Harvey Mills announced from his seat at the counter. "Charlie, why don't you come keep me company while your mom takes care of herself."

"Thank you, Harvey. We'll get your orders to you as soon as we can," Paige called to the customers.

"Never you mind them," Ursula said loud enough to have everyone from Oscar and Harold from the Cocoon Club to the town's new attorney, Leah Ellis, nodding in agreement.

The latter got to her feet and rounded the counter. "I used to waitress while I was in law school. I can lend a hand." She plucked the notepad out of Ursula's hand and waved them into the kitchen. "Go ahead. I can figure this out. And if I can't, Charlie can help, right?"

"Right!" Charlie nodded.

"Come back in here, missy." Ursula pushed her out of sight, making that tsking sound in her throat as Gil followed. The second Paige got her hands under the warm water, she felt as if she could breathe again. She'd forgotten how hard it was to get blood off her fingers. "Gil, don't you go bothering her."

"It's okay, Ursula." Paige had never seen the woman get so protective before. "I'd be more worried about Jasper right now. His leg's in bad shape." She avoided Ursula's inquisitive and oddly knowing gaze. "I don't think Fletch is going to make your meeting, Gil. Knowing him, he's going to stick close to the hospital until he's sure Jasper's okay. Willa." Paige gasped. "I need to call and tell her—"

"You can wait and call her when you know something," Ursula ordered. "Where's the boy been all this time?"

"We found him camped out near Calliope's farm. She realized someone had been in her shed recently. We found a trail of blood." She looked to Gil, who held out a towel for her. Given what Fletch had told her about the man wanting to put Luke out of a job, she didn't want to think well of him. "Thanks. Jasper isn't responsible for the break-ins. Fletch wasn't able to question him, but we think he was actually trying to find out who was behind them. We found video of him examining one of the crime scenes. I'm betting whoever whacked him in the leg with a nail-spiked two-by-four is really responsible."

"Fletch is at the hospital, then?" Gil asked.

"As far as I know. Look, Gil, I know you want someone arrested for what's been happening with these break-ins, but it's not fair to pin them on Jasper until he can explain himself. Please keep an open mind."

"No, you're right, of course." Gil looked a little green. "You know what, I have something I need to look into, back at the office. And some calls to make. Then I'll head over to the hospital to see how Jasper and Fletch are doing."

"Okay." Paige frowned. That wasn't even remotely close to the reaction she'd expected.

"I'm glad you're all right, Paige. Sounds like you're amazing under pressure. And with the sight of blood."

"Yeah, well." It wasn't as if she was going to admit to having been trained to respond to it. "We do what we need to do, right?" After he left, she turned to Ursula. "Can you give me another ten minutes to go upstairs and shower?" She plucked the stiffening shirt away from her skin. "This isn't exactly appropriate work attire."

"You go. And Paige?"

"Yes, ma'am?" Paige turned to look at the short, intense woman who not so long ago had her quaking in her shoes.

"Proud of you, girl. You did real good with that boy."

"How do you know what I did?" Paige countered.

"Doesn't matter. When the chips were down, you came through. Ain't nothing more we can ask of one of our own. Now scoot. I don't like that shade of red on you one bit."

"ARE YOU GOING to arrest me?"

Fletch glanced up from reading the last of the reports Matt had dropped off at the hospital. He sat forward, closed the paperwork and set it on the foot of the bed where Jasper O'Neill's heavily bandaged leg rested on a stack of pillows. "Welcome back. Your mom and sisters just went to get something to drink. They'll be back in a few minutes. How are you feeling?"

"Weird. Wired." Jasper tried to push himself up, but his arms gave out. Fletch leaned over and hit the button for the bed control to angle him into a sitting position. "Thanks." He squirmed on the mattress, his long dark hair falling in front of his face. He shoved it back, only to get his hand tangled around the IV lines. "You didn't answer my question. Are you going to arrest me?" His speech was slow, methodical almost. The painkillers, probably.

"That depends on if you did anything other than trespass on active crime scenes." Fletcher watched the suspicion creep into Jasper's dark eyes. "And let's not count the fright you put in your mom. Not cool, kid."

Jasper flinched, looked down at his hands, a sign Fletch took as guilt. Good. Guilt he could work with. Guilt he could put to use.

"I can't fix her," Jasper said.

"So you decided to try to fix something else? Something you have no training for or expertise in. Something that nearly got you killed. If Calliope hadn't called me, if Paige and I hadn't found you, your mother would be dealing with an entirely different situation right now. Why didn't you come to me or Luke?"

Jasper let out a light snort. "Like you would have believed me. I'm a joke in this town. Everyone's scared of me."

"Walking around town like the Grim Reaper doesn't exactly work to your advantage. You're a smart kid, Jasper. Smarter than me, that's for sure. All that science stuff, the analyzing of data and evidence, that takes special talent."

"I like solving things."

"Yeah, that's what I'm counting on."

Fletcher pushed to his feet. "In answer to your question, no, I'm not arresting you. What I am going to do is talk to Luke and, once you're back on your feet, you're going to start work at the sheriff's station. You won't make much money, not at first anyway. And a lot of it will be grunt work, but there will also be some things you can teach us. You're going to go back to school, you're going to keep your grades up and on the weekends you'll be volunteering at the community center or with me on whatever I think needs doing. You do all that, you keep straight, when you apply for college scholarships, you'll have enough recommendations to get the degree you want. What you're not going to do is sit around and feel sorry for yourself because life dealt you a crap hand. You wanted to change things, you wanted to make a difference. Here's your chance. You're done being a worry for your mother and sisters, you hear me? You're no longer the problem, you're part of the solution."

"You're giving me a job?" Jasper's eyes narrowed. "With the police?"

"Consider yourself a one-person pilot program. If Kyle Winters can turn his life around, so can you. And this—" he picked up the file and waved it in his hand "—is us clos-ing the case on these vandalisms. Thanks to you, we were able to get prints off the spray paint cans left behind, along with DNA evi-dence on the chunk of wood that did that to you. You did real good, Jasper. But you can do better. Agreed?"

"Can I have my own desk at the station?"

Fletch wasn't certain he'd ever seen Jas-per grin before. The sight made him smile in return. "We'll play it by ear. You heal up, okay? When you're feeling up to it, you get your butt into the station and we'll take it from there. A lot's changing in Butterfly Harbor, Jasper. We need all the good help we can find. Get some rest." He tapped the file against Jasper's uninjured leg before he grabbed his jacket and hat and walked out into the hall.

He scrubbed a tired hand over his face, around to the back of his neck. Could the day have been any longer? Spending most of it in first the ER and then in Jasper's room, he'd been determined to stay until he set things right with the kid. Paige had been right. About a lot of things, including the blood clot and the sepsis. Poor kid was going to be on antibiotics and bedridden for a long stretch. Good thing he liked to read.

She'd also been on target over him being willing to assume Jasper guilty simply because his being responsible was believable. Arresting Jasper, making a case against him in order to help his friend keep his job... Luke never would have forgiven him for that.

Fletcher wasn't sure he'd ever forgive himself for being willing to sacrifice one life for another. Especially a kid with so much potential.

The doctor had called it a miracle they'd found him when they did. Another hour? It probably would have been too late.

Too late.

Fletcher braced his hands on his thighs and bent over, squeezed his eyes shut until he saw stars. Would there ever come a time when those words—and that possibility—didn't leave him shaking from head to toe?

"Fletcher." Gil Hamilton headed down the hospital corridor looking surprisingly a little less than his confident, arrogant self. "Assumed I'd find you still here. How is he?"

"Ah, shoot." Fletch sighed and stood up straight, knocking his head a few times back against the wall for good measure. "Our meeting. I should have called. I swear I didn't forget on—"

"On purpose? I know." Gil waved away his concern with an envelope of his own. "Paige filled me in when she got back to the diner. Don't worry. I'm not in attack mode." Gil leaned to the side and looked into Jasper's room. "I owe you an apology, Fletcher. Both you and Luke. I was wrong. About a lot of things, it seems."

As strong as the desire to be flippant was, Fletch simply didn't have the energy. "Okay."

"I never should have pushed to have the investigation closed so quickly. I should have trusted you to do your jobs and recognize that the truth was the important thing."

"It always is," Fletch agreed.

"Then again, if I hadn't, maybe all of this wouldn't have come to light, right?"

Ah, there it was. He just never passed up an opportunity to grab credit. "Depends. All of what exactly?"

"What Paige said reminded me of something. Jasper was attacked by someone wielding a two-by-four studded with rusty nails."

"Yeah. Ozzy took the hunk of wood to the lab the other day. I've got the print results here. What's that?"

"I asked Sheriff Brodie to bring it by my office." Gil took a long, concerted breath, slapped the envelope against one hand. "Look, it's no secret I was pushing Sean for Luke's job. I'm not going to apologize for trying to make my life easier. Any chance those test results have a link to Chuck Nolan?"

"His sons, actually. I was just going to issue arrest warrants for both of them." Fletch flipped through his memories. "Hold up. Chuck Nolan had a few run-ins with your father over the years, didn't he? He and his family owned property on the other side of… ah." The light dawned. "They were part of the group of families you had us evict last year." About three months before Gil approved the razing of the entire community. The same property Gil was hoping to use as part of the new butterfly sanctuary.

"Ozzy's request for the property owner records got me to thinking. Then, with what Paige said…" Gil trailed off. "Chuck went after my dad once with the same kind of weapon after he turned down a refinancing loan. Guess his sons picked up where dad left off. Seeing as Chuck and his boys moved to a trailer park on the outskirts of Durante, I asked Sheriff Brodie to pay them a visit this morning."

"Did you?"

"Seems his sons had heard enough of Chuck's blustering and ranting about Hamilton Bank over the years that they decided to take matters into their own hands and get the revenge their father wanted. They wanted to cause as much damage to any property still owned by the bank. Poisoning the well, so to speak. Stop people from buying."

"Amazing what sons will do to get their fathers' attention." He'd bet those boys didn't have much of a chance from the get-go. Much like Gil. "Let me guess," Fletch said. "They're pretty proud of themselves."

"Oh, they bragged about it even as Brodie cuffed them. They also admitted to coming across Jasper in Kyle's house. They'd heard about it being abandoned from one of their buddies in detention, figured it was another blow they could strike for their dad. They didn't expect Jasper to be there. He gave as good as he got, apparently." Gil shook his head. "Gave one a serious shiner and the other a split lip."

"Where are they now?" Fletch asked.

"Being booked in Durante, but we can get

them transferred to our jurisdiction if you want. You can close out the case nice and tight. For Luke."

For Luke. Fletcher looked down at the file and envelope he held in his hands. It didn't seem like enough, given the machinations that had occurred. The Nolan boys might have committed these crimes, but it was Gil's father—and Gil himself—who had struck the first blow. There were all kinds of wars to be fought. And all wars had victims.

"You know, if I arrest them," Fletch said. "If Butterfly Harbor prosecutes and tries them, there's a lot of stuff that's going to come out. Like why they did it. I bet they'll relish their day in court. Chuck, too. I can picture him on the stand, talking about how your father's bank kept raising the interest rates on his loan and then refused to rene-gotiate. Knowing how slow the courts are running, the trial should start right around election time. That's not going to be good for you." He pinned Gil with a hard stare. "Espe-cially for a mayor still working on distancing himself from his father's tarnished legacy. That's going to be tough on a lot of people."

"It will indeed." Gil smirked and said, "Why do I think you have another idea?"

"Because you're a smart guy, Gil. Here's what we should do. Let Brodie have them. Let Durante's system deal with the charges, offer them a deal, whatever they think is the best tactic. I'll sign off on it."

Gil shook his head, his laugh sounding anything but amused. "You really are full of surprises, Fletch. You're the last person I'd ever expect to be cooperative."

"As I said, I'll keep my mouth shut about the fact you were willing to throw a sixteen-year-old kid under the political bus to save your reelection chances. Boy, what a story that would be. I bet Melina would love to write about that. You know how she's always looking for a way to get noticed."

Gil's eyes were like frozen steel. "And?"

"And you're going to right some wrongs because things have gone unchecked long enough. Starting with backing Luke in the election because that's how much faith you have in our sheriff. You know he's a good lawman and an honorable person."

Gil's jaw worked overtime. He gave a jerky nod, almost as if he was twitching.

"And we're going to need a budget increase for the sheriff's department. Another thirty thousand a year should cover things. I've just hired a new intern. A criminalist in training. You're a big fan. So big you're going to write him a glowing letter of recommendation for college when the time comes. He won't even have to ask." Fletch slapped a hand on Gil's shoulder as he started to leave. "Oh, and one more thing."

"You're using up all your currency in one shot?" Gil shook his head. "You really don't know how to play this game, do you?"

"Oh, I know. I've watched you play it for years. What I prefer is to get out of the mud as soon as possible. Your plans for where to build the butterfly sanctuary just changed. You've settled on your second site choice because you are determined to protect our agricultural community and most especially Duskywing Farm. You said the other day your main priority was whatever is best for Butterfly Harbor. Now here's your chance to prove it."

CHAPTER THIRTEEN

"PAIGE. GO HOME. Your shift ended a half hour ago." Ursula came out of the kitchen waving her spatula in the air before she aimed it at Paige then Twyla like a laser beam. "Now. Out."

"I have another hour to make up." Paige didn't look up from where she was refilling the salt shakers. The last thing she needed was to spill and end up with bad luck. She wasn't in any rush to head upstairs. In the silence all she'd be doing was thinking, and that was never good. "I was late this morning, remember?"

"Remember?" Twyla flipped her long red hair behind her shoulders and planted a manicured hand on a narrow hip. "Charlie's telling everyone about how you saved Jasper's life. You're a hero."

"Charlie exaggerates." The last thing Paige wanted was to be the center of anyone's—let alone the entire town's—attention. At least

Willa and Nina could put one worry out of their minds. For now at least. That was all that mattered to her. Well, that and the fact that the real culprits behind the string of vandalisms had been arrested. "I did what anyone else would have done in the situation."

"Not me. I would have passed out at the first drop of blood," Twyla declared. "How did you know what to do? Cutting his leg open like that?"

Paige shook her head. "I just did." She didn't want to think about it. She didn't want to think about how much she missed putting her training to use. Nursing was a calling; she knew that as surely as she knew her own name. It was what she'd dreamed of becoming growing up, the one thing that kept her going even when she wasn't sure where she'd be living or with whom. Not being able to practice her profession…she hadn't needed the reminder of just how painful that was.

"Your Charlie is already gone for the evening," Ursula said. "Go enjoy yourself for a change. Now that you and the good deputy don't have to go looking for that boy, you can enjoy yourself."

"Speaking of enjoying yourself." Twyla

pointed to the door as the bell jingled. "Hey, Fletch. Heard you had quite the day today."

Paige looked up so quick she spilled salt all over the counter. "Oh, sh—ugar."

Fletch sidled up to the counter and stood directly in front of her. "Now, is that any way to talk to the man who's in the mood to take you out to a celebration dinner?"

This flirty, determined man standing in front of her reminded her of the first time she'd ever seen him. She knew then she had to be careful around him, that all those swirly circles spinning in her stomach were a recipe for disaster. And yet here she stood, looking at him and pushing caution aside with more ease than she knew she should.

She pulled her hands down, wiped her damp palms against her apron. He really should come equipped with those spinning "danger ahead" lights. "You celebrate closing every case?"

Fletch grinned. "You know that job Jasper hasn't been able to get? He's got one now with the sheriff's office."

"Really?" Paige eyed him warily. "How much did that cost you?"

"Come out to dinner with me and I'll tell you."

Out of the corner of her eye, Paige saw Ursula wave Twyla away, then push her toward their only customer at the back of the diner.

"Fletch." Paige yanked the dish towel from under the string of her apron and swept up the salt. "I told you, I can't—"

"It's dinner, Paige. We aren't eloping. Look." He reached into his jacket pocket and pulled out a long, narrow envelope. "Apparently I won some kind of promotional contest from this new restaurant on the wharf. Two dinner tickets to some new place called the Soaring Dutchman. Right on the water." He waved them in front of her. "And don't say you have to think about Charlie because I already know she's staying with Simon and Abby. I've been informed it's space movie and pizza night."

"My kid is going to turn into a pizza. Or a space princess," Paige said, unable to stop the smile from tilting the corner of her lips. "I haven't been to Monterey since we moved here." Even as she said the words, her mind was screaming at her to run away. A night out—alone—with Fletcher Bradley? As appealing as the idea was, it was equally dangerous. The more time she spent with him, the more she wanted to spend time with him.

She didn't want to lie to him anymore. But telling him the truth wasn't possible.

Paige swallowed hard, looked at the tickets.

"If you don't go, I'm going to tell Holly you worked overtime without putting it on your time sheet," Ursula muttered under her breath as she swept behind Paige, a tray of just-washed fountain glasses in her arms. "A night off and a bit of fun, not to mention a meal out, wouldn't do you any harm."

"See? Even Ursula agrees with me, and she never thinks I'm right. Right, Ursula?"

"Hmm." Ursula gave him the evil eye.

"You're not really going to make me beg, are you?" Fletch asked. "I've had a rough day. Don't I deserve a break?"

He did. And no, she wasn't going to make him beg. But that didn't mean the idea didn't hold some appeal. "What time do we need to leave?"

His face brightened, as if that was possible. "I can be back here in an hour. Just have to change and drop Cash off with Matt. Should give us plenty of time to make the drive and not have to rush."

Even with her heart in her throat, Paige couldn't say no. "Okay. Fine. Dinner."

"Perfect ending to the day." He surprised her by leaning over the counter and pressing his lips against hers. For just long enough for her to want more. "See you in an hour."

"OH, WOW. HOW amazing is this!"

Amazing wasn't a word Fletch would use when describing the Soaring Dutchman. *Throat-tightening, stomach-clenching* for sure. *Nauseating* maybe. The short walk from the parking lot a block up from Cannery Row had been punctuated with the cooling ocean breeze snapping the nautical and colored triangular flags waving at the tops of poles. The setting sun glinted off the water and off the windows of stores and billboard signs along the makeshift boardwalk.

Monterey was easier than Butterfly Harbor. The water sounded softer here, calmer. He could almost tune it out.

Paige's thin sandals slapped against the plank boards. She caught her flyaway hair as it got tousled by the wind. She looked at him, then toward their destination. The restaurant housed in, of all things...

"You didn't tell me this was a dinner cruise." She faced him, her smile wide and fanciful as she practically danced backward toward the narrow gangplank.

"I didn't know." He didn't recognize his own voice. Okay. He slowed his pace, took long, deep, controlled breaths. He could do this. But with each step he took, his knees shook. He couldn't feel his feet, could hear only the phantom roar of ocean waves crashing up onto the rocks. He stopped walking, pulled out the tickets and reexamined them. There, on the back, in small print below the swordfish icon, he saw the words *Ocean dining experience*.

He thought that meant an extensive seafood selection. His skin went clammy. He could feel the collar of his shirt tightening, cutting off his air as he drew in shallow breaths. "Give me a second, will you?" He tried not to appear frantic as he looked around the collection of stores, his gaze landing on a gift shop with a dazzling array of butterfly gifts and offerings. A distraction. That's what he needed. Just a few minutes to get himself together.

There wasn't anything to worry about. It was perfectly safe. He was being ridiculous and yet…he may as well be thirteen again, standing on the shoreline frantically searching for a way to stop the past.

He felt like a robot with the way his legs jerked. How had he not looked into this place more carefully? Because he'd instantly thought it was the perfect evening out for him and Paige and he'd jumped at it. It really was the little details that killed you.

Fletch managed to make it to the shop before he grabbed hold of the window frame hard enough his fingers went numb. A view he'd figured he could manage. Even for a few hours if it meant spending the time with Paige. She was distracting enough. But forcing himself onto that vessel? Feeling it rock and roll under his feet? Hear the water slapping against the…he squeezed his eyes shut, willing the unease and panic to go away.

"Hey. Fletch."

He gnashed his teeth so hard his jaw hurt. He hated the sympathy and concern he heard in her voice. He didn't want it, didn't need it. And yet…

When she curled her gentle hand around his arm, he could finally breathe again. "You all right?"

"Fine." He couldn't look at her, couldn't do anything but force the memory of a little boy's suddenly silenced cry back into the recesses of his mind. "I'm not a real big fan of the water."

"What do you mean you don't like the water?" The teasing lilt in her voice did nothing to calm his nerves. "You live in an ocean-side town. You walk ten steps out your office door and it's right there."

"Yeah, really not helping." He squeezed his eyes shut. "And in case you didn't realize, I live on the farthest street away from the beach." Where he could barely hear the water. "Just..."

He pinned his focus on the string of three monarch butterflies dancing on thin, delicate wire. Flitting in their imaginary world as if they didn't have a care. "I'll be good in a few minutes."

"I don't think you will be."

She was right. The more he tried to breathe, the harder it became. He could hear his heart hammering in his own ears, drowning out the ocean sounds even as he knew they were just within reach.

"You need to sit down." Paige slipped her hand down his arm and entwined her fingers through his. "Come on. There's a bench right around the corner."

"Paige, please. Just let me—"

She kissed him. Quick, hard, enough to fry his rapid-fire synapses. "Nice to know it works both ways." He let her lead him, his male pride taking a significant hit as she drew him to the weathered bench. Traffic, he noticed. Pedestrians hoofing it from store to store, bags of goodies in their hands from the world-renowned aquarium a few blocks away.

Paige continued to hold his hand as she shifted on the bench, tucking her bare leg under her skirt as she smoothed her other hand over his hair. She looked so pretty in the pale pink summer dress, tiny white daisies running across the hemline at her knees. The white sweater lay softly against her shoulders, and unusually for her, she'd left her hair down, spilling around her face that for once, as she looked at him, didn't hold anything but concern.

Fletch looked away. This was not how he'd planned for the night to go.

"You get panic attacks like this very often?" Paige asked.

"That's not what this is." But arguing didn't make any sense.

"That's exactly what this is. Or it will be

soon if you don't get your breathing under control." Her fingers skimmed the side of his face, her soothing voice easing the spinning in his head.

"I don't think your touching me like that is going to help." His attempt at humor had her fingers stilling. She tugged her hand away, but he reached up, caught it in his and squeezed. "Sorry. That wasn't a criticism." If anything it gave him something to focus on other than his own weaknesses. "I didn't realize this place was a boat."

"No kidding." Now it was Paige's turn to joke as she tightened her hand in his. Both her hands in his. "We can go somewhere else. It isn't worth your making yourself sick over."

No, it wasn't, but the last thing he wanted to do was disappoint her. "It's so stupid." He leaned forward, still clutching her hands, and lowered his head. "Being afraid of the water."

"This isn't being afraid, Fletch." Now she did pull her hand free so she could stroke his hair again. "This is a phobia. And it's okay. I'm not going to make you do anything you don't want to."

"But I do want to." And he did. Seeing that expression on her face, how happy she was, knowing something he'd done, a place he'd brought her could make her smile like that, smile at *him* like that? It was all he wanted to see. For now, days, weeks…for however long to come. "I'm a grown man, Paige. There's nothing to be afraid of. I know that." He poked his finger against his temple. "I work next to the ocean every day, and it's never done this to me." At least not in a very long time.

"I would have thought living in Butterfly Harbor meant you were acclimated to the water. It is pretty much everywhere. I don't suppose you want to tell me what this is about. What started this?"

"I told you, seeing that boat—"

"That's not what I'm talking about and you know it. Something like this happened the other day with Charlie, didn't it? You didn't react that way because she scared you."

"Oh, she scared me."

"Then not *just* because she scared you. What happened, Fletch?"

"I told you, she just ran right into the wa—"

"Not Charlie." She leaned in, scooted closer. "Tell me what happened to you."

He shook his head, even as the words

pressed in on his heart. "It won't change anything."

"Yes, it will." She caught his chin in her hand and turned his face to hers. "It will change things for you. Tell me. Talk to me, Fletcher. Who did you lose?"

"How did you—"

"I've seen enough trauma patients to know. There was an accident? Something you couldn't control."

"No one controls the ocean," he said. "But it was my fault. Back when we lived in Florida, we, um, had a family thing at the beach. Me, my parents, Lori and…Caleb. My little brother. He was eight. And it was my job to look after him." He tried to look away, tried to pull free from her grasp, but she held on, inclined her head, silently urging him to continue. "I swear I was only gone for a few minutes. There were these surfers and they were offering lessons to the kids on the beach, and I'd always wanted to learn. I told him to stay with Lori, but Lori didn't know that and she went off with her friends. Caleb went exploring on the rocks. Witnesses said this huge wave hit and the next thing they knew he was gone." His breath shuddered in his chest. "I stood on that beach, with my parents, with

Lori, for hours. My feet froze in the sand. I can remember standing there, shaking so hard I thought my bones were going to break, and Lori, God, I can hear her crying sometimes even now."

His throat burned. He was finally able to duck his head and shut his eyes against the pain, but the memories only followed him.

"It wasn't your fault," Paige whispered, shifting closer and wrapping her arms around his. She held on tight, rested her head on his shoulder. "You were a child, Fletcher. There wasn't anything you could have—"

"He was my responsibility. I was supposed to watch him, take care of him. My father—" He broke off, cleared his throat. "From that day on, every time he looked at me, I saw that accusation in his eyes. And my mother, I think something inside her died that day. Nothing was ever the same. It was nearly two days before they found his body. I barely remember the funeral or what happened after. Only that everything seemed to stop until Lori and I came out here to live with our grandfather. My parents just couldn't cope. With anything after that."

"You didn't have any support system? No one to talk to, no one to lean on?"

"I had Lori." He nodded, then let out a soft laugh. "Thankfully I had Lori. I think we held each other together, but I don't know that we ever really talked about it. We only knew the other was our safe place." He couldn't remember the last time he and his sister had talked about their baby brother. "To this day, the closer I get to the ocean, the harder it is to function. It's like something inside me shuts down. So yes, that's why I panicked the other day when Charlie—"

"Stop. I understand." Paige squeezed his arm. "And it makes sense. You care about her. You didn't want anything to happen to her. No one, especially a child, should have to go through what you did without someone to help them. But now that you've talked about it, even a little, how do you feel?"

How did he feel? He lifted a hand to his face and felt mortifying dampness from tears he never should have let slip out of his control. "I feel like that stupid thirteen-year-old kid again."

"Because inside you still are that thirteen-year-old boy. The one who didn't get a chance to grieve properly. The one who, from that day on, has taken on everyone else's burdens. You know, ever since I met you, you've always been helping someone. Saving someone. I'd bet it's why you became a deputy. Because you want to save everyone you can. But you can't save Caleb, Fletcher." She lifted her head and stroked her finger down the side of his face. "As much as you want to, nothing you do can ever bring him back. And that's something you're just going to have to accept."

"If this is your way of telling me to test your theory so we can go on that dinner cruise—"

"Now you are being stupid. We aren't going on that dinner cruise." She slipped her hand inside his jacket and pulled out the tickets. "I'm going to go turn these in so someone can enjoy them, and then you and I are going to play tourist and find a nice, quiet restaurant off the oceanfront and have dinner. Sound like a plan?" Before he thought to argue, she kissed him again. One of those butterfly feathery-light kisses that made his heart flutter. "You know what else I noticed about you?" she asked after she stood up. "You've always been the life of the party. Everyone's friend and go-to person, but I have to wonder if maybe you've also always been a little lonely."

"I used to be." He smiled at her, his gaze falling to her lips. "Not so much anymore."

"WHAT DO YOU mean these tickets weren't won?" Paige stood beside the gangplank entrance as the young woman behind the podium pulled up the ticket information.

"We haven't had any promotional offerings like that." She tapped on her tablet, inclined her head capped with a muss of blond curls. Her brow furrowed. "What were the numbers again…oh, here we go. Amelia P. Cooper."

Paige's ears roared. "I'm sorry, what name did you say?"

The young woman repeated it, along with Paige's old address in New York. "No, wait, I'm sorry, how is this possible?" Paige grabbed for the tablet, ignoring the woman's startled gasp. "I didn't order these. I didn't pay—"

"Here's your credit card information." The woman leaned over and pointed to the digital transaction. "Is that correct?"

"Yes." She recognized the last four numbers, but she hadn't used that card for at least eight months. Paige couldn't even remember the last time she'd pulled it out of the to-go bag. "Maybe someone got a hold of my account information." And bought her and Fletcher dinner tickets? That was just… Even as the color drained from her cheeks, the rest of her body went hot. "Charlie."

"I'm sorry? Ma'am, would you like to speak with my manager? If this was a fraudulent purchase—"

"No." Paige shook her head and set the tickets on the podium. "No, I think I know what happened, and it's not anyone's fault." Except her own. How had she not seen this coming? Charlie had been so adamant about her and Fletch becoming more than friends, of course she'd have concocted some scheme— no doubt something to do with Simon—to get what she wanted. "Please, make sure someone can use these. Just…give them away."

She moved off to the side, tried to quell the panic rising up inside her like a tidal wave. She'd been so careful these last sixteen months. She purposely and deliberately had not left anything resembling a paper trail. No credit card transactions, no checks, nothing that could be traced back to her bank or address in New York. The arrest warrant that had been issued…it could easily have been sent nationwide. Or someone could just be waiting for her to slip up and expose her location.

"Oh, Charlie, what have you done?"

As unsteady as Fletcher had seemed a few minutes ago, that was how shaky Paige felt now. This wasn't happening. Not now. Not when things were going so well with… Fletch.

Her heart stuttered. Fletch. Tears burned the back of her throat. She didn't want to leave him. Didn't want to leave Butterfly Harbor and all the friends they'd made, but what choice did she have? In two, three days max, there was every chance Detective Diaz was going to be knocking on her door, keeping his promise to arrest her and drop Charlie into the foster care system; a system Paige might never be able to pull her out of.

"Everything okay?" Fletch was heading her way, the concern on his face no doubt a reflection of the expression she'd been wearing only moments before. "Were they able to use the tickets?"

"Yes." She swallowed the worry that settled in the back of her throat. The hope that she could finally stop running and make a permanent home for her and Charlie evaporated like smoke. But she wouldn't panic. She wouldn't give in. Not now. Not tonight.

No, she'd give herself tonight, one perfect night out with Fletch.

Then first thing tomorrow, she'd start packing.

CHAPTER FOURTEEN

"MOM, YOU'LL NEVER guess what Simon and I figured out!" Charlie burst through the apartment door, the wind from the unexpected storm pushing her inside. She shoved the hood off Simon's old raincoat Abby insisted she wear this morning, which sprayed rainwater all over the place. She couldn't wait to tell her mom the news! "We did some research on Abby's computer and we think we found—" She stopped. "Mom?" Her mind went blank when she saw the to-go bag open on the coffee table, the contents spilled out on the floor and chairs. That funky feeling in her belly started up again, the topsy-turvy swirling that she hated so much. "What's that out for?"

Her mom sat very still on the edge of her unmade bed. She looked tired, like she hadn't slept, and she was looking at Charlie in a way Charlie couldn't tell what her mom was thinking.

"Charlotte Rose, sit down please."

Uh-oh. She'd used her middle name. Charlie took a step back and dropped into the chair. She hooked her damp, mud-caked shoes in the rung of the chair and locked her hands tight together. "What's wrong, Mom?"

"You and I have never lied to each other. I don't want to start now, so I'm going to ask you a question and you're going to tell me the truth. Do you understand?"

Charlie nodded. Her throat hurt, like it did whenever she started to cry, but she swallowed hard. "Uh-huh."

"Did you use the credit card I had set aside in our bag for anything?"

Charlie's face went hot. She ducked her chin. She'd told herself if she got caught it would be okay, but she never thought her mom would be this mad. "Yes, ma'am."

"What did you use it for?"

"Dinner tickets on a boat for you and Deputy Fletcher."

"You did that on your own, did you? Found this new restaurant, signed up for their mailing list and ordered dinner tickets that cost what it takes me two days at the diner to earn?"

Charlie nodded again. "Yes." When her

mom didn't respond, Charlie wondered if she'd heard her.

"Why?" Her mom finally whispered, and it was then Charlie saw tear tracks on her mom's face. "Charlie, you know that card is only for very special emergencies. Why on earth would you do something like this?"

Charlie knew if she lied it would only make things worse. Besides, she might get in less trouble if she admitted the truth faster. "I wanted you and Deputy Fletcher to like each other. I don't want to leave Butterfly Harbor, Mom. Not ever, and this was the only way I could think to get the two of you to like each other. Did you go? Did you have a good time? Did you fall in love?"

"Fall in—" Her mom's eyes filled with tears in the second before she stood up. "Charlie, that isn't how things work. People need time to get to know each other. It's not a matter of you pushing them together and making it happen."

"But I didn't have time. And you said if you want something to happen you have to work at it. So Simon and I—"

"Simon!" Her mom spun to face her. "I knew it! He helped you with this, didn't he?"

"It was my idea." Charlie sank back in her

chair as she spoke. She might be in trouble, but she wasn't going to get Simon kicked out of school. "It's not his fault. What happened at dinner?"

"It doesn't matter, Charlie, because nothing is ever going to happen. Not now. Not… ever." She covered her mouth, shook her head so hard her hair slapped against the side of her face.

Not now? Charlie frowned. What did *that* mean?

"Where's the credit card?"

"In my room. Under the mattress. I was going to put it back, I promise."

"Get it, please."

"Okay." Charlie slid off the chair and went into her room. She kicked the coloring book out of the way, sent the crayons scattering across the floor and the pink-and-white butterfly rug. When she scooped the card out from under her mattress, she took her time returning to her mom. "What are you doing? Mom, no!" Charlie flung the card onto the table and threw herself at her mother, who was pulling the new pictures and frames off the shelf and putting them in the bag. "No! We can't leave. Not again. You're supposed to fall in love with Deputy Fletcher so we can stay!"

"I told you, things don't work that way, Charlie."

"But they did for Simon! Luke wasn't going to stay. He only came back for a little while, then he fell in love with Simon's mom and now they're a family." The words tumbled out in a rush, like she couldn't stop them. She couldn't catch her breath. "I'm supposed to start school next week! You promised me I could go to school like a normal girl!"

"Well, that's just not going to be possible now." She plucked Charlie's hands off her arms and turned her back to her room. "They can find us through that card, Charlie. They can track me down, and I can't let that happen. Decide what it is you want to take with you. We're leaving first thing in the morning."

"No!" Charlie couldn't breathe. Her entire body hurt and felt hot. She stomped her feet. "No. I'm not going!"

"I beg your pardon, young lady?"

Charlie hadn't heard that tone in her mother's voice before. She didn't know why, but she sure didn't like it. But she wasn't going to give in. "I said no. I'm not leaving. Not again. It's not my fault we have to keep moving, it's yours! Because you helped Robbie, and that's not fair! You weren't supposed to. You knew it and you did it anyway, and now I don't have a real home or a dad or anything I want. And now I won't even have a best friend because you're taking me away again and we'll never come back!"

Her mother's expression eased, and her eyes turned sad as she took a step toward her. "Charlie, you know this is how things have to be. Just for a little while longer, I promise. I swear, pretty soon we can stop moving and you can go to school—"

"I want to stay here!" Charlie yelled. She slapped a hand over her mouth. She'd never yelled at her mom before. "It's the only place I've ever wanted to stay. I want to stay here with Simon and Fletcher and Cash and…" She tried to catch her breath. "And you can't make me go with you!"

She ran fast and ripped open the door. She kept running down the alley, down the street, not even bothering with her bike. She didn't stop. Not at the corner, not down the street. Not at the bottom of the hill that would take her to the Flutterby Inn.

And the one person who could help.

"Mrs. Hastings." Paige pressed a hand

against her racing heart when her friend opened her door. "I don't suppose Charlie is here by any chance?"

"I've been expecting her, but no, my dear, I'm afraid not. Goodness, you look a fright. Come in." Mrs. Hastings reached out her hands and pulled a soaked Paige inside. "Take off that jacket and sit down. I'll make you tea. Warm you right up."

"No tea, thank you. I have to get to the diner pretty soon." But even as Paige shook her head, she allowed the older woman to push her into one of her kitchen chairs. "I'm sorry to bother you, but Charlie and I had a bit of an argument and I know you always make her feel better."

"I'm sorry, Paige, she hasn't been here yet this morning. What did you two fight about?" Evidently her refusal had fallen on deaf ears as Mrs. Hastings turned on her teakettle.

Paige dropped her head into her hands, scrubbed her palms hard against her face in an effort to stave off a new rush of tears. Everything was so messed up. She'd made so many mistakes, all to protect her daughter. Now she was coming to the conclusion she'd probably done more damage to Charlie by running than if they'd stayed in New York.

"We're leaving," Paige whispered when she folded her arms on the table. "In the morning. She came home, saw me packing and, well…" She waved a hand in the air. "She doesn't want to go."

"Of course she doesn't. This is her home. It's your home." Mrs. Hastings clucked her tongue and set a plate of sugar cookies in front of her.

Paige sighed even as she picked one up. "Mrs. Hastings, you shouldn't be baking with your diabetes."

"I'm old enough to do what I want when I want, and I wanted a cookie. Now tell me why you're leaving."

Paige shook her head, surprised she had the energy after yet another sleepless night. "I can't."

"Can't or won't?"

"Both." She took a big bite so she wouldn't have to talk.

"Seems to me you've got a bit of a trust issue when it comes to people, Paige." She poured the hot water into the pot, dropped in her favorite teabags and brought it over to the table to steep. "Always one to jump in to help, but not very forthcoming with the details. People do talk, you know. Guessing where you came from, what happened. Why you never stop long enough for anyone to ask you questions. Like who Charlie's father might be."

Paige rolled her eyes. "Small-town gossip. If that's all people want to know, feel free to spread the word. Charlie's dad died before she was born. Construction accident back in New York." She stopped, set her cookie down. Sat back in her chair. "What's in these cookies? Truth serum?"

"Love and understanding." Mrs. Hastings reached across the table and took a hold of her hands. "You've been running so long you don't know how to stop. You belong here, Paige. You and Charlie both. When are you going to trust us enough to let us help you?"

"It's not that simple." Paige leaned her head back. "It's complicated and difficult and…" Tears exploded in her eyes, blurred her vision, triggered the last of her anger. "Darn it, I'm not a crier! I don't do this!"

"Maybe it's time you did. You young ones just bottle everything up so tight inside. Holly with her dad's accident all those years ago, Abby trying to do everything she could to save that inn of hers, Fletcher and what happened with his brother—"

"You know about that?" Paige gasped. "He said he'd never talked about it."

Mrs. Hastings smiled shyly. "He didn't. Not with me. I was friends with his grandfather. Good man. Hated what happened to his son's family when Caleb died. Hated what his son and daughter-in-law heaped on both Fletcher and Lori afterward. Blamed them both. Turned on each other. It's why he brought those kids to Butterfly Harbor. Told you about that day, did he?"

"Mmm-hmm." Paige nodded. "It's so sad. So unexpected. He's such an amazing man, I can't believe he has that in his past." How had he remained so unjaded? So open and caring? How had he not closed himself off?

"Yes, well, he rose above his circumstances, didn't he? Made a life for himself. A life that, if I'm not mistaken, he'd like very much to include you and Charlie in."

"Oh, not you, too." Paige tried to pull her hands free. "It's bad enough I've got Charlie and Simon playing matchmaker—"

"Smartest ones in town, those two. Makes me glad I don't have to be their teacher, I can tell you. But you. Oh, Paige." Her hands tightened. "Think about what you'll be giving up if you leave. Whatever it is you've done, or think you've done, ask for help. Tell Fletcher the truth. He cares for you."

"I don't know that I can." But having someone to come to, having Mrs. Hastings to talk to, did ease her heart. Maybe she was right. Maybe… Paige bit her lip. "He's the most honest and honorable man I've ever met, Mrs. Hastings. What if he doesn't understand? What if—" Paige gasped. "Oh, no. Oh. No."

Mrs. Hastings tilted her head, gave her a nod and slow smile. "Figured it out, did you? Fallen hard for him, haven't you? Saw it that day in my yard. If you ask me, it was him eating that banana cake your girl made for him that did it."

"Yeah." Tears spilled onto her cheeks. It wasn't that she was afraid of telling the truth. She was afraid of Fletcher's reaction. That he wouldn't understand. That he'd blame her as much as she blamed herself. As long as she didn't say anything, she was safe. But the second she opened up… "Oh, this can't be happening. Not now." She didn't dare trust…did she? Every other time in her life when she'd taken a chance, taken a step onto a ledge, something always, *always* went wrong.

"Love never happens when you want it to, my dear. It appears when you need it most.

Have faith. In Fletcher. But most of all in yourself. You deserve to be happy. So go fight for it."

CHAPTER FIFTEEN

"Hɪ, CHARLIE!" ABBY called absently as Charlie raced through the front door of the Flutterby Inn and headed straight for the dining room. "Bye, Charlie."

"Simon!" Charlie didn't realize she'd shouted until the other people having breakfast jumped in their chairs and sent her disapproving looks. "Sorry," she mumbled, ducking her head as she hurried across the room to the corner table. "Simon, you have to help me. We need to go find the treasure. Now!" She threw herself across the table and grabbed his arms, knocking the book he was reading to the floor.

"Chill out, Charlie," Simon snapped with a frown that hurt her heart. "What's the matter?"

"She's packing. My mom. She's packing and she says we're leaving. Tomorrow." She refused to cry, refused to give in. They still had one chance, one hope. "We have to find that treasure box. Today."

"But it's pouring outside!" Simon looked out the window, back to Charlie. "Why so fast? Didn't their date go okay?"

Charlie shook her head and sent water spraying over the table. "She said the people who are after us are going to find us. Because…" Now the tears did burn her throat. "Because we used the credit card."

"What?" Simon's eyes went wide behind his glasses as he jumped to his feet. She took it as a good sign he was wearing one of his superhero T-shirts today. She'd need all his superpowers if she was going to fix what she'd done. "What do you mean people are after you?"

Charlie bit her lip. She wasn't supposed to tell. Anyone. But Simon was her best friend. And right now, he was the only person she could trust. "My mom did something that got her in trouble. But we left before she could be arrested."

"Arrested? What did she do?"

Charlie frowned. Was it her imagination or did he sound impressed? "We don't have time for me to tell you. Please, Simon. Let's go." She gripped his arm and tugged.

"Go where?" Jason asked as he came out of the kitchen with an oversize waffle he put in front of Simon. "Not without breakfast. And not while it's still raining like this."

"But we have to," Charlie said. "It's really, really important."

"I'm sure it is." Jason pointed to the chair next to Simon. "Sit, please. You can have something to eat before tackling whatever adventure you have planned next. No argument."

Charlie slumped into the chair, sagged back and crossed her arms, scowling up at the man in white. And here she thought Jason was so cool. "I'm not hungry."

"Pancakes it is. Simon, eat. As if I have to tell you." Jason pinned them each with a stern glare before he disappeared back into the kitchen.

"Okay, let's go." Charlie bolted out of the chair, but Simon grabbed her arm.

"Uh-uh. We wait. We take off now, Jason will only tell Abby, who will call your mom, and we don't know how long it's going to take us to find that treasure. We need all the time we can get."

Charlie scrunched her mouth. She really didn't like it when he made sense. "Fine. But

I don't care if it's still raining. That map we found on the internet only tells us where to start. It might take forever."

"Would you trust me?" Simon reached for his orange juice, drank half of it, then handed her the glass. "I'm not letting you move away. We'll find the treasure and take care of it, okay?"

"Simon, Charlie, you guys doing okay?" Abby asked as she tapped away on her tablet, moving toward the kitchen.

"Uh-huh," Simon said before Charlie could. "Is it okay if we hang out in one of the old cabins after breakfast? We're working on a special secret project."

"Go ahead. Anywhere but cabin number seven. They're still working on the remodel. You can get the key from Alyssa." She smiled at them before she pushed through the swinging door.

"Why did you ask that?" Charlie frowned.

"Because then she won't wonder why we aren't hanging around the inn today. And there's another path down to the caves at the end of the trail to the cabin. I told you." He slathered melting butter across the bacon-studded waffle and cut off a piece. "Trust me."

"Yes, no, Abby. Thanks for calling." Paige braced herself against the pounding rain as she climbed the steps to her apartment. At least the mystery of where Charlie had disappeared to had been solved. "She had a rough morning. Just tell her I called and that I'll come pick her up after my shift at the diner. Thanks." She stopped on the landing, disconnected and opened the door.

One part of her knew Mrs. Hastings was right. At some point she had to stop running long enough to trust someone. But then she remembered doing so could cost her the only thing she cared about in this world. Not that Charlie was particularly thrilled with her at the moment.

She stopped just inside the apartment, looking out at the mess she'd made in her frantic, panic-induced determination to pack. She loved everything about this place, every little detail she'd added, every bit that had been given to her. She didn't want to leave anything—any of it—behind. For the first time, what she'd thought of as a necessity would never fit in their solitary to-go bag.

She'd need at least another suitcase. Or two. And she needed to get it done.

Still, she didn't move.

Not until she heard the knock on the door. She turned and found Fletcher standing in the rain, his baseball cap soaked as he smiled at her in that way that had her breath catching in her chest. When had it happened? When was just the sight of him enough to make her feel better? When did that smile that was just for her make every other problem she had fade into the shadows? "Hey, Fletcher. Now's really not a good time."

"Hey yourself." He stepped inside, closed the door and Paige backed up out of his way as she slipped off her jacket and draped it over the back of a chair to dry. "Good thing we had our first official date last night and not today. It's a mess out there." He whipped his hat off, stuffed it into his pocket, his gaze circling the apartment.

Paige watched, silently, as he took in the mass of clothes, the unzipped duffel bag, the stack of cash and toiletries.

"Paige? What's going on?" The lightness she'd come to expect in his voice dulled, as did the light in his eyes. "You going somewhere?"

She hugged her arms around her waist, squeezed hard to remind herself she could still feel something and stood her ground.

"We're, um, leaving Butterfly Harbor. Charlie and me." Because she couldn't stand being under the spotlight of his shocked gaze, she moved around him, picked up one of the framed photos of her, Holly and Abby that she'd wrapped in a T-shirt. "I was going to come by later and tell you."

"No you weren't."

She closed her eyes. She never had been able to lie to him. "Look, Fletcher, I'm sure you think this is about you and me and last night—"

"Kind of hard not to. Here I thought things went great. Better than great."

He hadn't moved. Not an inch. Then why did she feel as if he had started to take up the entire room?

"It did. I had a wonderful time. I love spending time with you. I love—" Paige stopped herself before she dug herself into a hole of emotion she'd never climb her way out of. "I love that we could get away and have some fun. But something's come up. And we need to leave."

"Need to or want to?"

"Need." Because she didn't want to. She wanted to stay. With all her heart. "There's, um, something I need to um, do. Take care of. It'll take a couple of months. We might be back after that." She gasped when he walked over and took hold of her arm, spun her around to face him.

The look on his face was everything she'd ever dreaded seeing: confusion, betrayal, anger. And that was before she'd told him anything close to the truth about herself.

"You're a horrible liar, Paige. If you're running scared because of me, if you're willing to leave the one place you've come to consider your home because I'm in love with you and you don't feel the same, I'll back off. I'll keep my distance, from you and Charlie. For however long you want."

"That's not why I'm—" Whatever she was going to say next vanished out of her mind. "You're in love with me?"

"That can't come as a surprise." His hold on her loosened, shifted, and he slipped his hands down her arms, clasped her fingers between his and brought them up against his rain-dampened sheriff's jacket. "I fell in love with you the first time I saw you. It was all downhill from there."

Her chin wobbled as she looked up into the kind depths of his eyes. He was such a good man, such a good person. He'd made such an amazing stand-in father and…he'd fallen in love with a stranger. And that, when all was said and done, was the reality standing between them. "You don't love me, Fletcher." She tried to tug free, but he held on tighter. "Believe me, you don't. You don't know who I am. What I am." When he didn't give any indication of being convinced, she knew she had only one grenade left to lob. "You don't know what I've done."

"I don't care what you've done. I've seen you work your fingers to the bone ever since you got here to give Charlie a good life, a good home. I've seen you with Mrs. Hastings and Nina and Willa. I let you convince me to give Jasper the benefit of the doubt because I know you see the good in people no matter what. I do know you." He released her hands, and before she could dart out of reach, he caught her face between his palms and bent to press his forehead against hers. "I know and I love you. Please don't run away from me. Don't take Charlie away from me."

His last statement felt like a bucket of ice water to the face. "Don't you use Charlie in this. Don't you try to guilt me by using her." She wrenched herself free. "And don't negate my feelings or beliefs because you think you know who I am. Because you don't."

"Then tell me!" His blast of temper made her jump. "Enough with the cloak-and-dagger and innuendos about what a terrible person you are. If you want me to let you go, you'd better give me a good reason. Right here. Right now. What or who are you running from, Paige?"

"The police!" she yelled. "You wanted the truth. I'm running from the police. Sixteen months ago a material witness arrest warrant was issued for me back in New York. I'm a fugitive, Fletcher." To make certain there was no room for misinterpretation, she stepped closer and looked him straight in the eye. "I'm a fugitive."

Funny how when a grenade went off silence descended. Not the ordinary, peaceful ocean-town silence, but that nerve-racking, vibrating absence of sound that frayed every nerve ending in the body. Fletch didn't move. Not his body, not his face. Not even his eyes. They didn't flicker as they peered into hers. But she saw it: his faith in her cracked, like she'd slammed her fist into a mirror.

"What did you do?"

"Does it matter?"

"Yes." Fletch nodded almost imperceptibly. "Yes, actually, it does. Does this have something to do with Charlie's father dying? Were you trying to support her? Did you steal something? Hurt someone?"

If only. "I treated a teenager for a gunshot wound. I didn't find out until after that he was suspected of firing first in a drug bust. I didn't report it." If she'd hoped to feel a sense of having been cleansed by admitting the truth, she should have known better. The weight just pressed in harder. "I was a semester shy of my nursing degree. He was the grandson of our neighbor. He refused to go to the emergency room and his grandmother was terrified he was going to die. I did what I was trained to do. I saved his life."

"Was he guilty?"

"What does that matter? He was hurt and needed help. I took an oath, Fletcher. I did my job." And it had cost her everything. "For the record? Yes, apparently he did do it. And the detective he shot will spend the rest of his life in a wheelchair. Fifteen years on the job, married with two kids." A thought that still kept her up at night.

"You aided and abetted a criminal." The glint in his green eyes went as brittle as glass, shattering as he looked at her. "And then you ran."

In that moment, any hope she could stay, any hope Charlie could grow up in Butterfly Harbor, any hope Paige had of a future with Fletcher Bradley vanished. But she was done hiding. Done lying. At least as far as Fletcher was concerned. "Yes. To all of it. So tell me again how you love me, Fletcher. Tell me again how I should stay and risk losing my child because I helped someone."

"Someone who didn't deserve it. He shot a cop, Paige."

"So I should have let him die? That's not how things work in medicine, Fletcher. My job is to save every life I can. It doesn't matter who that life belongs to or what they've done. I don't get to make that distinction."

"But you can where the law is concerned. You break the law when it suits you. When it affects you."

Except it wasn't going to affect only her. It would have affected Charlie. It had affected Charlie. And that, Paige had to admit, was the real tragedy. Her daughter was going to be tarnished by this for the rest of her life.

"What are you going to do?" Paige asked.

"Are you going to turn me in? Or are you going to let me—"

"Or will I let you go?" Every word sounded like he was spewing ice. "What a choice that is. You were right. The Paige I love, she wouldn't do this. She wouldn't lie to everyone who's tried to help her ever since she got here. Does Holly know? Or Luke? What about Abby? Mrs. Hastings?"

"No." She shook her head. "You're the only person I've told."

"And with one foot over the city limits. Lucky me."

"Maybe now you understand why I tried to stay away from you. I didn't want to lie, Fletcher. I didn't want to pretend to be someone I'm not."

"Well, doesn't that just make me all kinds of stupid. Can't take a hint even when it's slapping me in the face."

"I'm sor—"

"Please, don't." He held up his hands, backed away. "You were right before. I really didn't know you at all." Every step he took away from her felt like a scalpel slicing her heart. "You really had me fooled."

She could tell him the rest, that it was Charlie who had been threatened, that she'd only been trying to protect her daughter by running, but just as she'd demanded he not use Charlie against her, she wasn't going to use her little girl against him. If the only way for her to leave was for him to hate her, so be it. She'd have to accept it.

"You didn't answer my question," Paige called from where she stood among the pile of her life, everything she had in the world. "What are you going to do?"

Fletch paused, his knuckles going tight around the doorknob. "What I have to."

He closed the door behind him.

Paige stared, wondering when, if ever, her heart was going to start beating again. The walls closed in on her. Everything she owned in the world seemed to take on a life of its own, accusing her, reminding her of everything she'd done wrong. Everything she wished she could do over. She'd done so much damage to her life, to Charlie's, and now to Fletcher's. The position she'd put him in was impossible.

She walked over to the kitchen table, sorted through the papers by her computer, found the card she wanted. She stared at the number for longer than she should have, her mind racing through the pros and cons, but circling back, always, to what was best for her child.

It was time to stop running. It was time to take responsibility for her actions, however well motivated they might have been.

She pulled out her cell phone and dialed. "Hi, Leah? It's Paige from the Butterfly Diner." She cleared her throat, blinked back the tears. "How long will it take to draw up an emergency custody agreement?"

CHARLIE HELD HER arms out at her sides and tried to keep her balance as she followed Simon's lead across the slippery, rain-slick rocks. She felt like they'd been walking for hours. She was wet, cold, tired and shaking so hard her teeth were chattering. She'd stopped wiping the rain from her face ages ago. It wasn't any use.

Keeping her head down, her hood laces pulled tight to protect her head, she wobbled this way and that toward what she and Simon hoped was a clearing on the other side of the beach.

"Simon!" Charlie called but her voice disappeared into the wind snapping at her jacket and sleeves. "Simon, slow down! I can't see you!" She squinted, tried to see through the raindrops.

"I'm over here!"

Simon's voice was faint, but Charlie felt her chest relax a little when she caught sight of his red raincoat off in the distance.

The wind billowed, blasting around her and driving her back. She cried out, ducked down and scraped her fingers into the slippery rock for balance. She waited, counting slowly until things calmed down. Her backpack was soaked, getting heavy and dragging her backward. Turning her back on the ocean, she unzipped her jacket, shimmied an arm free so she could take off the backpack. Feeling lighter and more in control, she put her jacket back on and, clutching the butterfly pack against her chest, made her way to where Simon had disappeared around a tall outcropping of algae-covered rocks.

"Simon?" she called when her feet hit sand. She sank down, ankle-deep, sand clumps dropping into her shoes, into her socks.

"This way! I found the caves!" Charlie set her backpack down and ran toward him. The small opening looked just like it did on the map they'd found online. Just like the map in the storybook she'd discovered on Mrs. Hastings's bookshelf weeks ago.

"Simon, you did it!" Charlie squealed and danced out of the way as a wave of water rushed up behind them and cascaded into the passage in front of them. "It has to be in there." She dived forward, but Simon caught her jacket.

"Wait." He dug into his pocket and pulled out a huge flashlight that took two hands to turn on. "It's one of those waterproof ones." The beam of light seemed pretty weak to Charlie, but when he aimed it into the narrow passage, she could see inside. "I should go first." Simon pulled her back.

"Why? Because you're a boy?"

"No, because I have the flashlight. Unless you want to go walking in the dark."

"I have to be the one to find it. Only the person who finds it gets their wish, and you already got yours." She held out her hands, which had gone bright pink and very stiff. It hurt to bend her fingers, but she couldn't stop now. She was so close. "Please let me have the light, Simon." She had to yell over the wind.

He didn't look convinced, but it was hard to tell given all the water on his glasses. He needed that impervious spell that wizard in the books used during his sporting matches.

"Please, Simon. It has to be me."

"Yeah, okay." He still didn't look happy about it as he handed the flashlight over.

Charlie bent down, aimed the light up, down and around so she could see what the best angle was. She ducked inside just as another wave washed in behind her, pushing her off balance, and rushed her into the cave far faster than she would have liked. But once she was inside…

She heard Simon splashing behind her as he followed. Her ears almost hurt at how quiet it was. She set the light down, pushed her hood off and turned in a slow circle as she noted what seemed like endless passageways erupting in front of her.

"Which way do we go?" She looked back at Simon, who was digging the map out of his other pocket. "I didn't think there would be this many to choose from."

"Neither did I. Hang on." Simon walked over and held the map over the light. "Should be the third one from the left." He pointed to the tunnel just ahead of them. "See? They're all here, and this has the dotted red line going forward. Sound good to you?"

"Yes." Except now she wasn't so sure this had been a good idea at all. It smelled really weird in here. Really dirty and stuffy and the water was spilling in from the ocean, dripping down off the ceiling as if it had been flooded not so long ago. "It's getting late. We should probably hurry up."

"Yeah. Abby told us to be back by three for your mom to pick you up."

"What time is it now?"

"Two fifteen." He squinted at his watch. "I think. My watch is really wet. Come on. Let's go." This time after Charlie picked up the light, he held out his hand. She took it. They walked side by side into the passageway, scrunching together as the walls shrank.

Her feet slapped in the water that was coming up around her ankles, splashing up around her knees. They kept walking, deeper and deeper. Simon slowed down, squeezed his hand around hers. "Maybe we need to go back."

"We can't," Charlie said even as she was thinking the same. "What if we're super close and we just walk away? Please just a little more? I promise, if we don't come to the end soon I'll—" Except the passageway did end.

And it opened up into a cavern that sloped

down. An outcropping of rocks jutted around the edge like a walkway.

Charlie aimed the beam around, looking up and down, for something, anything that looked like the magical wooden box the story talked about. The butterfly box that would fix everything she'd done wrong.

"I don't like this, Charlie." Simon held back when she took a step onto the ledge.

She heard a crack under her feet. Something shifted. But she kept moving, her eyes scanning until she caught the glint of something in the corner across the expanse. She looked down, felt her stomach drop as she realized just how high up she was.

"I think I see it!" She aimed the light across the way. "And I'm small enough to get around." The ledge was maybe a foot wide, if she remembered her first-grade math class on rulers correctly.

"Charlie—" Whatever else Simon said was drowned out by the rushing roar of water shooting through the passageway, circling and filling the bottom of the cave.

"It won't take me long!" She set the flashlight down on the ledge, aimed it across the way so she could see where she was heading. The sooner she reached the box, the sooner she could have her family and not have to leave Butterfly Harbor.

"Charlie, no! Come back!" Simon's frantic yell had her looking over her shoulder as another wave crashed into the space. She walked faster, curved around, sliding one hand against the sharp rocks on one side. She held out the other to stop herself from toppling over. It was like the balance beam, she told herself, in that gymnastics class she'd taken in Ohio. She just had to be very careful and very deliberate about where she stepped and how much weight she put on her...

"I see it!" The object she'd seen from the entrance glimmered. Shiny. It looked like polished wood, just like the treasure box from the story. When she stopped in front of it, she felt her eyes burn with tears. "It's here!" She bent down, reached out to touch it. All she had to do was open it and tell it her heart's deepest desire. Her fingers wrapped around the edges and she pulled. It didn't move. She tried again. Nothing. She grunted, shifted positions, pushed her hands deeper into the space between the box and the rocks. Water lapped up from beneath her, soaking her shoes.

"Charlie, come on! It's filling up! The tide must be coming in."

"Almost…have…it." There! She felt the other end of the box. She shoved her arm deeper to grab hold and… "I'm stuck!"

"What?" Simon yelled.

Charlie tried to pull her arm free, odd sounds exploding out of her throat as she could barely move. "I'm stuck! I can't get out." She tried again, felt her arm burning the harder she worked. "Simon, help!"

"Hang on! I'm coming!" She twisted around so she could see him heading around the ledge the same way she had, only when he got to the flashlight, she heard that same crumbling she'd heard before. And this time she knew what it was.

"Simon, go back!" Charlie yelled. "It's going to break!"

Simon looked across at her for a split second before he shifted back the way he'd come, the flashlight in his hand. "Maybe I can swim across."

"No." Charlie sobbed. Her entire body hurt. She twisted again, another direction, any way she could, but nothing was happening. "No. Go get help. But hurry!" Charlie looked down, and in the dim beam of the light she could see the water level climbing. "Please, Simon, hurry!"

"Hey, Abby, you have a minute to talk?" Once her shift at the diner was over, Paige found her friend in the kitchen of the Flutterby trying to sneak a taste of the chicken soup her fiancé had simmering on the stove.

"Jeez, sneak up on a girl, why don't you?" Abby fanned her mouth as she'd sipped too fast. "Ah, man, that's going to hit the spot tonight. What's up? If you're looking for the terrible two, they're in one of the cabins working on their secret scheme."

"I'll go down and get her in a few minutes." Paige shoved her hands deep into the pocket of her raincoat. She'd packed up as much as she could manage, surrendering to the need to use a few boxes, the smallest ones that would fit in her ancient car. "I let Ursula know a little while ago, and I need for you to tell Holly I'm sorry I couldn't tell her in person. I'm, um, I'm leaving. In the morning."

It should have gotten easier each time she said it. Instead, it was only becoming more difficult.

"What do you mean, *leaving*?" Abby stared

wide-eyed at her. "Paige, what on earth are you talking about?"

"It's not important, just wanted to let you know. You know, so you can tell, well, everyone." She couldn't bring herself to speak to Mrs. Hastings again. If for no other reason than to avoid admitting that the old woman's faith in Fletcher had been misplaced.

Not that she blamed him. She didn't. He'd reacted exactly as she'd expected him to. Exactly how she'd feared he would. It was her own fault for ever believing things would be different just because she'd fallen in love with him.

When she turned to leave, Abby ran to her and slipped in front of her. She stretched out her peach-sweater-covered arms and blocked her from exiting.

"No way do you get to drop a bombshell like that and slink away. What on earth is going on? Is it Fletch? Did he say something to upset you? He didn't dump you, did he?"

"No." Paige hated sounding so weepy. "If anything…he told me he loves me." She had to drop her head back to try to stop the tears from falling, but that didn't help. At all. "It's all just really complicated, Abby. It's just easier if I go and—"

"And what? Let your friends worry about you and Charlie for the rest of their lives? No way. Not happening. You're going to tell me everything. Right now. Jason, great. Make her sit down."

Jason stopped just inside the kitchen, his hands filled with empty serving dishes from the buffet he'd set out for Gil Hamilton's business friends. "Sure." He jerked his chin toward one of the stools at the stainless steel work counter. "Paige, sit."

"Big help you are," Abby muttered as she planted her hands on Paige's shoulders and spun her toward the stools. "I'm not letting you go anywhere until you tell me what's really going on. And don't even think about fighting me. I got this lug back here to agree to marry me, so you know what I'm capable of."

"This is true," Jason said, but as he set down the dishes and turned his attention on Paige, Paige noticed the concern in his eyes. "This have something to do with why you're leaving town?"

"How did you—?" Abby swung on him.

"She just quit the diner. Full house when she did, so…word's gotten around already." Jason poured three cups of coffee and set them in front of them. "Abby's right. We aren't letting you leave until you tell us what's going on."

"I don't want to." Paige's chin wobbled as she sank onto the stool. "I really don't think I can take any more disappointment from people I care about today. Please don't ask me to." It couldn't matter that the only thing she wanted right now was to feel safe, to feel wanted. To feel loved.

"Oh, honey." Abby wrapped her arm around her shoulders and squeezed. "It can't be that bad."

"It is." Paige brushed away the tears. "I made a really, really big mistake a while ago. Something I'm not sure I can fix. But for the first time since it happened, I don't know what to do." She rested her head on Abby's shoulder. "I don't think I could bear it if you all hated me, too."

"Who hates you?" Jason asked and looked as if he'd been struck with a stupid stick.

"Fletcher. I told him the truth about what I did and, well…" Paige shrugged. "Let's just say it went about as well as I expected." Her two months had turned into hours, and yet here she stayed…because part of her, the biggest part of her, didn't want to leave.

"How about you fill us in and we'll take it from there?" Abby said.

"Paige." Jason reached out his hand palm up and waited for her to take hold. "You know what I went through a few months back. You know what I was dealing with. It wasn't until I realized I had people around me to help that I was able to start to let go. You aren't alone anymore. You have us. I promise, whatever it is you've done, neither of us is going to judge you."

"Not even if I helped someone who tried to kill a police officer?" There it was. Again. Only this time it didn't hurt quite so much to say.

Abby's hand stilled from rubbing her arm. "Okay, I don't know if that's just you testing the limits of what Jason just said or if you're being honest."

"Oh, that's me being honest." She was down the rabbit hole now, wasn't she? "You really want the truth? Okay, you asked for it."

And she told them.

WELL, HADN'T THIS just been one horrible, soul-destroying, bottom-of-the-barrel day. And it wasn't even noon. Normally Fletch would embrace the unexpected storm.

Weather like this tended to shut the town down as people hunkered in their homes with roaring fires and pots of soup on the stove.

What he wouldn't give for a day like that.

He sat and stared at his computer screen, at the case Paige had gotten herself caught up in sixteen months ago. Sure enough, pretty much everything she'd told him was right on the money. All the way down to the material witness warrant that was still in effect against her.

"You stare any harder at that computer you're going to burn a hole in it." Ozzy's teasing didn't even result in a flicker of amusement. "You okay, Fletch?"

"Not remotely." He clicked through the reported details of the case, right down to the evidence against the fifteen- now sixteen-year-old repeat offender who had indeed been charged with shooting an NYC detective and left him paralyzed from the waist down. Detective Marty Diaz was still listed as one of the investigators; the former partner of the detective who had been shot. Diaz had commendations up to his neck, one of the best-thought-of detectives in his department. Hard-core, old-school, by-the-book cop.

"No wonder she ran." Diaz had probably

intimidated her. Didn't change what Paige had done, however. What had she been thinking, disappearing with a kid in tow and a warrant trailing behind? How was either of them supposed to have any kind of normal life? She should have just owned up to her mistake and been done with it. Instead…

Instead, now all of them were in a mess. Including him.

He looked at his phone for at least the tenth time. A fugitive was in his jurisdiction. He should have made the call as soon as he got back to the station. Instead, all he was doing was sitting here, looking for any and every reason to forget he'd ever heard of or met Paige, make that *Amelia* Paige Cooper. Amelia. He almost laughed. She didn't even look like an Amelia.

When his cell phone rang and he saw it was Abby, he debated about answering. Then again, he could use a good distraction.

"Hey, Abby."

"Don't you hey Abby me, you idiotic lump. What is the matter with you? When did you trade your brain in for a tinfoil hat?"

He sat up straight in his chair. Abby sounded…angry. Except that wasn't possible. Abby didn't get angry. There was a reason everyone considered her the town's personal good-luck fairy. She flitted around practically dousing everyone with pixie dust. "I might ask you the same question," Fletch said as he held the phone out to save his hearing.

"Well, then get over to the inn and ask me in person, you—hey! Jason Corwin, you give me that phone right now—"

"Fletcher?" Jason's voice floated oddly calm over the line. "I believe my gracious and genteel fiancée is requesting your presence at the inn at your earliest convenience. We have something we need to discuss with you. Regarding Paige."

"You've got to be kidding me." Fletch dropped his head into his hand. "What did she do, take out a full-page ad in the paper after she unloaded to me?"

"Well, she didn't unload everything on you," Jason said. "Hang on a second. Sorry. Needed to get away from Abby before she reclaimed the phone. Yes, Paige told us the story, Fletcher. The *whole* story."

"Let me guess, she left out the part where she robbed a bank on her way out of town?"

"Wow. You're so ticked at her lying about this, you don't see it at all, do you? What's the one thing that would have made her throw her entire life, years of training, everything she cared about away to protect?"

Fletch's entire body went numb. He almost dropped the phone. "Charlie."

"What do you know? Your brain is still functioning."

"What would she have to protect Charlie from—"

"An overzealous detective who, when it was discovered she hadn't reported the injury, retaliated by telling Paige he was going to throw Charlie into the foster care system once Paige was arrested for aiding and abetting a criminal."

"He did what?" The anger in his voice burned his throat.

"You heard me. Seems he'd looked into her background and found out she was a foster kid. Figured he'd get her locked down and on their side, but instead he scared her into disappearing. They've been running ever since. And if you think for one minute either Abby or I blame her one bit, think again. We're going to figure out a way to fix this and make things right. For her and Charlie. So might I suggest you get your priorities straight before I come over there and clobber you with my ladle?" He hung up.

Fletch held out his phone and stared at the blank screen. Was there even a word for how completely stupid he'd been? "Ozzy, I have to go."

"Yeah, sure. Everything—"

The door slammed open and Simon flew in, bringing half the storm with him. Leaves and branches swirled behind him, blowing inside.

"H-help. Need help." He pitched forward, but Fletch darted around the counter and caught him before he hit the floor. "Charlie." Simon's breath rattled as if he had water in his lungs. "Down at the beach. Arm caught. Water...rising." He grabbed on to Fletcher's arms and turned such panicked eyes to his, Fletcher felt himself falling into the past. "She needs help. She's going to drown!"

"Oz!" Fletch shouted.

"On it!" Ozzy was on the phone a second later, rattling off information to Matt, who was out on patrol.

"Jeez, kid, you're a block of ice." Fletcher carried him into Luke's office and grabbed the blanket off the back of the sofa, wrapped him up as tight as he could before he flicked on the space heater. "Simon, you need to tell me exactly where she is." He could barely hear his own voice above the jackhammering of his own heart.

"I have a m-m-map." Simon shivered so hard Fletch was worried his bones might snap. "In my p-pocket." He tried to pull it out, but he couldn't hold still.

"I've got it, buddy." Fletcher yanked it free. "Show me." Simon moved his finger around the map, mumbling about landmarks and where to look.

The beach and surrounding area was the one part of Butterfly Harbor Fletch held little familiarity with, but he committed the map to memory as if his life—Charlie's life—depended on it.

"Just checked with the weather service and there's a high tide warning in effect as of twenty minutes ago," Ozzy said from the doorway. "Matt's on his way to the diner and the hardware store to get reinforcements. Do we know where she is?"

"I do." Fletcher held on to the waterlogged printout as carefully as he could without smearing the ink, ran a copy on the printer and handed the damp one to Oz. "Simon can fill you in. You get everyone you can to follow me there as fast as possible, you hear me?"

"Wait! Fletcher!" Ozzy yelled and followed him to the door as Fletcher pulled on his hat and jacket. "You can't do this on your own."

"I'm not leaving her out there alone. Paige is at the inn with Abby and Jason. You make sure Simon gets over to them, fill them in. And tell Paige…" The words caught in his throat. "You tell Paige I'm going to get Charlie."

He ran out into the storm, turned his face into the pelting rain and raced down the path to the beach, not stopping, even when his feet hit the wet sand. If he stopped, he gave the fear time to catch up, time to overwhelm, and he didn't have time for fear.

Neither did Charlie.

CHAPTER SIXTEEN

PAIGE SIGHED, THE caffeine buzzing in her system causing her already out-of-control thoughts to race like an over-revved race car. She was being held hostage by a short, blonde innkeeper and her wickedly talented chef of a fiancé. If Paige even glanced at the door, she got the stink eye from both of them.

"Calling Fletcher won't have changed anything," Paige said. "You're only going to convince him to call the New York cops faster."

"He makes one call to that department and I'm going to make sure he lives to regret it." Abby hadn't stopped pacing since Paige had told them the whole—and this time it was the whole—story. From her years in foster care, losing Charlie's father, to her medical training. The whole pathetic story that ended with Paige becoming a wanted fugitive.

"I actually heard about the case you're involved in," Jason said as he dished out a bowl of noodle-heavy soup, set it in front of her, then retrieved a fresh-baked batch of biscuits from the oven. "It was all over the news at the time, but I don't remember hearing anything about you. Only that the kid had been shot during the crime, as well."

"He was shot twice." She could still remember having to dig out the bullets from his shoulder and side. "See what never saying no to someone gets you?"

"Doesn't mean Fletch gets to lord it over you," Abby mumbled. "I expected better of him. It's not like he's Mr. Perfect."

"Actually, he kinda is." For the first time since the credit card revelation last night, she found herself smiling. "Don't blame Fletcher, Abby, please. He's a police officer. I always knew this could happen." It was the main reason she'd tried so hard to stay away from him. "Of course he's going to side with the cops. What I did was a betrayal of everything he believes in." But she knew what her real crime was as far as he was concerned: everything she'd ever told him—told anyone— since she'd arrived in Butterfly Harbor had been a lie.

"What Fletcher believes in first is family, and he should have remembered that," Abby said.

Someone yelling out in the hotel lobby had all of them looking toward the door as it swung open and Ozzy pushed Simon inside. "Paige." Ozzy whipped off his rain-soaked hat as Abby raced forward to grab hold of a shivering Simon. Before he said another word, Paige felt her entire world screech to a halt. She got to her feet, hands fisted at her sides, as she looked at a dazed Simon, who blinked puddle-sized tears.

"Where's Charlie?" She sounded so calm, so in control. It was all an act. "Ozzy, where's my daughter?"

"Down in the caves," Ozzy said. "She got caught inside. We've got people getting ready to head down to help. The tide's coming in fast and we'll need sandbags, but it's going to take time. Fletch should already be there."

"Fletch?" Paige felt herself sway. "No, no. Oh, Ozzy, we have to go help him." She ran forward to the doorway. "He's not good around water, around the ocean. His little brother drowned when Fletcher was a teenager. He gets panic attacks—" Realizing she'd revealed a secret Fletch had kept most of his life, she slapped a hand over her mouth. "Oh, no. Fletch." Despite his phobia, despite the fear, he'd gone after her baby. Even after all she'd done, all the lies she'd told, he'd done what he'd always done: he hadn't hesitated to put Charlie first. If something was going to happen…to either of them… "I need to get down there."

"Let's go." Jason had already come to stand next to her. "Ozzy, you're with me and Paige. Abby, you stay here with Simon and run point. Start making coffee and phone calls. Don't worry, Paige." He stopped long enough to squeeze a comforting hand on her shoulder. "This is Butterfly Harbor. We've got this."

FLETCHER MANAGED TO stave off the full-blown panic until he started making his way up the outcropping of rocks. His heart pounded so hard it physically hurt. His head was filled by the overwhelming echoes of the tide and crashing waves as they sprayed over him. Every step he took felt weighted down like he was wearing cement socks. But he couldn't stop. He didn't have the luxury of surrendering.

He was not going to be too late. Not again.

"We're going to find her and she's going to be fine." Fletcher repeated the mantra to himself as he maneuvered around, over and through the slippery patches. He forced himself to slow down, to stand up and take in his surroundings, get his bearings. For a moment, it was as if he was hovering outside himself, the terrified part of him breaking off to let him grab hold of whatever control he could muster.

He didn't dare look out in the water. Focusing on the rocks, on the sand, the lichen and algae around him; those he could handle. Staring out into the empty vastness of the unending ocean might be enough to stop him dead in his tracks.

A flash of color from on top of the cliffs caught his attention. Brilliant color, long red hair, the faint sound of tinkling bells as Calliope Jones stretched out her hands as if worshipping the obscured sun beneath the pounding rain.

A flicker of movement dropped from her hands, a blur, barely noticeable as the object flitted and bounced against the wind. He followed the sight, and as he did, he saw a path breaking through the rocks and there, at the base of the path, just around the corner, a familiar fabric butterfly wing.

"Not far," Fletcher whispered as he regained his thoughts and focused on that wing.

As far up as he'd climbed was as far down as he descended. He scrunched his toes hard into his work boots with every step, gripping for balance as he forced himself onward. He swore, as soon as this was over, once Charlie was home safe and sound—and severely grounded if he had anything to say about it—he was putting warning signs back up from here to the coast to stay off the rocks. "Stupid budget cuts."

He jumped off higher than he should have, hit the sand harder than expected. But he was back on his feet and racing to where Charlie's drenched backpack sagged against the bottom of the cliffs.

There, right in front of him, the rocks had a big break, an opening that was going to challenge whatever strength he had left.

"Fletcher!"

The voice called from behind him, from the same path he'd taken, and he stepped back to find Jason, Ozzy and Paige making their way toward him.

"Fletcher, where is she?" Paige cried as she sat on the biggest rock left and slid down to the sand. She ran full bore at him, reaching for the backpack that he held out. "Fletcher?"

"Simon said they went inside."

"Inside there?" she screeched. "What on earth were they…" She went silent, anger and fear battling it out in her glassy eyes. "The treasure box. She's looking for that treasure box."

"Let's hope she either found it or got it out of her system."

"How are you so calm?" Paige asked. "How can you—"

"Because it's Charlie," Fletch said with more bravado than he felt. He had to focus on her, not see the ocean beyond her, not hear the crashing waves or…that flicker of something that seemed to stop at the opening of the cave. "We need to get in there."

"I have flashlights and some air tanks." Ozzy scrambled down the last of the path. "Harvey's leading a huge group behind us. We'll start filling sandbags as soon as they get here. See if we can stop the water…"

Paige grabbed his arm. "Fletch, I have to go with—"

"No, Paige. Please stay. I need you to understand this. It's too dangerous. And when Charlie comes out, she'll really need you…"

Paige looked as if she wanted to argue, but she set her jaw and nodded.

Fletch led the way, squeezing himself

through the narrow cave opening, the rough rocks scraping against his skin.

"Gotta hand it to these two," Jason grunted as he slithered in behind him. They inched their way forward, the water both helping and hindering their progress. "I really thought the stories about Simon's extracurricular activities were exaggerated, but this exceeds even my expectations."

"I'm thinking Charlie's reputation is about to be upped," Fletch agreed, grateful to be distracted by the conversation. Once they were in the main cavern, he clicked on the waterproof flashlight, looking for the third passage that Simon had described to him.

Thoughts of Charlie returned. She was all he cared about. He'd been too late one too many times in his life already. Which was why he barreled through the passage so fast his feet barely hit the ground. When he skidded to a halt at the opening and saw water had filled the cavern up over the ledge Simon told him about, he felt his stomach drop. "Charlie. I don't see her." His hands shook as he flashed the light around. Where was she?

"There!" Jason pointed off to the side, the flash of pink, Charlie's head and shoulders still above the waterline.

"Charlie!" Fletcher yelled.

"Deputy Fletch! I'm stuck! I can't get my arm out. The water—" she sputtered.

"It's okay, Charlie, I'm coming."

Water rushed in behind him, knocked into the backs of his knees and nearly drove him over the edge. His entire body went clammy. He could barely move, but he kept his focus on the pink spot across the distance.

"You want me to go?" Jason set a reassuring hand on his shoulder. "Paige said she thought you might have some…issues."

"Issues?" Fletcher could feel the fear building inside him. Fear he needed to face. "Guess my secret's out. I appreciate the offer, but I need to do this." Before he could think it through, he stepped forward and into the water.

He dropped…farther than he expected, the unfamiliar rush of water around him driving the air from his lungs.

Another plume of water rushed in, hitting Fletcher square on the top of his head before he pushed out from under it. He forced the air out of his nose and found himself floating free for what felt like minutes. The silence was oddly calming. He didn't have to breathe. The faint light from the flashlights reflected off the surface of the water as he sank, falling…until the sound of a child's cry ripped through his ears, shaking him loose from his fear. He kicked, rotated and propelled himself up. When he broke the surface, he could hear Charlie crying, screaming his name.

"I'm here, Charlie," he gasped as he swam over to her. "Jason, aim that light over this way! I'm not going anywhere, Charlie. You're safe now." He arced his arm over his head, found the ledge and grabbed hold to haul himself up beside her.

"I thought you'd gotten drowned." Charlie's face was damp with the ocean and tears, her lashes spiked. She kept tugging at her arm. "I can't get out. I only wanted to find the box and have my wish. I'm so sorry, Deputy Fletcher. I know I'm not supposed to go to the water alone. Please don't yell at me again."

"I'm not going to yell, but we will talk about this later." First thing he did was kiss the top of her head, if only to prove to himself she was okay. "I want you to hold still for a second, okay? Just let me see if I can get my hand…in…here…" He forced his hand in under her arm, tried to find enough space to pry her free, but she'd gotten her jacket hooked on something sharp around back.

And her fingers… "Charlie, you need to let go of the box."

"I can't." She shook her head. "If I do that I lose my wish. I want to stay. I don't want to move again."

As stubborn as her mother. "Charlie, listen to me." He grabbed hold of her chin and forced her to look at him. "You're not going anywhere, do you hear me? You'll get your wish, I promise, you won't have to leave. But you have to trust me. You have to let go."

Charlie narrowed her eyes. "You're just saying that so I'll do what you want."

They did not have time for a philosophical debate. "I don't lie to the people I love. Now let go of the box."

"Fletch! The water should be slowing soon!" Jason's voice exploded through the cavern. "You got her? She okay?"

"Almost! Charlie, please. Just relax your hand." He felt the tension in her arm ease, and he tugged as gently as he could. The water lapped up, slapped him in the face, sharp as a razor. He hated it with every fiber of his being.

He wasn't going to let it win again.

"It's not working." Charlie got that determined look on her face. "Maybe if you broke my arm?"

"I know you thought his cast was cool when he broke his, but stop competing with Simon." The very idea of her breaking anything made him sick to his stomach. "How about you close your eyes and make a new wish. A butterfly wish. Have you heard of those?" He must really be father material if he was making up spur-of-the-moment stories to distract a child. "You imagine a butterfly fluttering around your head, reading your every thought. You doing that, Charlie?" He tried to move his arm around hers, but there was so little space and he'd already ripped through the fabric of his shirt.

"Uh-huh. It's a pretty butterfly. A monarch. They're my favorites."

"Like the ones on Calliope's farm, right?" He tried to keep his voice light. "Now, you tell that butterfly your wish. That you want to leave, that you want to be free, just like the butterfly is." There. Her arm moved. He could almost hear the rock giving way as he pushed his own arm against the sides. He felt her fingers, so cold and stiff, against his hand.

"There it is," Charlie said, awe in her voice. "Deputy Fletch, look! It's a butterfly!"

As he gave one final pull and looked up to where Charlie's gaze landed, he saw the flitting, glistening wings of the orange-and-black-winged creature, hovering, the imperceptible sound of wings beating brushing against his ears.

For a moment he wondered...was that the same butterfly that had guided him to her?

Charlie's arm pulled free. She almost floated away before Fletcher grabbed her and wrapped her arms around his neck. He couldn't stop looking at the butterfly as it drifted down, almost to eye level, before leading the way back across the cavern's flooded expanse.

"She's so pretty," Charlie whispered. "My magic butterfly. She gave me my wishes."

"And with so little effort on your part," Fletch gasped, trying to remember how to swim on the surface while carrying someone else. "When we get back outside, remember your mom's going to be upset. She's going to be crying and she's going to be mad. She gets to be, you understand? You let her work through whatever she needs to."

"M'kay." Charlie kicked her legs, probably

thinking she was helping, but ended up kicking him in the thighs. He went under more than once, but finally, he reached out and grabbed the ledge under Jason's feet.

"Okay, you could have timed that a little better." Jason reached down and hauled Charlie off Fletch's back. "You okay, Charlie?"

"Five by five!" She grabbed his flashlight and aimed it at the butterfly as it flitted into the passage. "I'll go on ahead. You wait for my dad."

"Kids. They get what they want and then they just leave you behind." Fletcher threw himself forward onto the ledge. Dad. Huh. Luke was right. That did have a nice ring to it. "I think I need a vacation."

"You've earned it." Jason slapped him on the back. "Let's get you back to your family."

PAIGE STARED AT the opening to the caves, her body numb with cold and fear, the warmth and support of her friends surrounding her. Dozens of people had joined them on the beach, from Abby and Simon, to Charlie's soon-to-be teacher. Store owners, inn employees, Harvey from the hardware store along with his team of workers, who had filled enough sandbags to keep the tide at bay despite the sudden clearing of the storm. Comforting hands held her, encouraged her, positive thoughts being murmured from the circle. Gil Hamilton and his staff from the mayor's office had joined the effort, and now they all stood…waiting.

"She'll be okay," Abby whispered as she clung to both Paige and Simon. "Fletch won't let anything happen to her."

"I know." And she did know. But she also knew a person's worst enemy was often themselves. He had a lot of demons that went into the cave with him. She could only hope and pray that they wouldn't overwhelm him.

"There!" Simon yelled as a flash of color shifted in the opening of the rocks. "That's her! Charlie!" He started to run forward, but Abby tugged him back, then gently pushed Paige forward as she stumbled toward her daughter.

"Mom!" Charlie burst free, soaked to the skin, scraped up and looking as wide-eyed excited as she did every day of her life. "Mom!" She ran into Paige's arms as Paige sank to her knees. Never in her life had she felt such relief, such a rush of love as she did holding her child. Safe. Uninjured. Alive. Thanks to Fletch.

Jason emerged next, followed by Fletch. The roar of applause and cheers overtook any sounds the ocean might have made as Paige lifted her head to look up into Fletch's strained face. He sagged against the rocks, was instantly surrounded by friends and neighbors as they congratulated him. But he didn't once, not even for a fraction of a second, pull his gaze from hers.

"Thank you," she mouthed and hugged Charlie even tighter.

"Mom, I can't breathe," Charlie mumbled against her chest.

"I don't care." She rocked her back and forth, kissed her head, smoothed her hair. "Charlotte Rose Cooper, you are in so much trouble I can't even think straight."

"Yeah, I know." Charlie sighed. "Deputy Fletcher said so. I called him dad. I hope he didn't mind."

Paige squeezed her eyes shut so hard they hurt. "I don't think he minded at all."

"Can we go home now? I'm hungry."

"You bet, let's get you home," Paige whispered. As she got to her feet and pulled Charlie with her, she looked up. A flash of color near the top of the rocks caught her eye, as the butterfly her daughter couldn't stop watching flitted toward Calliope Jones's outstretched hand, landing on her finger. Calliope dipped her head, the gentle breeze sending the sound of tinkling bells down to the shore. And then she and the butterfly were gone.

"I thought butterflies didn't fly in the rain, Mom." Charlie squirmed in her grasp as Simon ran over to hug her. "How did it get in the caves if it can't fly in the rain?"

"I don't know," Paige said as she turned into Abby's hug and thanked all those who had come to support her and Charlie. She didn't know how a butterfly could fly in the rain, but she did know one thing for certain: Paige might not be able to stay in Butterfly Harbor.

But she was going to make sure her daughter would.

CHAPTER SEVENTEEN

"WE'RE GOING TO need to hire more employees if you're going to keep having days like this," Ursula grumbled as she banged on her service bell for pickup. "Didn't expect a dinner rush after a major rescue like that. Look at your girl over there, hustling the deputies at cards. Never knew she put the scare of a lifetime into all of us earlier today."

"No, you wouldn't." Paige looked over from her seat at the counter, a seat she hadn't been allowed to leave ever since she and Charlie had come down after long hot showers, a change of clothes and a new attitude. She had a lot to take care of, a lot she'd been putting off, but it couldn't be put off any longer. Mrs. Hastings, perched on her own stool at the end of the counter, sent her one of her knowing looks.

The diner was filled to the gills, but whatever impatience there might have been was overshadowed by the relief everyone felt that Charlie's explorations hadn't resulted in something tragic. Paige had spoken to just about everyone, including the mayor and his guests, who had been thoroughly impressed with the town's support in a time of need.

It was as if she'd given the mayor some extra-good PR without even meaning to. Melina Sorento was scribbling in her notebook, talking to people, even interviewing Simon for his take on the entire event to feature in next week's paper.

Next week. Paige took a deep breath and finished her coffee. Too bad she wouldn't be here to see it.

The door chimed as it opened, and Paige almost choked on her coffee. "Holly! Luke! You weren't due back until Tuesday."

Holly pushed through the crowd and pulled her off the stool for a hug. "Abby called and told us what happened. We couldn't very well sit around knowing what you and Charlie had been through." She squeezed hard. "Are you doing okay? Charlie's okay?"

"We're both fine." Paige returned the hug, casting an accusatory look Abby's way, but Abby only shrugged and hopped up to hug her friend next. "You didn't have to come back, honestly."

"Oh, please. We can take another vacation. Especially now that Luke knows this place is in good hands without him. Seems like you're in good hands, too," Holly said as she wrapped her arm around Paige's shoulders. They watched as Luke joined his deputies, then bent down to talk directly to Charlie. "He was more worried than I was about her. She's infectious, that kid. But then you know that, right?"

Paige smiled and nodded, then she caught Leah's eye and motioned her over. She hadn't planned to do this now, but, as she'd learned in the last few days, there wasn't any time to waste when it came to making the most of her life. "Can I talk to you and Luke in the kitchen for a few minutes? It's important."

"Yeah, sure."

"No, no, you both go on. I'm fine here," Abby called. "I'm going to get a milkshake. I've earned it."

"You have indeed," Paige agreed. "Twyla, strawberry shake for Abby, please."

"You got it!" came a voice from the crowd.

Plates of onion rings, French fries, jalapeño poppers and burgers bigger than a person's head kept flying through the serving window at Ursula speed. As Paige led the way toward the back of the kitchen, she felt her body tighten back up as Leah joined her, Holly and Luke. "Holly, this is Leah Ellis. She's taken over her uncle's law practice here in town."

"Oh, you must be Benjamin Ellis's niece." Holly reached out to shake her hand. "He was one of my best customers for years. I hope he's enjoying his new job."

"He is, thanks." Leah reached into her bag and pulled out the large manila envelope. "On the house, Paige. And so's any advice you might need in the future." She tucked a stray strand of blond hair behind her ear. "I'll let you all talk."

"Abby filled us in on the last year," Luke said with nary a glimmer of resentment in his eyes. "I wish you'd told us what was going on. We could have helped."

"I know." Paige gave a weak smile. Now that she had this in her hands, she couldn't seem to stop shaking. "I made some deals with the universe while Charlie was in that cave. You know, mom deals," she said to Holly, who nodded. "I'd already asked Leah to draw these up, but now I know it's for the best. I'm heading back to New York tomorrow afternoon. I'm going to turn myself in, accept whatever consequences they deem appropriate. I'm, um, not sure when I'll be back." She handed Holly the envelope. "I know this probably isn't the best thing to spring on someone, but I've named you and Luke as Charlie's legal guardians. I want—I need her to stay here. With people who love her. With her family."

Holly's eyes watered instantly as she took the papers. "Paige, no. This has to be over-thinking things. Surely it isn't necessary—"

"I've never had the best of luck with these kinds of things. But I ran from this because I couldn't bear the thought of Charlie being caught up in the foster care system. All I've ever wanted was for her to feel safe and pro-tected, loved. And most of all wanted. That's something I never had. I know she'll have that with you. She'll have everything she's ever wanted here. Please tell me you'll take her."

Holly opened her mouth, no doubt to pro-test again, but Luke took hold of her hand. "If this is what you want, of course we accept."

"I want her to have a relationship with Fletcher, too," Paige said. "However much he wants. They deserve that. I'll tell her the truth before I leave, so you won't have to deal with that. If she's going to be angry with someone I need it to be with me." She wiped the tears off her cheeks and backed away when Holly moved forward to hug her again. "No, please. I need to take some time to myself for a while. Just…take care of my baby."

Before either of them could say a word, she hurried around them, back out into the diner, and, before she could change her mind, she walked out the front door to start packing.

IT TOOK HER until two hours before her flight to New York the next day to get up the courage to tell Charlie what was going on. Being the center of attention all of yesterday had worn her little girl out, and now, as Paige zipped up her to-go bag, she knew it was time.

Expecting to be booked and processed as soon as she turned herself in at the police station, she'd chosen the simplest of clothes; packed only the bare necessities. Shoes laced up, hair locked down in a braid, she knocked on Charlie's bedroom door before she pushed it open. There her daughter sat at her small desk, drawing what had to be the tenth picture she'd made of the butterfly treasure box she was convinced had given her all she ever wanted.

"Charlie? I need to talk to you about something."

"Sure, Mom." Charlie colored faster so she could finish, then held up the paper. "Good one?"

"It's perfect." Paige held out her hand. "Come out here with me, please."

Charlie frowned, picking up on the grief in Paige's voice, certainly. "Is something wrong? I'm not in trouble again, am I? I didn't do anything else, I promise."

"No, you're fine. There's something going on that I need to tell you—"

Someone knocked on the door. Paige sighed. She didn't have time for any interruptions. "Whoever it is, can you please come back…" She pulled open the door. "Later. Fletch. Luke. What are you doing—" Her voice broke. She reached back and grabbed Charlie, holding her against her as she started to shake. The dark-haired man with the familiar piercing, accusing eyes stood off to the side. "Detective Diaz. What are you—"

"Mom?" Charlie started to sound as scared as Paige felt. "What's going on?"

"Hey, Charlie." Luke held out his hand. "Simon's downstairs at the diner. Why don't you go keep him busy for a while."

"Mom?" Charlie turned her freckled face up at Paige.

"Um." She looked to Fletch, who gave her an encouraging nod. "Yeah, go ahead. I'll come get you in a bit."

Charlie stepped away, walked down the stairs, looking over her shoulder as she went. Paige stepped back and waved them inside. "Please, come in. Sorry it's such a mess. I've just finished packing." She couldn't seem to stand still. "I'm sorry, but what are you doing here? I don't understand." He wasn't going to arrest her here, was he? In front of everyone in Butterfly Harbor? In front of the town Charlie was going to live in? "Please don't do anything in front of my daughter."

"Please, Ms. Cooper." Detective Diaz glanced to Luke. "Sheriff Saxon called me yesterday afternoon. After speaking with both him and Deputy Bradley, it seems I owe you an apology. Which is why I'm here. They insisted I take the red-eye out to San Francisco last night so I could talk to you in person."

"The red-eye? An apology? What is going on?"

Fletch must have taken pity on her as he walked around to wrap his arm around her shoulders in support. "The charges against you have been dropped, Paige. Detective Diaz was able to make his case without your testimony. Something, it turns out, he actually did months ago. The Brennan kid is going to cut a deal for early parole."

"But, I checked just last week. My arrest warrant was still active." She looked up at him. "How is that possible?"

"I made a mistake, Paige," Detective Diaz said. "When my partner was shot all I wanted was to make the person who had done it pay along with anyone who helped him. I was out of bounds threatening to take your daughter away. I let my anger get the better of me and let things go on longer than I should have. By the time I could drop the charges—"

"Sometimes it's hard to let go of certain cases," Luke explained. "You not reporting the gunshot wound was a misdemeanor, Paige, and while it technically violated the oath you would have taken upon getting your nursing license, you were still in school at the time. We've made a few calls, called in a few favors and, with Detective Diaz dropping all the charges against you, you'll be allowed to finish your classes and earn enough credits to graduate. It's over, Paige. You don't have to give us custody of Charlie. You don't have to go back to New York and turn yourself in. It's over."

Paige couldn't believe her ears. "And you flew all the way out here to tell me in person?"

Detective Diaz said with a wry smile, "I wasn't exactly given a choice. But yes, I owed you that much at least. I never expected you to run, Paige. And I'm so sorry you felt as if you had to."

"I appreciate that." She pressed a hand against her chest. The breath she'd been holding for the past sixteen months escaped and, with it, all the fear and worry over what was to come. "How's your partner doing?"

"Better." Diaz nodded. "He's been chosen as part of a case study on spinal injuries. There's a good chance he might regain partial movement in his legs. Thank you. For asking."

"Of course."

"Let's get you that burger we promised you," Luke said as he backed up and opened the door. Before he left, he walked over to Paige, drew her into a hug and set her back in Fletch's arms. "When this all hits you later, just go with it. And when you're ready to decompress and celebrate, we'll be here."

He closed the door behind them.

"How is this even possible?" Paige couldn't move. All these months and…it was over? Just like that? She looked up at Fletch, too afraid to think…too afraid to hope.

"Holly and Abby went on a bit of a rant yesterday after you left the diner, told us everything. And this time I do mean everything. That you were willing to give up Charlie—"

"Don't." Paige's knees wobbled. "Oh, please, don't remind me." She dived for her couch and sank onto the edge. "My little girl. I get to keep my little girl." The tears started again, but this time she didn't even try to stop them. "I got her back twice in the span of a day. Both times thanks to you."

"Well, me, Luke and Jason."

"Jason?"

"Who do you think flew him out here? Sent a car for him and everything."

"I'm going to bake him the biggest banana cake he's ever seen." Paige laughed. But the laugh turned into a sob. "Oh, Fletch. I'm so sorry for everything. For lying to you, for not trusting you—"

"Stop, Paige." The way he said it, the way he looked down at the floor as he stepped toward her. Was she going to regain her life, regain her freedom, only to lose him? "You don't owe me anything. Not an explanation, not an apology. If anyone owes anyone anything it's me. For not being the kind of man you thought you could trust. I'd like to change that. If you'll let me."

"If I'll let you? Fletch, of course… I mean I…" She couldn't seem to get the words out. She held out her hands, waited for him to take them. "I love you, Deputy Fletcher Bradley. I love every honest, frustrating, stubborn bit of you. And if you'll have us, Charlie and I would very much like to be part of your family."

"Yeah?" There was that grin, that silly crooked grin that she now realized was all for her.

"Yeah." She jumped to her feet and locked her arms around his neck, reveling in the feel of his arms wrapping around her, holding her close. "With everything that happened, the running, the lies, everything, I wouldn't change any part of it." She pulled her head back far enough to look into his eyes. "You know why?"

"No." He kissed her on the tip of her nose. "Tell me."

"Because I never would have come to Butterfly Harbor. I wouldn't have found you." She curled her fingers into the thick curls of his hair and kissed him gently. "I wouldn't have found my home."

"In that case, Paige Cooper..." He spun her in circles until she couldn't stop laughing. "... welcome home."

EPILOGUE

"You can stop staring at it." Fletcher chuckled at the way Paige couldn't take her eyes off the ring on her finger. "I can promise it isn't going anywhere."

Paige hadn't been able to wipe the smile off her face for the past week. It had taken that long to come to terms with getting her life—her entire life—back. With a very nice bonus. "It's beautiful." She loved how the sparkling diamond caught the light through the car window.

"It's small," Fletch said and not for the first time.

"It's simple. Like me." She turned and looked at him, placed her hand on his arm and squeezed. "I don't need fancy jewelry, Fletcher. I just need you."

"And me!" Charlie bounced forward from the back seat as Fletcher parked in front of Mrs. Hastings's house. "Thank you for my engagement present." She clasped the butterfly pendant accented with two tiny diamonds in its wings between her fingers and slid it across the thin gold chain. "It's so pretty!"

"A special occasion calls for a special gift," Fletch said and kissed the back of Paige's hand. "Can we discuss wedding dates now?"

"I thought it was the bride who was supposed to be anxious." Paige laughed. She was still trying to figure everything out. Where did she finish school? Did she get a job at a hospital? She loved working at the diner, and for Calliope, but the idea of being a nurse filled her with more hope than she'd had in years. The possibilities were endless.

Out of the corner of her eye she saw the front door open and Mrs. Hastings step onto the porch to wave to them. "Charlie, why don't you—"

Charlie shoved out of the car and slammed the door behind her, but she didn't get much farther. Not when her attention appeared to be snagged by something across the street.

"Mom!" Charlie motioned over her shoulder, her eyes wide with something akin to panic. "Mom, look! The sign's gone."

"What...sign?" Paige followed Charlie's gaze to the cottage home with the butterfly glass window above the door. Her stomach dropped.

Not only was the For Sale sign missing, but the front yard had been tamed, the trellis painted and the weeds removed and replaced with thick, lush sod. "Oh, no." Paige jumped out and joined Charlie at the newly painted fence. She rested her hands on Charlie's shoulders and hugged her. "It looks like it's been sold."

It was silly, Paige thought, given all the good that had happened to her, to be sad about a house that was by all rights never going to be hers. She didn't want to be greedy, not after everything she'd been given recently. She pressed a hand against her chest. It was still the most beautiful house she'd ever seen.

She blinked moist eyes up at the vintage stained glass window.

"Who bought our house, Mom?" Charlie asked.

"No one bought it." Fletch slipped an arm around Paige's waist and held tight. "The owners decided to keep it in the family."

"Oh." Charlie sighed and rested her chin on the top of the fence post. "I guess that's okay."

"I certainly hope so." Fletch dug into his

back pocket and pulled out a set of keys. He dropped them in front of Charlie's face and jingled them. "Welcome home, Charlie."

Charlie gasped, grabbed at the keys and spun around, the huge smile on her face exposing her back teeth. "Really?" She squealed so loud Paige flinched. "Really and truly? We'll get to live here?"

"Really and truly." He reached around her and pushed open the gate. "Go on inside and check it out. Especially upstairs, the second door on the left."

"You bought us a house," Paige whispered. "You bought our house."

"Not exactly." Fletch drew her in front of him, wrapped his arms around her as Charlie's squeals echoed from inside. "This was my grandfather's house. He built it himself. It was his pride and joy. My grandmother made the window." He pointed to the brilliant monarch butterfly shimmering in the sun. "All these years I wondered why none of the offers ever felt right. Now I know. It's been waiting." He pressed his lips into her hair. "For you and Charlie."

"And you," Paige whispered as she stared at her new home. "There's nothing left,

Fletcher. You've given me everything I've ever wanted."

Charlie squealed again, prompting Paige to think it was time to join her daughter. And then she heard something else. Something that sounded an awful lot like a…

"Was that a bark?" Paige glanced over at a suddenly innocent-looking Fletch. "That was a bark. Fletcher Bradley, you did not."

He grinned. "Now is probably a good time to remind you just how crazy you are about me."

The second-story window slid open and Charlie leaned out, her arms filled with puppy. "Thank you, Daddy! He's perfect!"

"She!" Fletch called out, as a laughing Paige dropped her head forward. "Be back in a sec." He hurried over to Mrs. Hastings to say they would be by for tea in a little while.

Paige waited for him at the front door, and when he joined her, she held out her hand.

So they could walk inside.

Together.

* * * * *

If you liked this story,
don't miss the other books in Anna's
BUTTERFLY HARBOR *miniseries:*
THE BAD BOY FROM
BUTTERFLY HARBOR

RECIPE FOR REDEMPTION

Available now from Harlequin.com!
And watch for Anna's next romance,
coming in spring 2018 from
Harlequin Heartwarming!

Get 2 Free Books,
Plus 2 Free Gifts—
just for trying the Reader Service!

Love Inspired®

Get 2 Free Books,
Plus 2 Free Gifts—
just for trying the
Reader Service!

HOMETOWN HEARTS ♥

YES! Please send me **The Hometown Hearts Collection** in Larger Print. This collection begins with 3 FREE books and 2 FREE gifts in the first shipment. Along with my 3 free books, I'll also get the next 4 books from the Hometown Hearts Collection, in LARGER PRINT, which I may either return and owe nothing, or keep for the low price of $4.99 U.S./ $5.89 CDN each plus $2.99 for shipping and handling per shipment*. If I decide to continue, about once a month for 8 months I will get 6 or 7 more books, but will only need to pay for 4. That means 2 or 3 books in every shipment will be FREE! If I decide to keep the entire collection, I'll have paid for only 32 books because 19 books are FREE! I understand that accepting the 3 free books and gifts places me under no obligation to buy anything. I can always return a shipment and cancel at any time. My free books and gifts are mine to keep no matter what I decide.

262 HCN 3432 462 HCN 3432

Name	(PLEASE PRINT)	
Address		Apt. #
City	State/Prov.	Zip/Postal Code

Signature (if under 18, a parent or guardian must sign)

Mail to the **Reader Service:**
IN U.S.A.: P.O. Box 1867, Buffalo, NY. 14240-1867
IN CANADA: P.O. Box 609, Fort Erie, Ontario L2A 5X3

Get 2 Free Books,
Plus 2 Free Gifts—
just for trying the
Reader Service!

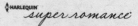

YES! Please send me 2 FREE LARGER-PRINT Harlequin® Superromance® novels and my 2 FREE gifts (gifts are worth about $10 retail). After receiving them, if I don't wish to receive any more books, I can return the shipping statement marked "cancel." If I don't cancel, I will receive 4 brand-new novels every month and be billed just $6.19 per book in the U.S. or $6.49 per book in Canada. That's a savings of at least 11% off the cover price! It's quite a bargain! Shipping and handling is just 50¢ per book in the U.S. or 75¢ per book in Canada.* I understand that accepting the 2 free books and gifts places me under no obligation to buy anything. I can always return a shipment and cancel at any time. The free books and gifts are mine to keep no matter what I decide.

132/332 HDN GLWS

Name   (PLEASE PRINT)

Address   Apt. #

City   State/Prov.   Zip/Postal Code

Signature (if under 18, a parent or guardian must sign)

Mail to the **Reader Service:**
IN U.S.A.: P.O. Box 1341, Buffalo, NY 14240-8531
IN CANADA: P.O. Box 603, Fort Erie, Ontario L2A 5X3

Want to try two free books from another line?
Call 1-800-873-8635 today or visit www.ReaderService.com.

* Terms and prices subject to change without notice. Prices do not include applicable taxes. Sales tax applicable in N.Y. Canadian residents will be charged applicable taxes. Offer not valid in Quebec. This offer is limited to one order per household. Books received may not be as shown. Not valid for current subscribers to Harlequin Superromance Larger-Print books. All orders subject to approval. Credit or debit balances in a customer's account(s) may be offset by any other outstanding balance owed by or to the customer. Please allow 4 to 6 weeks for delivery. Offer available while quantities last.

Your Privacy—The Reader Service is committed to protecting your privacy. Our Privacy Policy is available online at www.ReaderService.com or upon request from the Reader Service.

We make a portion of our mailing list available to reputable third parties that offer products we believe may interest you. If you prefer that we not exchange your name with third parties, or if you wish to clarify or modify your communication preferences, please visit us at www.ReaderService.com/consumerschoice or write to us at Reader Service Preference Service, P.O. Box 9062, Buffalo, NY 14240-9062. Include your complete name and address.

HSRLPI7R

READERSERVICE.COM

Manage your account online!

- Review your order history
- Manage your payments
- Update your address

---

*We've designed the
Reader Service website
just for you.*

Enjoy all the features!

- Discover new series available to you, and read excerpts from any series.
- Respond to mailings and special monthly offers.
- Browse the Bonus Bucks catalog and online-only exculsives.
- Share your feedback.

Visit us at:

ReaderService.com

Get 2 Free Books,

Plus 2 Free Gifts—

Love Inspired HISTORICAL

just for trying the
Reader Service!